The Tribune Temptation

Roman Heirs, Book One
Jenna Bigelow

To the Latin teachers and Classics professors who first sparked my interest in all things Ancient Rome. I hope you don't mind what I've done with the place.

CHAPTER 1

T HERE WAS A WOMAN in his lap, and Aelius had no idea how she'd gotten there.

It must have happened when he'd closed his eyes to take another gulp of strong wine. Her weight had settled against him, making the stool beneath him creak, and he opened his eyes to meet a flirtatious smile. A pair of kohl-shadowed eyes gazed at him.

The crowded tavern resounded with the noise of men engaged in drinking games, gambling, or general carousing. A few women, colleagues or competitors of the one in his lap, filtered through the throng in search of business.

"Excuse me," he said, attempting not to slur. "I'm not interested in your services."

His friend Catullus, on the other side of the rickety tavern table, leaned forward with a grin. "Come on, let her distract you from your troubles. You'll feel better after, no doubt."

"I will guarantee it." The woman cast an appraising glance at Catullus. "I do offer a favorable rate for two at a time."

Catullus's eyes lit with interest, and he raised an eyebrow at Aelius hopefully. "That's a good deal. I'm game if you are."

"I am not," Aelius said. Catullus was quite flexible with his amorous exploits and while Aelius was no prude, he drew the line at consorting with his own friend. In any case, he did not engage with prostitutes as a rule. Most of them were slaves, and whatever enthusiasm a skilled practitioner might affect, he refused to lie with a woman who couldn't say no. He remembered too well the oppressive feeling of living a life that wasn't truly his own.

He gently pushed at the woman's shoulder, but she didn't budge. His irritation sharpened. He could have removed her more forcefully, but he would not shove a woman, even one who had deposited herself in his lap without invitation.

With a sigh, he thrust a hand into the leather purse securely belted at his waist and drew out a bronze coin. "For your trouble."

She rolled her eyes and snatched it up, finally climbing off him. "Well, I'm here most nights, if you're ever in a better mood."

"Thank you," Aelius muttered, and she swayed over to greet some men at a nearby table.

Cheers exploded from the other side of the tavern as someone won a drinking game. Aelius glowered at the knot of revelers. Such happiness felt miles away after the day he'd had.

His cup was empty, so he reached for the wine jug, but Catullus got there first and moved it out of reach. "I think you've had enough. Drowning your sorrows is all well and good, but really, it's just a minor setback."

"Minor setback? I lost an election." The loss still pierced him, as fresh and humiliating as it had been when the magistrates announced the results a few hours ago.

Catullus took a casual swig of wine. "There will be other elections. Besides, no one expected you to win. Frankly, I was shocked *anyone* voted for you."

"You really know how to make me feel better."

"I meant it's a testament to your charm, and your future potential. For someone like you, to win as many votes as you did? It's encouraging." Catullus's eyes flicked to the mark on the inside of Aelius's left wrist.

Reflexively, Aelius moved his arm so the brand was no longer visible. He usually wore a thick silver bracelet to hide it, but he'd taken it off before embarking on this drinking excursion to lessen the chances of being mugged. "I don't know what else I can do. I practiced every speech, I—"

"Listen, you didn't lose because your speeches weren't practiced enough. You lost because the people who matter either don't know who you are or don't care. Elections aren't won in the Forum or at the ballot-box. They're won in dining rooms on the Palatine Hill."

A hopeless weight pressed down on Aelius's chest. Perhaps he'd underestimated how competitive the election for tribune of the plebs would be. It was the only political office reserved for men of plebeian rank, meant to curtail the dominion of the patrician class.

More importantly, it was a crucial stepping-stone on the path to Aelius's true goal: to be Rome's first freedman consul. Winning the most powerful position in Rome would ensure no one could afford to look down on him or his mother ever again. It would also allow him to enact policies that would benefit the lives of slaves and freedmen like him. He just needed to keep that part of his plans a secret for now, or else be branded a radical without hope of winning a single vote.

But the powers of a consulship were of no consequence if he couldn't even win a low-level tribune election. "I'm afraid no well-to-do families are inviting me to their dinner parties."

"But they are inviting me." Catullus gave him a significant look that Aelius couldn't decipher. "I have some thoughts that may be of use for your second attempt, but let's discuss further when you're sober. I need to get you home before midnight, or else your mother will skin me alive. Though to be fair…" He rose to his feet and tugged Aelius up from his stool. "There's not much I wouldn't let your mother do to me."

Aelius groaned, both from Catullus's infatuation with his mother and from the way his head spun at the sudden change in position.

Catullus hooked a lanky arm around Aelius's shoulders and maneuvered him through the tavern to the door. "Are you sure she entertains no callers? A beautiful widow like that shouldn't be spending her nights alone. I'd expect you to be like Telemachus, fending off his mother's suitors."

"Am I supposed to get that reference?" Aelius's education had been condensed, and the finer points of literature often eluded him. He'd only received four years of tutelage between the ages of fourteen, after being freed from slavery, and eighteen, when he'd joined the army to complete the ten years of military service required to stand for political positions.

Catullus sighed. "The *Odyssey,* you barbarian."

They left the tavern and emerged into the cool night air. Catullus kept a steadying arm around Aelius's shoulders as they traipsed—or stumbled, in Aelius's case—through the streets.

Aelius felt a rush of gratitude. Despite Catullus's often inappropriate remarks, he was a good and generous friend. Befriending him had been one of Aelius's better decisions since leaving the army and pursuing political office. Catullus cast a wide social net, fraternizing with people of all classes to gather material for his popular poetry, and didn't mind being seen with a freedman.

The journey home was hazy, but soon they were entering the atrium of Aelius's home on the Esquiline Hill. The atrium contained a small pool to collect rainwater, flanked by columns with square-carved tops. A few decorative items, inherited from his late stepfather, Herminius, adorned the perimeter of the room. A stone pedestal held an antique red-and-black vase depicting a group of prancing satyrs. Near the front of the room, there was a small cluster of portrait heads, each representing an ancestor of the Herminius family.

The newest head showed his stepfather's countenance. It was a good likeness, but the marble made him look more dour than he had been in life. Herminius, a successful grain merchant, had been quick to smile and always the first to offer someone a kind word. He'd married Aelius's mother, Gaia, shortly after the two had been freed, and had died of an illness two years ago.

Catullus jabbed him in the ribs. "Try to look just a little bit sober in case we should see—"

A shadow moved, and Aelius's mother rose from a bench set between columns. She pulled a shawl closer around her slender shoulders and regarded them with an icy stare. "Good evening, boys."

Catullus straightened up at the sight of her. "Good evening, lady. I have returned your son to you."

"Didn't mean to wake you," Aelius said, willing his words to come out crisply.

"You didn't wake me." Gaia raised her chin. "It's rather difficult to sleep when one knows her only son is out carousing, at the mercy of every thief and brigand prowling the streets at night."

Guilt stabbed at Aelius. He shouldn't have made her worry. "I'm sorry, Mama. I just needed…" *To forget. To escape.*

Her gaze softened. "Well, I'm very glad you've returned safely."

"I made sure to look out for him, Gaia." Catullus stepped forward and took her hand, planting a gallant kiss on it. "I would not have such a lovely brow creased in worry."

Aelius rolled his eyes, which made him dizzy, but Gaia smiled. "Flatterer."

"It's not flattery if it's true, lady. I wish you would let me write a poem to—"

"Clearly we have both had too much to drink." Aelius attempted to elbow Catullus but missed. "I think it's time for bed."

Gaia nodded. "Catullus, you must stay here for the night. You live across town, and it's dangerous to walk alone at this hour. I will have a room prepared for you."

"Your beauty is matched only by your generosity, lady."

She gave him another smile, then beckoned Catullus to follow her to one of the spare bedrooms. Aelius retired to his own room. He collapsed into bed without undressing and stared up at the ceiling. The room spun, and he closed his eyes, which only made it worse.

Now that he was alone, all the unpleasant feelings he'd been trying to escape came flooding back. What if he couldn't do it? What if his dreams to climb the political ladder and become consul were truly foolish?

A knock sounded at his door. "Aelius?"

His mother's voice. He struggled into a sitting position, a hand pressed to his forehead as if that could stop the spinning. "Yes?"

The door eased open, and Gaia slipped through. She carried a small clay lamp which cast a glow of flickering light into the darkened room, illuminating the whitewashed walls. "I wanted to see how you were doing. I was worried about you."

"I'm fine. Catullus kept an eye on me, as you can see."

She shook her head and came to sit on the edge of his bed, the lamp nestled in her lap. "Not that. I meant I know how upset you were by the election." She laid a cool hand against his forehead, just like she used to do when he was a child.

Aelius turned his face away. He'd tried to hide his devastation from his mother, but as usual, she saw right through him. "Every politician loses at some point. I'll run again next year."

"Are you sure that's wise? Maybe you should take some time to think about it."

"You don't think I can do it?"

"I'm certain you can. But I question if this will make you happy. This constant striving, scheming…Once you attain one position, you will only want the next thing. If it's money you're worried about, you know Herminius left us with plenty to live on. We could leave the city and take an estate in the country. Somewhere by the sea, or maybe a little vineyard in the hills. Wouldn't that be nice?"

"Would leaving the city make you happy?" Her happiness, after all they had suffered, meant everything to him.

She shrugged. "It would be a lovely place to raise a family." She gave him a meaningful look. "We have a name now. You can't let that disappear."

Her right hand went to her left wrist, covering the brand that matched Aelius's own. T, for their former master. Aelius usually hated the fact that they were both permanently marked with a relic of their past shame, but there were times when the twin marks were almost comforting. The brands now signified that he and his mother belonged only to each other.

"I know," he murmured.

She released her wrist. "Besides, you know how much I want grandchildren."

He could see the life his mother wanted: happy children running through the gardens of a quiet country estate, peaceful days spent enjoying the fresh air. It tempted him, but he shook his head. "There is no point in having an heir without a legacy for him to inherit. I will build a legacy first, and then I promise I will give you as many grandchildren as you like." He was only thirty-two. Plenty of time for all that.

Politics, on the other hand, couldn't wait. Men had to be at least forty-two to run for consul, and there was a huge prestige in attaining the rank at the minimum age. He needed to win more influential positions nearly every year in order to be eligible to run for consul when he turned forty-two. Losing this election meant he was already behind.

She smiled. "I will hold you to that, my love. Now, rest. Things will look brighter in the morning." She kissed him on the forehead, then rose from the bed and left the room.

Aelius adjusted the pillow behind his head, considering his mother's words. What if he just gave up? It was tempting to leave the city behind and start a quiet life in the country where no one knew them.

But something in him balked. He had spent too long ignored and overlooked, slighted and disdained. Freedmen were citizens, yes, but they were never allowed to forget the stigma of their pasts. Most freedmen weren't even allowed to run for office. Aelius had been lucky to be officially adopted by Herminius, which allowed him to pursue politics. He'd been given a great gift, and now he needed to prove himself worthy of it. Achieving political success was the only thing that would prove he was more than his past.

He would be Rome's first freedman consul, no matter what he had to sacrifice. After that, maybe he would be happy.

Aelius woke to a pounding headache and a mouth that felt as if he'd eaten sand. He lay in bed, cursing every drop of wine that had passed his lips last night, then gathered the energy to heave himself into a sitting position. His room had a curtained window out onto the atrium, and the amount of sunlight blazing through the sheer fabric told him it was already late morning.

He rose with a groan and stumbled to the pitcher and basin which rested on a table against the wall. He splashed his face with water. The cold shock made him feel slightly more alive. Then, he changed into a fresh tunic and ran a hand across his chin, feeling the prickles of fresh stubble. Malchio, one of their household slaves, could help him shave later, but for now, breakfast was his first priority.

He left his room. Immediately, the sound of laughter and conversation reached his ears, echoing from the other side of the atrium. He followed it to see his mother seated across from Catullus at a small table next to the central pool. Catullus was tucking into a bowl of porridge topped with sliced dates. He glanced up as Aelius approached. "Good morning. You look, er...well."

Aelius was sure he did not look any such thing, but he returned the greeting. Gaia jumped up from her chair and offered it to Aelius. "Sit and eat, dear." Without waiting for him to agree, she grabbed his shoulders, sat him down, and filled a dish with porridge from the serving bowl, then piled a small plate high with cheese and fruit. She pushed the food in front of him. "I will leave you two to eat together. I must attend to some household matters." She bustled off.

Catullus craned his neck to watch her walk away. Aelius tossed a date at him. "Watch yourself."

Catullus caught the date and ate it. "Get some food in you. Your mood will improve, no doubt."

Aelius grumbled but obeyed. He did feel better after a few spoonfuls of hearty, warm porridge, washed down with a swig of well-watered wine. "Last night, you seemed to think you knew a way for me to win the next election."

"I might have some ideas. You're probably not going to like them."

"I draw the line at poisoning my political opponents, and I'm not going to waste my inheritance on bribery."

Catullus chuckled. "Good to know your limits. No, my idea was less expensive than bribery, but perhaps as permanent as poisoning. And possibly as disagreeable." He leaned forward, planting his elbows on the table. "Marriage."

Aelius's eyebrows shot up. "Have you been talking to my mother?"

Catullus ignored the remark. "You need connections. The strongest way to make connections is through marriage. You need a wife whose family is well-positioned among the patricians you need to impress."

"But tribunes are elected by the plebeian assembly. Patricians don't even vote in those elections."

"Yes, but their influence is still great. Plebeians vote as their patron tells them to, don't they? Get a few patricians on your side and you'll get the votes. And the easiest way to get patricians on your side is to marry one of them."

Aelius frowned. "You think any patrician father would let his daughter within an arm's length of me?"

"That is the trickiest part of my plan, of course," Catullus said. "But, for all your faults, you have no lack of charm. Find a man with daughters to spare, charm one of them, and make your case. The patricians could benefit from having a man on the inside with the plebs to make sure they don't get up to anything too radical."

Aelius's lips tightened. The office of tribune was intended to protect the plebeian citizens from the abuses of the patricians—not extend their influence. And Aelius's ideas were more radical than most. He wanted to introduce a bill banning the sale of pregnant slaves, so fathers couldn't be separated from their children, and another to waive the inheritance tax on men who freed their slaves in their will.

But if he couldn't win this election, his ideas were meaningless, so for now, he would listen to Catullus. "And where am I supposed to meet these patrician daughters?"

"That's where I come in." Catullus smiled smugly. "By virtue of my poetry, I've become one of the most sought-after dinner guests in the city. I can get you in anywhere. In fact, there's a party two nights from now at the home of a senator. You'll come with me. Perhaps your future wife won't be in attendance, but you can start building a reputation for yourself as the sort of charming man all the girls will want to meet. Make yourself...palatable." His gaze ran over Aelius, lingering on his left wrist.

Aelius drew his hand into his lap, furtively flicking the edge of a napkin over his wrist. He'd forgotten to put his wristband back on after taking it off last night, and his brand was clearly visible in the daylight.

The idea of a freedman marrying a daughter of the elite was laughable, truly. Besides, he had no desire to marry, even for political gain, but right now Catullus's plan seemed his best chance at setting himself up for a future victory.

"All right," Aelius said. "I'll accompany you to the party."

CHAPTER 2

TWO NIGHTS LATER, AELIUS accompanied Catullus to a grand townhouse on the Palatine Hill. His finest toga lay heavy and unwieldy on his shoulders, and he kept adjusting it as he followed Catullus into the atrium.

He tried not to look too impressed by their lavish surroundings but couldn't help craning his head up at the carved capitals of the columns surrounding the room, painted in red, blue and green. Intricate mosaics of colored tile spread beneath his feet, and lanternlight sparkled on the water of the central pool. A collection of elaborately painted antique vases, each on their own carved pedestal, surrounded the perimeter of the room. They must be worth a fortune.

Sounds of music and laughter grew louder as a slave escorted them toward the dining room. With anxious fingers, Aelius twisted the silver wristband on his left wrist. He strove to tamp down his nerves. He'd have to get used to mingling with the elite if he wanted to be consul one day. At least no one here knew his true background. They'd take him for a plebeian, not a freedman.

They entered the dining room. Colorful frescoes were splashed across the walls. In the flickering light, the figures almost looked as if they were moving. It was some sort of mythological scene, but Aelius couldn't make out which one.

Catullus introduced him to their host, a gray-haired senator named Crispinus, and his wife, a woman with a simpering smile and cold eyes. Then they took their seats on the low couches placed around the three-branched table. Slaves brought around silver platters of appetizers. Catullus piled his plate high, but Aelius was too distracted to eat much.

Catullus shoved a poached fig into his mouth and nudged Aelius. He tilted his chin toward two young ladies sitting with an older woman who had to be their mother at the opposite wing of the table. "Two contenders over there. I know for a fact their family has two more daughters at home. They'll struggle to find suitable husbands for all of them. Might be willing to sacrifice one to your cause."

One of the young ladies caught Aelius's eye and smiled, her appreciative gaze skimming his body. Aelius smiled back.

The girls' mother noticed and shot Aelius a glare sharp enough to pierce metal. She spoke a firm word to her daughter, who redirected her gaze elsewhere with a chastened look.

"Perhaps not," Aelius muttered. Even a plebeian was not good enough to smile at a pretty patrician girl, apparently.

Catullus shrugged and reached for his goblet of wine. Aelius scanned the other guests. He glanced over several wives seated next to their husbands. His gaze landed on another seemingly single young woman. "What about that one?"

Catullus shook his head. "Engaged to a magistrate."

Aelius kept looking. His gaze paused on a young woman seated next to their host, Crispinus. She must have slipped in after they'd entered, because he hadn't noticed her during their introduction to Crispinus and his wife. She seemed a few years older than the other unmarried girls. A vibrant blue palla was pinned to her head, covering her hair, and she wore no makeup. Even in the dim room, Aelius could see deep shadows beneath her eyes. She sat stiffly upright, her mouth frozen in a dissatisfied frown, her eyes fixed on the empty plate before her. She sat so still she could have been carved from marble. *A statue, fit to worship.*

Aelius couldn't seem to shift his gaze from her. He caught a hint of glossy dark hair beneath the sapphire fabric. A sudden, inappropriate urge overtook him to know what that hair would feel like twined through his fingers.

"Who's that?" Aelius murmured, tilting his chin toward the woman.

Catullus raised his eyebrows. "Why, that's Crispina, of course," he said, as if that should explain everything.

The name did explain one thing. "Our host's daughter?"

Catullus nodded. "Don't you pay any attention to gossip?" When Aelius shook his head, Catullus leaned forward, lowering his voice. "Crispina's husband divorced her last month. It was a considerable scandal. For a senator's daughter to be sent packing, disgraced…"

That explained her unhappy bearing. "What did she do?"

"It's what she *didn't* do," Catullus said. "She was married for three years, and couldn't provide her husband with a child. So he divorced her to find a more fertile wife, and now every man in Rome knows she's barren. I hear her parents are very displeased with her, and they won't be making her life easy now that she's back. She's either got a life of solitude ahead of her or a marriage to some decrepit old man who just wants a pretty wife for his last few years. Maybe she can snag a priestess-hood if she's lucky. A terrible waste, isn't it?"

Aelius's interest piqued. He took another long look at the young woman. Could she be what he was searching for? He couldn't hope for better than a senator's daughter, and she had no better options. Her father would be desperate to get her off his hands, and he might even be willing to contemplate someone like Aelius as a suitor.

"Shouldn't I consider her, then?" Aelius asked. "She could be exactly what I need."

Catullus's mouth tightened. "I thought about suggesting you go after her, but I think she should be a last resort. I know her. She was prickly at best before her divorce, and since then I imagine her temperament has only soured further. To make matters worse, she's extremely well-read and intelligent. She can recite Homer backwards and forwards, and I think she even knows Aramaic—"

"What, you don't think I can hold my own with an educated woman?"

"With all due respect, my friend, you're not exactly an academic." Catullus lowered his voice even further, speaking close to Aelius's ear. "Crispina dared to correct me—*me*!—at a party a few months back when I was reciting Sappho. In front of everyone, can you fathom it? It was horribly rude."

"Ah, so you just don't like her because she embarrassed you," Aelius said. "Well, I don't know any Sappho, so she can hardly repeat the offense."

Motion flickered where Crispina had been sitting, and Aelius returned his gaze to her. She rose from her couch with brisk but graceful movements and headed for the door.

Aelius seized his chance and rose as well. Speaking to her alone could be his best opportunity to create a good first impression.

"If you're not back by the time the next course is served, I'll assume the atrium has a new statue," Catullus said.

Aelius blinked at him. "What?"

Catullus let out a long-suffering sigh. "I was comparing her to Medusa. It was quite clever."

Aelius rolled his eyes and made for the door. He kept his movements casual, so anyone watching would think he was only going to relieve himself, but as soon as he left the dining room, his pace quickened.

Ahead of him, Crispina's palla fluttered behind her like a sail seeking a sea breeze. Aelius jogged a few steps until his foot flashed out and caught the hemmed edge of the fabric. It pulled loose from her head and fell, revealing shining dark hair bound into a sleek bun at the nape of her neck.

Aelius immediately bent to pick up the fallen palla. "I beg your pardon, lady," he said as Crispina turned.

She snatched the fabric from his hands. "Are you following me?"

"No, I was just..." He struggled to gather his thoughts, thrown off-kilter by her directness. He'd been expecting the coy manners of a well-bred patrician girl—not a question so forthright it could have come from his commanding officer in the army. "Going where you were going. To take a breath of air in the atrium."

"I was going to relieve myself. Are you going to follow me there?" Without waiting for an answer, she turned and continued walking down the colonnaded hallway.

Idiot. They'd exchanged barely a dozen words, and somehow he'd managed to cock it up already. He should have listened to Catullus. But he wouldn't give up so easily.

He followed at a slower pace, keeping a safe distance so she wouldn't notice him. He entered the atrium; she continued through it and disappeared into another part of the house. Aelius lingered by the central pool. She'd come back this way, and then he could try to salvage the situation.

Aelius waited in the cool evening. Distant noises of the party filtered to him from the dining room, but the atrium was quiet. A few minutes later, a figure appeared on the other side of the atrium.

Crispina had pinned her palla back atop her head. It flowed over her shoulders down to her ankles in a wave of deep blue. She paused as she entered the atrium and cast Aelius a suspicious glance.

Aelius summoned every ounce of his charm. He knew women found him attractive, as he often caught lingering stares or flirtatious smiles from ladies he encountered in passing. He curved his lips into a smile. "Pleasant evening, isn't it?"

She approached slowly, clasping her hands on her bare forearms. "I suppose." She glanced in the direction of the dining room, and her mouth tightened.

He sensed she wasn't eager to return to the party, which he could use to his advantage. "I don't think we've been formally introduced. I'm Aelius Herminius." His full name was Marcus

Trebonianus Aelius Herminius, but he hated using it. It was customary for freed slaves to take the name of their former master, but he preferred to be known by his own name, Aelius, and that of his stepfather, Herminius.

"How do you know my father?" She did not introduce herself.

"Er, I don't actually. I'm here with Catullus."

"The poet."

It wasn't a question, but Aelius nodded. "He spoke very highly of your taste in poetry."

An eyebrow lifted. "I doubt that."

Silence stretched. Aelius's mind whirled, trying to think of something else to say. She wasn't moving to return to the party, but she wasn't saying anything either. Instead, she regarded him with a steady, cool gaze that made his skin crawl with anxiety.

He decided to try a compliment. All ladies liked compliments, didn't they? "You look most beautiful tonight, lady."

She glanced over at the pool next to them as if bored.

A gentle nighttime breeze flowed over them, wafting the floral scent of perfumed oil to his nose. Her scent, he realized. It brought to mind a disquieting image of her lithe body being massaged all over with oil. His mouth opened, seeking words to distract him from the images running through his head. Then he was talking, his mouth sputtering words before his mind could catch up. "Catullus tells me you are recently divorced."

Her gaze flicked back to him, sharp as a freshly honed blade.

The words kept spilling out. "In fact, I was relieved to hear it—"

"Were you?"

Aelius realized how idiotic his statement had sounded. "Forgive me, I didn't mean it that way...I just...I found you to be so striking, lady, and…" His disjointed words hung in the air. Aelius cringed. How was it that he could speak with confident eloquence to a hundred men in the Forum, but he'd managed to so thoroughly botch a single conversation with one woman?

"Please, do continue," Crispina said, her voice dripping vinegar.

Aelius braced himself. Too much had been said already. The only way to possibly salvage this disaster of a conversation was to be forthright and honest. "I am in search of a wife, and I thought you…well, you…"

She stared at him with a blank, flat gaze, with no hint of reaction at his bumbling words.

"…you might be interested in marrying me," he finished lamely. He waited for the shock, disgust to fill her face at such a horrible, unexpected proposal.

Her eyes flashed, like firelight on obsidian, and her features hardened. She wasn't shocked or horrified by him, Aelius realized: she was angry.

"What a funny joke." Her voice was soft, but an edge of menace thrummed behind it, like a cat poised to strike. "Such an easy target I've become. The disgraced divorcée, the butt of dinner party pranks. Did Catullus put you up to this? Is this fodder for one of his overwrought poems?" She took a step toward him. He moved back, his calves hitting the stone edge of the pool at the center of the atrium.

He realized with a surge of horror that she'd thought he was mocking her. "No, you have the wrong idea—"

In a fluid motion, she bent down to the pool and raked her hand through the water. A wave sprang up and drenched the left side of Aelius's body. He stumbled away in shock, spluttering.

Crispina turned on her heel and left the atrium. Aelius cleared water out of his eyes. Well. He could hardly blame her: he deserved that.

He dried himself as best he could with the folds of his toga, then returned to the dining room. Crispina had resumed her seat next to her father. She did not look up as Aelius walked past her and rejoined Catullus on their couch.

Catullus gave him a long look. "Did she try to drown you?"

"Nearly," Aelius said ruefully. Luckily the room was dark enough that he hoped no one else would notice his soaked toga. He took a long swig of wine. "I've made a mess of it all."

"I warned you she can be peevish. What did you do?"

Aelius cringed at the memory, painfully fresh. "She made me nervous. I tried to explain why I wanted to talk to her." He closed his eyes. "I may have attempted to propose to her. She thought I was mocking her."

Catullus let out a whistle. "Gods below, you're an idiot."

"Yes, you were right, and I should have listened," Aelius admitted. "How do I apologize? Should I approach her again tonight?"

"Not unless you want to actually end up floating face-down in the impluvium, I fear," Catullus said. "A groveling letter is the way to go. I've written plenty. I can help you with the wording. And don't worry, there's another dinner party next week I can take you to. There is sure to be a different crop of girls in attendance."

The prospect of a different pool of candidates didn't fill him with the optimism it should have. An hour ago, he hadn't even known Crispina existed, but now, something in him was convinced she could be the solution to his problem.

Aelius could benefit Crispina as well. He eyed her, sitting silently next to her parents at the other wing of the table. They both ignored her, apart from the occasional disdainful glance from her mother. Crispina's mother regarded her with a look that Aelius was more used to seeing directed at himself when someone realized he was a freedman: scorn mixed with contempt.

A hint of sympathy welled in Aelius's chest; though he'd never known his father, he'd never had to suffer the coldness of a disinterested mother. One loving parent was better than two indifferent ones.

Yes, he and Crispina could help each other. He could offer her a marriage that would free her from the shame of her divorce and the evident unpleasantness of living with her parents, and she could get him access to the elite that he needed.

Unfortunately, he seemed to have made himself detestable to her, but hopefully Catullus's help with a groveling letter could fix that.

A sudden buoyancy filled him, as it always did when he came up with a plan. True, he still had no desire to get married, but now, he wondered if Crispina's blue-veiled figure held the key to the only future that would make him happy.

CHAPTER 3

S UNLIGHT FILTERED INTO CRISPINA's bedroom from the open door, which let in light from the atrium. Crispina leaned against the doorframe, taking advantage of the light to glance over the letter that had just come for her. Life had been markedly boring since returning to her parents' house, and while the letter wasn't exactly welcome, at least it was interesting.

Aelius Herminius to Crispina:

Please accept this humble apology for my behavior at your family's dinner party last week. I hope you will take it as a compliment if I say, with all sincerity, that you made me nervous. I regret that you mistook my ineloquent words for a joke or prank. Nothing could be further from the truth. I was heartfelt in my proposal, even if it was ill-timed and poorly delivered. You likely think I'm mad, but if you would allow me to see you once more to explain more fully, I'm certain you will understand.

Crispina read the letter twice. Her eyes lingered on *you made me nervous*. She'd never imagined a man might admit a mere woman had unsettled him. It was at odds with her impression of Aelius as brash and arrogant.

And it seemed he really did want to marry her. That was the most intriguing part. She almost wanted to hear him out just to find out why. He was handsome enough—more than handsome enough, if she was honest with herself—and he likely would have no shortage of willing brides. She allowed herself to remember how he'd looked standing in the atrium last night, lamplight flickering on his coppery skin.

So why her?

Whatever motive he had, it could be nothing good, but she still wanted to find out. Curiosity had always been her weakness. She would consider a reply later, but for now, she had more important matters to attend to.

She slid the letter into the back of a drawer in her cosmetics table, then pinned her palla to her hair and fetched her basket from its hiding place under her bed. She covered it with a cloth to hide the contents from view. Moving on light feet, she left her bedroom and crossed the atrium. If she could just make it to the front door without being noticed…

Her mother emerged from one of the rooms off the atrium. "Where are you going?"

Crispina froze and turned to face her mother. "To Horatia's," she lied. She hadn't loved her ex-husband, but marriage had brought with it a degree of freedom. She'd been accountable to no one but her husband, who rarely cared what she did or where she went. Now, after returning to her parents' house, she was caged.

Mother approached. "What's in your basket?"

Crispina suppressed a sigh. "I sewed some items for Horatia's child." Her best friend's second child was due in about a month.

"Can't you have a slave bring them?"

"I want to see her. She's too pregnant to go anywhere."

"Very well, but take the litter. I can't have you traipsing about the streets like a plebeian." She snapped her fingers. Immediately, a slave appeared. "Have the litter prepared for Crispina."

The slave rushed off. Crispina's fingers curled in frustration. There was no way she could get where she wanted to go now, not under the supervision of a squadron of litter-bearers. They might obey her, but they'd tell her mother, and then she'd be barred from leaving the house for good.

But a visit to Horatia might do her good. Crispina had barely left the house since her divorce last month, and she missed Horatia. She would only have to reckon with the jealousy that would choke her at the sight of her pregnant friend.

Crispina allowed herself to be helped into a litter, and it lurched into motion. The litter's curtains blocked her view of the streets, but she knew each house they passed belonged to a senator or magistrate or former consul. The families who ran Rome lived clustered in this neighborhood, insulated from the noise and crowds of the rest of the city by vigilant guards who shooed away any unfortunates who dared loiter near their estates.

After a short ride, she was entering Horatia's townhouse. A slave escorted her to the sunlit sitting room off the atrium where Horatia reclined on a couch.

Horatia glanced up with a smile at Crispina's entrance. "My dear! What a surprise." She started to struggle to her feet, but Crispina waved a hand.

"Don't rise on my account. You look ready to burst." Crispina took a seat in a chair opposite.

Horatia ran a loving hand over her protuberant stomach. "Only a month to go. Decius won't stop hovering." She smiled.

Crispina forced a smile. She would have given anything to have a kind, gentle man like Decius for a husband, not to mention one son already born and another child on the way.

It wasn't that she was desperate to be a mother. She enjoyed children, but they were quite loud and messy. Horatia's five-year-old son, while amiable most of the time, could screech loud enough to make the roof tiles shudder.

But it had been made clear to her that her inability to conceive a child was a failure, and Crispina did not like failing.

"And you, my friend? How have you been?" Horatia's gaze grew sympathetic.

Crispina heaved a sigh. "Trapped. Bored. I was trying to get to the Aventine Hill today, but Mother caught me." She showed Horatia her basket, which contained a stack of wax tablets and a pile of writing styluses. "The children will be wondering where I've got to these past few weeks."

"I can't believe how long you've kept that up." Horatia smoothed a hand over her stomach. "It started when we were girls, didn't it?"

Ironically, Horatia's loathsome older brother had been the catalyst for Crispina's love of teaching. He had been the sort of young man who believed women were innately less intelligent than males. As a girl of fifteen, Crispina took pleasure in proving him wrong by challenging him to things like reciting lines from Homer or listing the years in which each of Rome's seven kings ruled. Crispina invariably won all of these little contests.

Horatia's brother also believed that slaves, even those who hadn't been born into servitude, had less capacity for intellect than citizens. Thus, according to him, female slaves were the lowest of the low in terms of intelligence. Crispina, wanting to prove him wrong once and for all, challenged him to a bet of one hundred sestertii that she could teach a female slave child to read and write at same level as a citizen male child within three months.

By the time she succeeded, using the seven-year-old daughter of one of her parents' slaves as her student, she barely cared about the bet. She had discovered teaching lit a fire within her, giving her a sense of purpose and satisfaction she had never felt before. She split her winnings with the little girl, whose dedication and enthusiasm were essential to Crispina's victory, and immediately wanted to do it again.

But that was right before her marriage to Memmius, and his household hadn't contained any children. So, exploiting her new-found freedom as a married woman, she had taken her enterprise one step further. She found a group of poor plebeians on the Aventine Hill who, with some subtle bribery, allowed her to teach their children for an hour or so each week. The children lived in squalor, but Crispina was convinced that if they could attain an education, they could create a better life for themselves and their families. She'd visited them every week without fail until her divorce. Horatia had even accompanied her at the start, though she didn't fully share Crispina's enthusiasm, and her interest had faded after her first pregnancy.

"It's important to me. I have little enough else to look forward to." When Crispina had been disappointed month after month by her lack of conception, her students had been her solace, her fulfillment. Without them, her life felt useless.

"Come now, I'm sure some suitor will materialize before long," Horatia said. "There are plenty of widowers who already have heirs."

"I don't want to be some old man's third wife," Crispina muttered. But marrying again might be the only way to regain a degree of autonomy and return to her students on the Aventine. Better to be a wife with her own household than a daughter perpetually under her parents' thumbs.

Her mind went to Aelius, his proposal, and his letter. She cleared her throat. "I did have an interesting conversation at my parents' dinner party last week. There was a man in attendance. Aelius Herminius. Do you know him?"

Horatia shook her head. "Don't think so. What about him?"

Horatia knew everyone in their circle, so her unfamiliarity with Aelius was both concerning and intriguing. "He tried to propose. Of course I assumed it was a prank."

"Did you tell him off?" Horatia asked.

"I splashed him," Crispina admitted. "In the atrium pool."

Horatia covered her mouth amid a peal of laughter. "I wish I could have seen that!"

"But he sent an apology today and asked me to hear him out."

"Interesting. What's he like?"

Crispina shrugged. "I don't really know. He was there with Catullus, the poet. He's not bad-looking." An understatement, but Horatia didn't need to know that. "He's young. Younger than Memmius, at least." Aelius looked to be in his early thirties, so he was still more than a decade older than her, but her former husband had been in his forties when they wed. "There must be something wrong with him if he wants to marry me."

"Hear him out," Horatia suggested. "Marriage isn't perfect, but at least you won't be trapped in your parents' house for years on end."

"Indeed." An idea struck her. No doubt Catullus knew what Aelius was about with his marriage scheme. The poet lived close by, so she could pay him a visit on her way back from Horatia's. She wanted to gather as much information as possible before deciding whether to reply to Aelius's letter.

Light footsteps pattered into the room. Horatia's five-year-old son, Paullus, trotted in. He tried to climb up onto the couch with Horatia, but she gently spun him around toward Crispina. "Go sit with Crispina, dear. Mother is simply too big right now."

Without hesitation, the boy climbed up into Crispina's lap. She patted his head. "Hello, Paullus." He could be a terror, but when he was in a gentle mood, his sweetness never failed to tug at her heart.

A moment later, Horatia's husband, Decius, entered the room, looking frazzled. "Paullus, don't disturb your mother. She's in a very delicate state!" His gaze landed on the boy, securely nestled in Crispina's lap. "Oh, hello, Crispina."

Crispina smiled. "Hello, Decius. Congratulations on your imminent new arrival. Are you praying for another boy?"

"I wouldn't mind a girl, to be honest," Decius said. He crossed to Horatia's couch and glanced anxiously down at her. "How are you feeling, my darling? Are you hungry? Shall I call for some lunch?"

"Thank you, my dear, but I'm quite all right. Crispina is looking after us."

He bent to kiss her forehead. "All right." He nodded to Crispina. "Good day, Crispina. Give my regards to your hus—I mean, your parents." Flushing, he left the room.

Horatia's mouth twisted into a rueful smile. "Sometimes he speaks before he thinks."

"It's all right." Crispina gazed at the doorway where Decius had vanished. A surge of jealousy rose in her chest, but she was well-practiced at tamping it down.

Horatia turned the subject to the latest trend in wall paintings, and the rest of the visit passed pleasantly. Paullus fell asleep in her lap like a kitten. When it came time to leave, she gently shifted the boy onto the couch with his mother. She whispered a goodbye to Horatia, then left.

Outside, her litter carriers were waiting for her. "To home, lady?" one of them asked as he helped her into the litter.

"Not yet. Take me to the home of Gaius Valerius Catullus. I believe it's two streets south of here." They'd met often enough at parties to claim a basic acquaintance, so it was not completely improper for her to visit him unannounced. The litter bearers would no doubt tell her parents she visited the poet, but she'd keep the visit short enough to avoid scandal and could claim an interest in his poetry.

A few minutes later, she entered Catullus's home. She lingered in the atrium for a moment while one of his slaves went to fetch him.

The lanky poet emerged from a room off the atrium, presumably his study, and bowed to her. Ink stained his fingertips, and his hair was rumpled. He eyed her with curiosity. "Good afternoon, Crispina. I hope I wasn't expecting you?"

"No, I apologize for the interruption. I was in the area and thought I would drop in. I had a few questions for you."

His eyes narrowed. "Haven't come to quiz me on my Sappho, have you?"

"You're still miffed about that?"

"Only a little. But please, tell me what I can do for you today."

"It's about your friend, Aelius Herminius."

His eyebrows lifted. "I gathered the two of you did not have the smoothest introduction the other night."

"So you know he tried to propose."

Catullus nodded. "And made an ass of himself. Will you give him a second chance as he's requested?"

"You know about the apology letter too?"

"I helped write it," Catullus said, looking smug. "Did it work?"

"I would have preferred more groveling."

"He must have cut a few lines. I wrote in plenty of groveling." He waved a hand. "In any case, I'm guessing the fact you're here asking about him means you're considering it."

"I only want to find out why he wants to marry me."

Something shifted in Catullus's gaze, growing cautious, and Crispina had a feeling that whatever he was about to say wouldn't be the whole truth.

"Aelius is running for tribune of the plebs," Catullus said. "Running again, rather. He lost the last election. He's decided he needs to foster powerful connections to gain the votes he needs, and marriage is the best way to do that. Which was my idea, of course."

"So he's a plebeian." That wasn't entirely a surprise. Neither she nor Horatia had recognized his name, which indicated he wasn't part of the exclusive patrician set they'd been born into. "And a politician." He certainly had the brash confidence for it, not to mention the voice. Even when delivering an ill-timed and idiotic proposal, his voice had been smooth and rich, and she imagined it would sound quite pleasant booming over a crowd in the Forum.

She had never considered marrying outside her class, but even a plebeian husband could give her the freedom she longed for.

Catullus nodded slowly. Again, he seemed to be thinking something he wouldn't say out loud.

Crispina pressed further. "But the tribune position is reserved for plebeians, so presumably none of them are well-connected among the patricians. Why is he different from any other plebeian candidate?"

Catullus opened his mouth, considered for a moment, then closed it.

"There's something you're not telling me."

"Yes, there is," he admitted. "But it's not my place to tell you, so you'll just have to agree to meet Aelius one more time if you want to get the whole story."

Crispina huffed. "Fine. I'll bother you no longer."

"One more thing," he said as she turned to leave. "I realize this must all seem very strange, but I know Aelius well. He's ambitious and determined to make a success of himself. Any woman would be lucky to have him as her husband."

She didn't entirely trust the poet, but his words rang with sincerity. "I appreciate the endorsement," Crispina said, then bid him goodbye and left.

Perhaps it was just the stifling boredom of life after a humiliating divorce, but Aelius Herminius, plebeian politician who made impulsive proposals of marriage and had a mysterious secret, was becoming very intriguing indeed.

CHAPTER 4

ELIUS GLANCED OVER THE wax tablet Crispina had sent in reply to his letter. The tablet itself was not a promising sign; she didn't want to waste her papyrus on him. And she'd made him wait two days, but at least he had a response.

Crispina to Aelius Herminius:

Thank you for your apology. I would have appreciated more groveling. If you would like to grovel in person, you can find me at the Salonius house next Thursday night. I trust your poet friend can get you in.

A curt reply, but altogether not as bad as he'd hoped. She was willing to see him again, which was encouraging. He dashed off a quick note to Catullus to tell him about the party and ask if he could snag an invite for them both.

His plan now seemed to have a reasonable chance of success, which sent a strange flutter of optimism mixed with trepidation through him.

It's just marriage, he reassured himself as he paced in his study, thinking over what he would say to Crispina the next time he saw her. *People get married all the time. I was going to have to marry anyway. Might as well get something out of it.*

"Aelius?" His mother opened the door to his study. "Dinner is being served. You must have worked up an appetite with all that pacing."

He flushed. "I didn't realize you could hear."

"Is something bothering you? I hope you're not still distressed about the election. You did everything you could."

"It's not about the election—well, it is, but not the last one. The next one." He took a deep breath. Now was as good a time as any to tell her what he was planning. "There's something I wanted to discuss with you, Mama. Er, to tell you."

She clasped her hands together. "Should I be worried?"

"No. At least, I hope not." He shifted from foot to foot, trying to feel more like a grown man and less like a boy confessing to stealing figs from their master's kitchen. "I plan to marry."

"Oh!" She flung her arms around him and pulled him into a crushing hug. For such a slight woman, her hugs always seemed strong enough to crack a marble column.

She pulled back and kissed him on the forehead. "Who is the bride? Is she from a good family? Why haven't I met her yet?"

"Well, it's because she hasn't agreed," Aelius said. "I know you want me to settle down and take a wife, but this isn't quite what you think."

Gaia frowned. "I hope you haven't gotten some poor girl in trouble. Haven't I warned you, it's all well and good to have your fun, but the worst thing you could do is to—"

"No!" He waved a hand to cut her off. She had always been frank with him about the realities of life for women, which made him approach his infrequent encounters with reasonably priced courtesans with caution and respect. But that had nothing to do with his current situation. "It's about the election. Marrying is the easiest way to forge the alliances I need. Catullus has introduced me to a senator's daughter who might be open to a match."

Her frown deepened. "Patricians do not marry freedmen."

"Not usually, but this one might." He explained briefly about Crispina's divorce. "She doesn't know about my…well, upbringing, but I will tell her soon."

Gaia did not look reassured. "Even if this girl does agree to marry you, do you really think it wise to base a marriage on nothing but political gain? And she can't even give you children. You must continue our line."

Crispina's infertility did complicate his plan, but a solution rose quickly to his mind. "We'll be married for a fixed term, perhaps through the election and six months into my term as a tribune, if I win. Then, we'll quietly divorce, and I'll marry someone else who can give you as many grandchildren as you desire."

Gaia met his gaze. "I know you feel this is what you have to do, and I won't stand in your way, but I don't like this side of you, Aelius. What of the young woman you plan to cast aside?"

His mother's misgivings sent a stab of uncertainty through him, but he pushed it aside. This marriage scheme was his best chance at gaining enough votes to win the tribune election, which in turn was essential to winning a consulship in the future. And gaining political influence was the only way to enact true change.

"If she consents, I will make the parameters of our relationship perfectly clear to Crispina," Aelius said. "She'll be under no illusions. It is a mutually beneficial arrangement. Nothing more."

Gaia folded her arms across her chest. "It still seems rather mercenary, but I trust you to do what you think is right."

He kissed her on the cheek. "Thank you, Mama."

Aelius was once again grateful for Catullus's friendship, as the poet easily obtained an invitation to the dinner party Crispina had mentioned and brought Aelius along with him. Guests milled around the atrium at the beginning of the party, served by slaves bearing trays of appetizers.

Aelius scanned the crowd. He spotted Crispina's parents, but she wasn't with them.

Catullus nudged him. "There she is."

Crispina stood in the shadow of a column on the far side of the atrium. She wore a green palla this time, covering her from the top of her head to her ankles over a burgundy dress. The deep emerald color set off her glossy hair and dark eyes. She looked beautiful—despite the fact that her face was pulled tight in an angry frown. She was glaring at someone.

Aelius followed her gaze, which seemed to be directed at a cluster of four people standing a few feet away: a middle-aged man, a young woman, and a couple who seemed to be the young woman's parents. "Who are they?"

Catullus squinted at the people. "That's Memmius, Crispina's ex-husband. I believe he's courting the young lady, and those are her parents."

That explained why Crispina was glaring at the man so hotly his toga should be charred. "I see."

"It was insensitive of the host to invite them both," Catullus murmured.

"She will welcome a distraction, then." Aelius took a deep breath and crossed the atrium to approach her. Luckily they were a good distance from the pool, so he hoped to avoid another soaking.

He nodded to her. "Good evening, Crispina."

She tore her gaze away from her ex-husband and nodded to him. "Aelius."

"Are you enjoying the party?"

"No."

Her straightforwardness gave him a strange thrill of delight. Especially in the world of politics, people rarely said what they meant. "Thank you for agreeing to speak to me again. We got off to a poor start the other night. Let me apologize again, as I never meant to cause offense."

"I have been told I take offense too easily. I probably shouldn't have splashed you."

"Oh, I found it most refreshing. Saved me from paying for a trip to the baths."

His quip was rewarded with a twitch of her lips that might have been a smile. "You did succeed in piquing my curiosity," she said. "I have always been too curious for my own good. Tell me why you proposed."

Given her frankness, he didn't bother with flowery promises or words of affection, but laid out his case in clear, forthright terms. "I'm running for tribune of the plebs in the next election. I need to win this election if I want to stand for the consulship in ten years."

Her eyebrows lifted. "How ambitious."

"I need to spend the next decade building as much influence as I can. Your father is well-connected. If we were to marry, I imagine he would want his son-in-law to be successful, and I'd be able to utilize his network to influence the votes I need."

Crispina folded her arms over her chest. An emerald bracelet flashed on her wrist. "But why marry me? You're handsome enough, surely an up-and-coming politician, even a plebeian, can find himself a better match than a barren divorcée."

Handsome enough. A flush crept over his cheeks. He knew women generally found him attractive, but hearing it from Crispina felt especially gratifying for some reason.

But her words led him to what he was most nervous to share. "There is...something else." He'd practiced this, but it was hard to look into her eyes and say the words. "I'm a...I was..."

She waited patiently for him to spit it out, her gaze never leaving his face.

"I'm a freedman," he finally said. "I was born a slave, and freed after my master's death, when I was fourteen."

Shock rippled across her face. Her gaze flicked up and down his body, as if looking for some sort of visual marker to confirm what he was saying.

He gave it to her. Gritting his teeth, he removed his armband and showed her the brand on his wrist.

She stared at it for a long moment, her face inscrutable. Finally, she spoke. "Freedmen can't run for political office."

"My mother married after we were freed, and my stepfather adopted me. Legally, I am no different from a freeborn citizen." He replaced the armband, feeling exposed and vulnerable without it.

She let out a long, slow breath. "I knew there had to be something," she muttered.

Aelius waited for her to turn away, to tell him never to speak to her again.

But she didn't. Instead, she met his gaze. "Now I understand why you want me. So tell me, why should I want to marry you?"

Relief flooded him: she was giving him a chance. He opened his mouth, and the words rose easily to his tongue. "It must be galling to be returned to your father's control when you were once mistress of your own household. So I offer you freedom." He hoped he had correctly assessed that this was what she most desired, based on Catullus's comments about her parents and his observations of their evident disdain for her.

"Marry me and you can do as you like, go where you like, conduct your life as it pleases you. And…" He glanced toward Memmius. "You won't have to face your ex-husband and his young bride alone at a party ever again."

Her gaze returned to her ex-husband, then flicked back to him. "I see. You know I cannot give you children." She spoke matter-of-factly, but a shadow lurked behind her eyes.

He nodded. "I will need an heir eventually, so I propose a temporary arrangement. Marriage through the election at least, and a few months into my term if I win. Then we may go our separate ways."

"I have no desire to be twice-divorced. Once was quite enough."

Dis, why hadn't he thought of that? His mind raced to find a solution he could offer. She wanted freedom. What could he use to negotiate?

An idea struck him. "In the event of our divorce, I'll gift you a property of your choosing, anywhere in Italy. You will have the freedom you desire, both during our marriage and after it." The inheritance from his stepfather would be enough to cover a purchase like that.

She considered. "You offer me freedom, yet you must know a woman is always beholden to her husband. I find it difficult to agree to shackle myself, even temporarily, to someone I've only spoken to twice."

He nodded. "We barely know each other. Will you allow me to call on you a few times?"

She shook her head. "My parents would not permit that. But…" She thought for a moment. "I'll be at the games next Thursday. My parents will be distracted. I'll save you a seat in our section."

His heart leaped. He was one step closer to winning her. "I look forward to it." Though gladiatorial combat was not exactly the most romantic setting, he reminded himself this was a courtship in name only, and their marriage would be the same.

CHAPTER 5

ON THURSDAY, AELIUS ENTERED the crowded stands of the arena. The noise of thousands of spectators laughing and chatting swelled up around him. This was one place, at least, he did not need Catullus for admission. All he had to do was sidestep the sellers hawking skewers of roasted meat and fried chickpea fritters, then make a small bribe to be allowed into the exclusive area on the lowest level where the patricians had their seats.

He spotted Crispina by virtue of the flame-orange palla she wore. Her family's box was large, spanning three rows of seats, and several other people occupied it in addition to her parents. They were all socializing toward the front rows of the box, sharing plates of grapes and figs, and no one noticed Aelius slip in and take the empty spot next to Crispina in the back row. "Hello," he said.

"Hello."

It was the first time he had seen her in daylight, and for a moment he couldn't look away from the way the sunlight threaded her dark hair with gold. He grasped for something to say. She wanted them to get to know each other, after all. "Do you enjoy the games?"

"Not particularly. You?"

He shrugged. "I saw enough fighting in the army." His ten years in the army had taught him discipline and allowed him his first chance to make friends, but he had not relished the violence. It had also taught him the importance of physical fitness, and he still visited the gymnasium at least twice a week to maintain his physique.

"Where did you serve?"

Progress: she was asking him questions. "Gaul and Spain, mostly."

Her eyes brightened. "I've only ever been between Rome and our summer villa at Baiae. What are the provinces like?"

Aelius began to tell her of the mountains in the north, treacherous and snow-capped even in summer, and the rolling hills of southern Gaul and Spain. The voice of the arena's announcer boomed over the stands. Aelius doubted it was audible to anyone outside these privileged front rows, but the crowds roared anyway as the two gladiators emerged and paraded around the arena.

Crispina paid the entertainment no mind, but tipped her ear closer to Aelius. He moved nearer to her on the bench until he could smell the perfumed oil she wore.

A breeze blew over them, catching the edge of her palla and blowing it back to reveal a round white shoulder and slender arm. Aelius broke off in mid-sentence. He had never found shoulders particularly erotic, but the sight of Crispina's bare skin made him itch to run his hands down her arm.

Crispina caught the edge of her palla and brought the thin fabric back into place, hiding herself from view. "You were saying?"

Aelius struggled to pick up the thread of their conversation. "Something about a river?"

"Ah, yes." He'd been relaying a humorous incident in which a disliked comrade had fallen into a freezing Alpine stream while fording.

The arena filled with the clanging and grunts of combat, but he and Crispina kept talking. He couldn't directly face her, sitting side by side as they were, so he stared down at her hands, folded neatly in her lap. She wore several rings—emerald, carnelian, even pearl—but the fourth finger on her left hand was bare. Would she wear his ring there one day?

The prospect sent a jolt of nerves through him. He ignored it, focusing instead on asking her how she'd managed to learn Aramaic. But the feeling remained, fluttery in his stomach. Crispina was everything he could want in a wife—beautiful, intelligent, and most importantly, born under a weighty name. So why did the prospect of marrying her send a strange shiver down his spine?

The shouts of the spectators rose to a fever pitch. Aelius spared a glance into the arena and saw that one gladiator was standing over the other one with his sword outstretched, prepared to finish the other one off. Crispina drew in a sharp breath. "Oh, I hate this part." As the sword drove down, she hid her face against Aelius's shoulder.

His arm came up to circle around her, as if he could build a barrier between them and the arena. His fingers brushed her back, feeling the solidity of her body beneath the delicate folds of her clothing.

She lifted her face from his shoulder and stared up at him. Their eyes met, their faces a handspan apart. The roars of the audience faded to a dull rumble in his ears, as if they were several streets away.

Someone making an early exit squeezed in front of them, jostling Aelius. He glanced away, and the moment was broken. The dead gladiator was being dragged from the arena on a hook by two slaves. "It's done," Aelius said.

Crispina straightened up. Her cheeks were flushed as she looked out over the arena. He wondered if she was the kind of woman that fainted at the sight of blood or gore. "Are you all right?" he asked.

She shot him a sharp glance. The softness in her eyes vanished, her prickly exterior back in place. "Quite."

They sat through another match in near silence. Aelius found himself hoping for a gruesome death so Crispina might hide her face against him once more, but the losing gladiator surrendered and was spared.

As the games drew to a close, Aelius recalled the reason he'd come. Had this been enough to convince Crispina to accept his offer?

He leaned close to her as the crowds cheered after the last match. "May I speak to your father?"

She kept her focus on the victors parading through the arena. She said nothing for a long moment. "You mentioned your mother," she finally said. "Does she live with you?"

"Er, yes," Aelius said, thrown by the non-sequitur.

"You promise me freedom, yet can a woman be truly free if she lives under the same roof as her mother-in-law?"

Aelius smiled. Of all the hurdles she could throw at him, his mother would be the easiest. "My mother, Gaia, is the kindest, sweetest woman in all of Rome. Come visit and I promise you'll see."

"All right." She nodded. "But the invitation will have to come from her. My parents will let me visit a respectable matron. Not a bachelor."

"Understood."

"Speaking of that, you should go before my parents notice you've been here the whole time." People were starting to make their way out of the stands around them.

"Very well. I'll have my mother invite you straightaway." Aelius slipped from the box and joined the crowds flooding out of the arena. Hope buoyed him as he walked home. He was one step closer to winning her hand in marriage. He only hoped that would be enough to win him the election in turn.

CHAPTER 6

C RISPINA STEPPED OUT OF the litter onto the street in front of Aelius's house. It was in a different part of town from her family's house. She doubted any patricians lived here, but the street seemed clean and quiet, filled with respectable homes. Humbler than what she was used to, but the distance was refreshing. Maybe she would have a chance to live her own life here.

A slave escorted her into the house. She wondered if it was awkward for a freedman to own his own slaves. She still hadn't quite wrapped her head around the fact that Aelius was a freedman. The brand on his wrist stood out vivid in her mind. She'd thought marrying a plebeian was the worst she could do, but she'd managed to find an even lower level.

But despite his ignoble origins, Aelius was well-spoken, ambitious, and sure of himself. He'd shown a trace of hesitation when telling her about his past, but hadn't apologized for it or exhibited any great diffidence. His confidence was compelling, and despite herself, she was looking forward to seeing him again. She'd enjoyed his stories about army life at the games. She'd just been reading a history of the Punic Wars; maybe she could lend it to him.

She glanced around the atrium. It was plainly furnished with flagstone floors—not a mosaic in sight—and whitewashed walls.

She walked toward a group of three marble portrait heads mounted on waist-high plinths in the corner. Every family of lineage displayed images of their ancestors in the atrium, both to honor them and brag about their far-reaching roots.

These portraits shared a large nose and heavy jaw, bearing little resemblance to Aelius. But of course: they must be his stepfather's family, of no relation to him. She found herself grateful that Aelius himself must have inherited more balanced features from his mother and whoever his father was. Had he known his father?

Footsteps sounded from the other side of the atrium, and Crispina straightened up, skimming a hand over her palla to make sure everything was in place.

It wasn't Aelius who came to greet her, but a woman who must be his mother, Gaia. Crispina drew in a breath. Despite being at least fifty, Gaia was one of the most beautiful women Crispina had ever seen. Her skin shone a warm gold, a shade darker than Aelius's, and her features were delicate and refined. She had a slim, lithe build her son had inherited. *No wonder Aelius is so handsome, with a mother like this.*

The thought made her blush, and she struggled to gather herself as Gaia approached.

"Crispina, my dear, how lovely to meet you." Gaia's smile was full of such warmth that Crispina felt as if a thick blanket had been draped around her after a day in the cold. Gaia held out an arm to beckon Crispina closer. A white-scarred brand showed on her inner wrist, a twin of the one Aelius bore.

Crispina bowed her head formally. "Thank you for inviting me to your home."

"It may be your home soon, I gather. May I show you around? Aelius is out, but he said he would join us later."

"That would be nice." She felt an unwarranted pang of disappointment that Aelius wasn't here to greet her, but reminded herself the whole point of this visit was to get to know his mother.

She followed Gaia on a tour of the house. It was certainly small, and the décor a bit old-fashioned, but it was furnished comfortably. "How long have you lived here?" Crispina asked as Gaia showed her the dining room.

"Eighteen years, if you can believe it. I first lived here with my husband when Aelius was about fourteen."

"That must have been after...er..." Crispina broke off. She'd been about to say *after you'd been freed*, but realized too late that would be tactless to bring up.

Gaia led her out of the dining room and around the other side of the atrium. "After we were freed, yes."

Crispina's face heated. As she always did when she was uncomfortable, she reverted to sharpness. She needed to test Aelius's assertion that his mother was the kindest woman in Rome. "The décor in the dining room is terribly outdated. I should like to update it. It would be improved with a fresco."

She expected Gaia to become irritated—what woman wanted to be told her taste in decorating was outdated?—but the woman merely smiled. "I would like that as well. I've never had an eye for such things."

Crispina tried again. "And the floors in the atrium. Mosaics would be more fashionable." Painting a wall was one thing, but ripping out a floor to replace with a mosaic would certainly ruffle feathers.

"A mosaic sounds very lovely," Gaia said. "You must do just as you wish with the whole house. It must feel like your home, after all. Now, come this way, dear. There is one room in particular I wanted to show you."

Crispina followed Gaia, slightly astonished by her grace and goodwill. Crispina's last mother-in-law had been so critical that Crispina couldn't even rearrange a display of vases without incurring a lecture.

Gaia led Crispina to a small room that faced the atrium, furnished as a spare bedroom. "Aelius mentioned you enjoy literature, so I thought you could turn this room into a library. Aelius already has his study, so it would be all your own."

Crispina stared at the room. A library of her very own. She let out a long, shaky breath. Her father and Memmius had both been of the opinion that education was only relevant for a woman so far as it made her an entertaining dinner companion. She learned Greek, of course, and she'd even managed to secure an Aramaic tutor for a few years during her marriage, but the detailed military histories and risqué love poetry she most enjoyed incurred nothing but disapproval.

For years, her reading had been confined to whatever scrolls she could pilfer from her father or husband's library and hide under her bed or among her clothes. To have a room of books, all her own…

"Aelius would not mind?" Though Memmius hadn't expressly forbidden her from reading, he sniped at her whenever he found her with her nose in a book, feeling she should spend her time weaving and sewing like other wives. To avoid his displeasure, she'd taken to hiding the habit.

"Of course not," Gaia said. "He will want you to be happy. He's quite taken with you, you know."

He is? "He's made it very clear his interest in me extends only as far as the influence that my father can provide."

"Yes, I'm sure that's what he thinks. But I know my son, and if you marry him, he will do what he can to make you happy. And if he doesn't, he'll have me to answer to."

"Do you support this scheme of his, then?"

They moved away from the potential library and around the other side of the atrium. Gaia was in front, so Crispina couldn't see her face. "He believes he needs political success to be happy, and he believes you are the key to that. Of course I want my son to achieve everything he wants."

"With respect, I don't think you answered my question."

Gaia paused and turned to face Crispina. She lifted her gaze to meet Crispina's. "I will be honest with you, as that is what you deserve if we're to be family. I think marrying for political gain is foolish and short-sighted, and I worry this arrangement will make both of you miserable. Even if it's temporary."

"Oh." Crispina couldn't think of anything to reply. She was used to being the one who threw people off-kilter with her forthrightness, and it was disconcerting to be on the other side of that.

"That doesn't mean I won't embrace you as my daughter-in-law if you marry Aelius," Gaia said. "My son is everything to me, and if you become his wife, I will love you as if you were my own daughter."

"Oh," Crispina said again, rendered wordless once more. She had never heard anything close to a promise of love from her former mother-in-law. Hardly even from her own mother, in fact.

"Now, there is just one more room you should see." Gaia beckoned Crispina to follow, and led her into a large bedroom. "This is Aelius's room. I expect you'll want to redecorate in here as well?" Her voice held a joking lilt.

Crispina glanced around the room. It was neat and tidy, with few personal effects visible. Her gaze landed on the big bed, and her cheeks heated. That was the bed she'd share with her husband…if she agreed to this.

But there was no reason for blushing. Aelius already knew she was barren, so they could have no reason for any sort of activities that would make her blush.

A moment later, the cause of her blushes poked his head around the half-open door. Crispina tensed, feeling as if she'd been caught somewhere she shouldn't be.

He nodded to her and kissed his mother on the cheek. "I see a tour is in progress. Are you finding the house to your satisfaction?"

"It's smaller than what I'm used to, but I imagine the reduced size makes the household easier to manage." The comment came out sounding more cutting than she intended. She winced, glancing at Gaia to see if she'd offended.

"Crispina has already suggested many improvements," Gaia said smoothly. "Our house shall be the most fashionable on the block by the time she's done." Then she moved toward the door. "Let me ask the kitchen to prepare some refreshments for us." She disappeared, leaving Crispina and Aelius alone.

Alone in a bedroom with a man she barely knew. Her mother would choke if she ever found out about this. The thought made her feel strangely brave.

"Your mother is quite lovely," she admitted.

Aelius smiled with only a trace of smugness. "I told you."

"I do have a question. I'm sure it's inappropriate."

His eyebrow quirked. "I relish inappropriate questions."

The heat returned to her cheeks. "Not like that. No, it was about the household." She hesitated. "Isn't it odd for you to own slaves?"

He leaned against the wall next to the door. "Sometimes. But it's better for them to work for me than someone else, and I've committed to freeing them after ten years of service. We keep their number to a minimum. There's Ajax, who minds the door, Malchio, Hector the cook, Cassandra who helps in the kitchen..." He rattled off a few more names.

Crispina doubted her father or Memmius knew the names of more than two or three of their slaves. "You're missing a Paris."

He looked at her blankly. "Excuse me?"

"The Trojan brother of Hector and Cassandra?"

"Ah, right. Forgive me, I don't read Greek. Well, I learned the alphabet, but I never mastered the tongue."

"You mean you've never read Homer? Or Sappho? Or..." She had never met an adult man of even the meanest social standing who didn't know Greek. Before meeting Aelius, she would have assumed anyone illiterate in Greek was ignorant and backward, but there was no way she could assign that judgment to Aelius. Maybe he wasn't the most learned man in the city, but she couldn't deny her respect for his ambition, especially considering the near insurmountable obstacle of his birth.

"None of it." He did not look as embarrassed as she thought he should. "So, now that you have been assured that my mother is not a bloodthirsty harpy, may I speak to your father?"

Crispina allowed her gaze to wander over him. Was she ready for this man to become her husband? Even marriage to an unpleasant husband could not be worse than her life now, trapped in limbo between being a maiden and a wife, an empty, lonely future stretching before her.

She drew in a steadying breath. "I have a few conditions."

"As do I."

She doubted his conditions would be the same as hers. "You go first."

"As we have discussed, you will have complete freedom to go where you wish, see whom you wish, do what you wish. I will make no demands on your time except for accompanying me to the occasional dinner party."

"No more than once a week," Crispina stipulated.

The corners of his mouth lifted. He liked this bargaining, she realized. "Thrice a week during the height of my campaign."

"Which shall be defined as the three week period between when the magistrate officially announces the election and the day the voting takes place."

Aelius nodded. "Agreed. And there is a customary banquet thrown by election winners the day after the election."

Crispina dipped her head. "Yes."

"So, as I was saying, complete freedom, with the exception that I require fidelity. I cannot be made a cuckold."

A reasonable request. She acceded with another nod. "And it will go both ways, I trust?"

His eyes skimmed over her in a way that made her wish she'd worn a few more layers of clothing. She could feel the thin linen of her dress clinging to her curves, and heat bloomed in the wake of his gaze.

"I could be satisfied with that." His voice dropped lower.

The heat moved to her face. She realized she had miscalculated with her question. She had only intended to show him that she wouldn't be held to a double standard of fidelity, but now she'd given him reason to believe they would fully enjoy the marital bed. Which Crispina had no intention of doing.

She hurried to clarify. "My condition is that there will be no need for any sort of…carnal activities." She glanced toward the bed meaningfully.

He followed her gaze, brow furrowing. "No need? But you just said we were to be faithful to each other."

She shrugged. "You know I cannot bear children, so what's the point?"

He raised an eyebrow. "I can think of several." His voice took on a huskiness that made her stomach flutter, but she stood firm.

"That is my condition." She was no innocent maiden. She knew the marriage bed held only obligation, discomfort, and disappointment. This marriage would be on her own terms as much as possible.

"You realize you're condemning us both to celibacy?" he said. "If we are to be faithful to each other, and yet also never lie with each other?"

"If matters of the flesh are so important to you, we can end this negotiation and never see each other again." She took a step toward the door, but he was blocking it, so she only succeeded in putting herself within an arm's length of him.

He crossed his arms, jaw tensing as he considered. "Is this because you think you're too good to share your body with a freedman? Because if you think so poorly of me, I will find another bride. I know what I lack, but I won't marry someone who thinks I'm scum."

"No!" The immediate denial came without thought. "That's not what I think." It pained her that he could entertain that idea even for a moment. What slights and insults he must have endured. *He deserves better.* "It's because I've been married before. I know as much as I ever want to about the marriage bed."

He met her gaze for a long moment. The defensiveness that had flared in his eyes receded, replaced with something softer. "Very well. I accept your condition on the premise that we leave room to renegotiate."

"Under what circumstances?" Perhaps he should have been a lawyer instead of a politician.

He bent down to her and put his mouth next to her ear. "When I eventually seduce you."

A hot flush spread from the place on her neck where she could feel his breath all the way down to her toes—mostly anger at his arrogance, but with an undeniable undercurrent of something deeper.

She grasped onto the anger, willed the other thing to wash away, and lifted her gaze to meet his, his face as close to hers as it had been that one long moment at the games. "You're very lucky there's no pool of water beside you this time."

A grin lit his face, and he pulled away, putting a respectable distance between them once more. "Now that that's settled, let's discuss the term of our arrangement. We must stay married at least until the election is over. Even if we make each other miserable, I can't have the scandal of a divorce when I'm trying to campaign."

Reasonable enough. The election was less than a year away. How miserable could they make each other in that amount of time? "I agree."

"And if I win, we should remain married for at least a few months after. It would draw too much attention to divorce right after winning. I propose that the maximum duration of our marriage be six months into my term as tribune."

That seemed fair to her, so she nodded. There seemed to be only one thing left. "You may speak to my father at your convenience. He's usually at home in the mornings on days when the Senate is not in session."

His face remained neutral, but she detected a light of triumph in his eyes. "I'll call on him at the earliest opportunity. Now, some refreshment?" He stood back from the door and held it open for her. She swept past him and left the bedroom.

She knew she should have been nervous upon entering into an agreement like this, but instead, a sense of calm certainty filled her. Finally, she had a future to look forward to that didn't spell endless days sitting at home, trapped in her parents' house. She could return to what truly mattered: her lessons on the Aventine. And when her marriage to Aelius inevitably ended, she'd walk away with a property all her own. Freedom was finally within her reach.

CHAPTER 7

CRISPINA PAID A VISIT to Horatia the next day to relay the recent developments with Aelius. She told Horatia about Aelius's kind mother, the small but cozy house, and the heated conversation with Aelius in which they had both laid out their conditions.

"Did he really say that?" Horatia's eyes were alight with interest. "*When* I seduce you? How deliciously pompous." She did not look as outraged as Crispina felt.

That moment had been replaying in Crispina's mind too often. Especially last night. She couldn't stop remembering the tenor of his voice, the look in his eyes as he spoke those words. "I should have slapped him. In any case, he's made certain he'll not so much as hold my hand in future."

Horatia rolled her eyes. "If he's as handsome as you say—"

"I said no such thing!"

"I can hear it in your voice. Can it hurt to allow a bit of pleasure at night? Especially with your, er…you know." She waved a hand in the direction of Crispina's womb. "Children are a blessing, of course, but they are dreadfully inconvenient." She gestured to her own swollen abdomen. "It would be nice to lie with one's husband without fear that you were risking nine months of *this*. But, then again, I suppose I can't blame you, under the circumstances."

"What do you mean?"

"Well, he's a freedman, of course. It would be like lying with a slave." Her mouth twisted.

"He's not a slave." The words came out sharper than she expected. "His stepfather adopted him, so he's a full citizen, and he's going to be consul one day, so you may want to reconsider your disdain."

"Consul." Horatia laughed. "Romans will never elect a former slave to rule over them. He may find success in the tribune election, because plebeians are rather less picky about who represents them, but I'd stake a bet now he'll never go further than that."

Crispina bit her tongue against the surge of defensiveness that came over her. Horatia was right. Aelius's dreams of a consulship were far-fetched, though his ambition was admirable. "In any case, he's promised me a property after we divorce. So it makes no difference to me whether he becomes consul in ten years or not."

Horatia leaned forward as far as her belly would allow, lowering her voice to a conspiratorial whisper. "Does he even know who his father is, I wonder?"

Crispina wished Horatia would drop the discussion of Aelius's background, but she remained polite. "It has not come up." In truth, she had wondered, especially after meeting Gaia. There was a clear resemblance between mother and son, but also several differences. Aelius's skin was lighter, his build taller, and his eyes hazel rather than amber-brown.

"What if it was his former master? Then he would be half-Roman, which isn't too bad, I suppose. Do you know who he belonged to? Is it someone we know? Wouldn't that be awkward?"

"His master is dead. It feels improper to discuss such things." Crispina tried to imbue her voice with finality. She wasn't naïve, and knew it was likely that Gaia had been obliged to lie with her master during her servitude, and it therefore followed that a child might have resulted. A child that could be Aelius. Her stomach twisted at the thought of Gaia, so sweet and kind, being degraded in such a way.

In truth, Crispina had been trying not to think about Aelius's past. It forced her to consider too closely the dozens of slaves that attended to her needs and wants every day. They did her hair, mended her clothes, cooked her meals, and cleaned her home.

How strange to think that if any of them were freed, they might turn into a charming, ambitious politician within a matter of years. Slaves were often released from servitude, yes, but freedmen were supposed to be content with occupying the murky middle ground between slaves and freeborn citizens. They were not supposed to develop ambitions of political success that could turn Rome on its head.

Aelius and his aspirations threatened everything she thought she knew about the social structures which dictated her life, which both discomforted and intrigued her.

Horatia finally took the hint and changed the subject. "Is there a date for the wedding? I doubt I'll be able to attend, but I'll make sure to send a gift."

Crispina shook her head. "Aelius still must gain my father's consent." And for that, he would need every ounce of his charm and persuasiveness.

Aelius paced in the atrium of Crispina's home, mere steps from the spot where they had first spoken. He remembered his ruse with her palla to get her to speak to him, their disastrous first conversation, the soaking that had followed. Now that he knew her better, he could look back on her displeasure with rueful incredulity at his stupidity.

He'd only met her a handful of times, but already things felt so different from that first encounter. She was still prickly and uptight, and no doubt their marriage would be fraught at times, but they were more similar than he had initially expected. They each had their struggles, things beyond their control but which society scorned them for: her infertility, his freedman status. That shared adversity created a certain kinship between them, a kinship which, hopefully, would form the foundation of a respectful marriage.

His potential wife was nowhere to be seen today. Likely she was in her room pretending not to know he was here. It was safest for them to conceal their level of acquaintance and the degree to which they'd schemed this together. Aelius would be just another man asking to marry a woman he barely knew.

A few other men had filtered in and out of the atrium on their way to visit Crispinus. These men were the reason Aelius needed Crispina; they were Crispinus's network of clients, plebeian men who promised their votes to their patron's candidate of choice in exchange for favors and influence. If Aelius could get a handful of patricians like Crispinus on his side, the tribune election would be his.

Finally, a slave emerged to conduct him into Crispinus's study. Crispinus was seated behind his desk, rifling through a pile of papers.

"Good morning, sir." Aelius sat in the chair opposite the desk without waiting to be invited to do so. Rather presumptuous, but he was no supplicant come to ask for a loan or legal aid in the courts. He would be the man's son-in-law if all went well.

Crispinus squinted at him. "Aelius Herminius, is it? Do we know each other?"

"I was at one of your recent dinner parties, sir. With Gaius Valerius Catullus."

"Ah, yes, the poet." His brow wrinkled, and Aelius wondered if he'd made a misstep by mentioning the poet. While Catullus's works were generally admired, plenty of people found them prurient and frivolous.

Aelius changed the subject and got to the point. An eminent man like Crispinus would have a morning full of appointments, and he'd appreciate brevity and efficiency. "I come to you on a matter of importance, sir. I would like your consent to marry your daughter."

Crispinus's gray eyebrows rose. "Crispina?"

Does he have another daughter? Aelius nodded. "Yes, sir. Crispina."

The man's eyes narrowed. "You must know she's barren."

"I'm aware, sir." Aelius had made a list of all possible objections or concerns that Crispinus could raise, and had practiced a rebuttal or counter-point to each. Now was the time to put his preparation to the test. "I met her at your dinner party and was quite taken with her."

Crispinus's frown deepened. "I know my daughter, and I know she goes to no effort to endear herself to anyone. I find it doubtful she has so enraptured you. I suppose I should ask if you've violated her, though it hardly matters."

"No!" Aelius said hastily. He didn't like the casual way Crispinus spoke of his daughter's possible dishonor. No wonder she was desperate to get out of this house. "I assure you, I hold Crispina in the highest regard." He leaned forward. Now was the time to lay it all out. "I intend to mount a campaign for tribune of the plebs in the next election. The support of your family name would be instrumental to my victory. And once I am victorious, it can only benefit you to have an ally in the plebeian assembly." Aelius had no intent of compromising his victory by becoming a puppet of the patricians, but that was a problem for after he won the election.

"So you are a plebeian, then." The distasteful expression returned to Crispinus's face.

"Yes, and a freedman, sir." He spoke the words as dispassionately as possible, as if he were telling Crispinus his address rather than revealing the shame of his birth.

Crispinus made a noise of disgust. "How low we have sunk, that because of one disgraced daughter we must entertain proposals from freedmen," he muttered.

Aelius pretended not to have heard the remark. "I am sure you will be happy to have Crispina installed in her own household."

"Yes, she has been a nuisance moping around the house. She drives her mother to distraction."

Aelius strove to keep his expression neutral. He could barely get through one conversation with Crispina's father without wanting to snap. With each word, he understood even more why Crispina wanted to escape so badly she'd agree to marry a man she barely knew. "Indeed. And because we will have no children to provide for, it's only natural for the dowry to be reduced. Perhaps half of what you outlaid for her first marriage." He had no idea how much Crispina's dowry to Memmius had been, but judging by her family's status, he bet it was a small fortune. The money didn't matter to him. Dowries were returned in the event of a divorce, so it wouldn't be his to keep anyway.

Interest lit in the man's eyes at the prospect of saving money. "A quarter, and you'll have the votes from all my plebeian clients."

"Agreed."

Crispinus gave a swift nod. "My scribe shall draw up the paperwork. You may consult with the augurs to determine an auspicious day for the wedding."

Triumph lit a warm fire in Aelius's chest. He'd done it. He'd secured the hand of a senator's daughter. *Crispina is going to be my wife.* The unsmiling woman who splashed him when he offended her, who hid her face against his shoulder at a gladiator's death—she was really going to be his wife.

Not forever, he reminded himself.

He still had a lot of work to do, but now he had a real shot at winning the election. "Thank you, sir. When will you inform Crispina?"

"Now is as good a time as any." He rapped an inkwell on his desk. The door to his study opened, and a slave poked his head through. Crispinus issued a brusque order to fetch Crispina.

A minute later, Crispina appeared. Her head was bare, as she was in the privacy of her own home, and her dark hair tumbled in loose waves over her shoulders. She looked lovelier than ever, unadorned with jewelry, garbed in a simple gown of light green that clung to her slender figure.

Her face remained blank as she glanced from her father to Aelius. "You asked to see me, Father?"

"I have decided that you will marry this man," Crispinus announced, gesturing at Aelius, "on a date of his choosing. You are very lucky I have made this match for you, considering your…difficulties."

Crispina bowed her head, the picture of a demure daughter. "Yes, Father. Thank you."

Aelius imagined that in any other circumstance, Crispina would have spat fire at being informed she'd been promised without her consent, but luckily this situation was of their own making. He had never imagined she could look so biddable. He vastly preferred the Crispina who doused him with water and spoke her mind.

Crispina turned to Aelius. "I shall need at least a week to prepare my bridal garments and pack my things. Please inform me of the date you choose at your earliest convenience." Her voice rang with formality.

"Of course."

Her father scoffed. "Already making demands of your bride-groom, I see." He glanced at Aelius. "I recommend a firm hand. Of course, I said the same thing to Memmius, and look how that turned out."

Crispina's eyes flashed, but she didn't lose her composure. Aelius admired her for it; his fists itched to clench tighter with every word her father spoke.

"Excuse me, Father, I must begin the preparations." Crispina nodded to them and slipped from the room.

Aelius made a hasty goodbye and left also. He hoped to catch Crispina in the atrium and steal a word or two, but she had already vanished.

The evening before the wedding, Aelius attended a small dinner party Catullus had put together to celebrate the success of their scheme. And Aelius's last night of freedom, according to Catullus as he led a toast to kick off the party. Aelius found the remark to be rather ironic, given his history, but he merely rolled his eyes at his friend. Three weeks had passed since Crispina's father gave his consent, and now only a matter of hours remained until Aelius would be wed.

The party was comprised of a handful of Catullus's friends, with whom Aelius had a passing acquaintance, as well as several fashionably dressed women whom he bet were courtesans. Aelius participated in a drinking game, in which he somehow escaped getting overly soused, but demurred joining the next round when it finished. He glanced around the room to find Catullus, who hadn't joined the game. It was getting late, and Aelius didn't want to spend his wedding day exhausted and hungover.

Catullus was seated on a couch flanked by one of the courtesans, a pretty woman with hair the color of wheat, and an even prettier young man. The poet kept glancing between them, as if he couldn't decide which he preferred.

Aelius bent down to speak to him. "I think I'd better be going."

"Going?" Catullus shot to his feet, dislodging the slender arm of his female companion. He grabbed onto Aelius's shoulder for support. "But you haven't enjoyed all the festivities yet."

"I've eaten, drank, conversed, and gamed," Aelius said. "It's been a wonderful evening, and I thank you for it. But I need to be rested and alert for tomorrow."

"I meant *festivities*." Catullus cast a significant glance down at the man and woman on his couch, then gestured to a woman across the room. "See that lady over there? I invited her especially for you. Thought she looked like your bride."

The woman had fair skin and dark hair, but that was where the resemblance ceased. She had none of Crispina's straight-backed poise, but was relaxing on a couch, laughing with abandon at something one of the other guests had said.

Aelius shook his head. "Thank you, but I'm not interested." It felt wrong to consort with another woman the night before his wedding.

Catullus's eyebrows lifted. "Have you forgotten you're about to enter a marriage with a wife who won't let you touch her?"

"I haven't."

"And let me ask you for the thousandth time *why* you agreed to that."

"I don't know," Aelius admitted. "It seemed…fair." He recalled the conversation in which he and Crispina had negotiated the conditions of their marriage. His mind had become a rushing whirlpool as soon as they'd started talking about sex, even in veiled terms. The fact that they were in his bedroom, steps from his bed, hadn't helped matters. And then he'd made that ridiculous, thoughtless remark about seducing her…He couldn't believe he'd escaped without a slap.

Worse, the remark made him realize how much he *wanted* to seduce her. Not to claim her or possess her, but to show her enough pleasure to melt her icy façade. What would she look like, flushed and mindless with lust?

"Well," Catullus said. "At least she's no great beauty."

Aelius blinked. "No great beauty?" He had found Crispina stunning from the first moment he saw her.

Catullus shrugged. "I mean, I wouldn't turn her down—that would be rude—but she seems so cold and stiff. I imagine it would be like bedding a corpse."

"A corpse? Are you insane? Crispina is…is…" He struggled for words. "Quite beautiful."

"I prefer women who smile."

The revelation that not every man found Crispina beautiful was shocking. Though Catullus had a point: Aelius had never yet seen Crispina smile or laugh. "I appreciate her dignity. She carries herself like a goddess."

"One of the meaner ones, perhaps."

Aelius rolled his eyes. He glanced back at the couch Catullus had left. The woman and young man were in each other's arms, kissing. "I think your friends are getting started without you."

Catullus followed his gaze and swore. "All right, off with you. I'll see you tomorrow." He clasped Aelius's hand, then returned to his couch, pushing his way between the two. They made room easily.

Aelius left the party with no regrets about the pleasures he was leaving behind. Yes, he was turning his back on such pursuits by marrying Crispina. But he stood to gain much, much more from their temporary marriage: victory in the next election, the tribuneship, a shot at the consulship one day. Respect, influence, and the power to enact change. A chaste marriage, even to someone as alluring as Crispina, would be an easy sacrifice.

CHAPTER 8

The gold ring laid heavy on Crispina's finger as she sat at her wedding feast. The party was small. Her parents must have been too embarrassed at her marrying a freedman to invite many people, and Aelius's social circle was not large. Beside her, Aelius conversed with Catullus on his other side. Gaia sat next to Crispina's mother, and her father was chatting with Decius. Horatia was too pregnant to attend, as she expected to give birth any day now.

The ceremony had happened at her parents' house earlier that day. Then, they had journeyed in a procession to Aelius's home, where the feast had been prepared. She and Aelius spoke only a handful of words to each other throughout the day. It had been like that at her first wedding, too. She'd hardly spoken to Memmius until they were alone in their bedroom for the first time. She had spent her whole wedding day consumed with excitement and nerves, certain she was entering a union that would last until death.

This marriage would not even outlast the three years she'd spent with Memmius, but at least she'd have a measure of freedom at the end of it. Aelius had promised her a property, and she'd never return to her parents' house in disgrace again.

Gaia, smiling, leaned over to say something to Crispina's mother. The other woman ignored her, pivoting her body away and feigning absorption in her husband's conversation on her other side. Gaia's smile faded.

A sudden swell of rage tightened Crispina's throat. How dare her mother snub Gaia, especially as a guest under Gaia's roof? Crispina rose and came around the table. She lowered herself onto the couch where Gaia sat and shot a withering look at her mother, who ignored her.

"Thank you so much for organizing this feast," Crispina said. "It's lovely. The food is delicious. You have a very talented cook."

Gaia's smile returned. "I was very pleased to do it. And yes, Hector outdid himself in the kitchen. You look so beautiful today, by the way."

Crispina's cheeks flushed. "Thank you." Her own mother had only criticized the wrinkles in her white gown and orange veil. She wore the same clothing from her first wedding, and the woolen garments had spent several years in the bottom of a chest.

"Have you given any more thought to the improvements you suggested to the house?" Gaia asked. "Perhaps you know some artisans to engage?"

"I fear I was rather pushy about that the other day. Really, the house is fine just as it is. It's your house, and I don't need to make a disturbance."

Gaia laid her hand on top of Crispina's. "It's *our* house. You must do as you like. Aelius will only have to approve the expenditures."

At the mention of her new husband's name, Crispina glanced at him to find he was no longer conversing with Catullus but gazing at her. He quickly looked away.

Crispina turned back to Gaia, who offered her a fresh serving of duck from the platter in front of them. They continued chatting, and Crispina made a point to lavish attention on her new mother-in-law in front of her own snobbish mother. It wasn't hard to talk to someone as warm and forthcoming as Gaia, and a flicker of optimism flared. As a wife, Crispina would likely spend more time with Gaia than with Aelius, so it was promising that they could enjoy each other's company.

As the feast wound down, slaves passed out small bowls of nuts. Crispina shifted uncomfortably. That meant it was near time to retire with her husband. She knew nothing would happen tonight per their agreement, but it was still awkward to go to bed with a man she barely knew. A man she had only married for self-serving reasons. A man she had no intention of forging any attachment with, no matter his charms.

A shadow fell over her, and she looked up to see Aelius, standing behind her couch.

"Are you ready to retire?" he asked.

She nodded. Best to get this over with. He extended a hand, and she allowed him to help her to her feet. Amidst a hail of nuts thrown by the guests and an array of shouted good wishes, they left the dining room.

Shouting and laughter echoed after them from the dining room. Aelius dropped his wife's hand as soon as they were out of view. They made their way in silence to his bedroom. *Our bedroom now.*

Aelius closed the door behind them. He cleared his throat. "Thank you for being so attentive to my mother." Crispina's parents' behavior had enraged him, though he'd pretended not to notice. No matter how hard he and his mother worked to raise themselves from their pasts, they would never be good enough for some people. But if he became consul one day, this behavior would cease. No one would dare snub a consul's mother.

At least Crispina had shown favor to Aelius's mother in front of everyone. A small gesture, but powerful. It had warmed his heart.

"I should have known my parents would be horrible to her." Crispina unpinned her red-orange veil and pulled the crown of flowers from her head. She kicked off her leather slippers and stretched her toes with a sigh, which made him smile. The wedding finery didn't suit her. The colors were too garish; her beauty required only subtle adornment to shine.

Aelius disentangled himself from his toga and laid it over the back of a chair, still wearing the tunic beneath. "How does it feel, being married a second time?" he asked. "Any different? I'm only a first-timer, after all."

Crispina fiddled to untie the complicated knot in the embroidered sash around her waist. A rueful look passed over her face. "I was naïve before. This time, I know exactly what we are to each other." She tugged at the sash, digging her fingers into the knot with a grimace.

"Do you need help?"

She sighed and released the belt. "Perhaps. You can cut it off me if all else fails."

Aelius approached. A bride's belt was traditionally tied in a complicated knot that only the husband was supposed to undo, meant as a precursor to consummation. But none of that would be happening tonight.

He had to stand very near to her to take hold of the knot. With his head bent, his face was so close to hers his nose would brush her cheek if she turned. The problem of the knot flew from his mind, replaced by the smooth ivory skin of her neck, the curve of her shoulder, the delicate valley of her collarbone. At this angle, he could see the shadow between her breasts, extending temptingly beneath the neckline of her dress. His mouth went dry.

Focus. He forced himself back to the task at hand and fumbled with the belt. *You're making that blasted knot worse, idiot.*

He took a deep breath to steady himself and dropped to his knees, hoping the change in position would help him focus. But that only put his head level with the swell of her breast.

For a moment, he wished he'd taken advantage of Catullus's offer at the party. Perhaps he wouldn't be so overcome if he'd lain with a woman last night. But somehow, he knew: he didn't just want a woman. He wanted *Crispina.* And she had been painfully clear that what she wanted from this marriage did not extend to his body.

"Just cut it off," Crispina grumbled. "I'm tired."

"That's bad luck." With effort, Aelius shut out his awareness of her body and focused only on the knot. He managed to loosen it in the right places, and with a few strategic pulls, it came undone.

"Thank you." Freed, Crispina walked over to a trunk of her belongings which had been delivered earlier. She rifled through it, pulling out a light linen tunic.

Aelius went to the basin and splashed water on his face, hoping to extinguish his lustful imaginings, then got into bed. He usually slept naked, but he didn't think Crispina would appreciate that tonight, so he left his tunic on.

He eyed her as she unfolded the tunic from her trunk. He wanted to remain respectful, but he also *definitely* wanted a glimpse of her bare body as she changed.

Crispina must have sensed the dishonorable direction of his thoughts, for she issued a sharp "Close your eyes," as she shook out the tunic.

He shot her a brief glower, but obeyed. The rustling of fabric followed. He squeezed his eyes shut tighter. His wife was naked, in the same room, and he wasn't even allowed to look at her.

"You can open them." Crispina, now clothed in the plain tunic, sat at the dressing table and began to unbraid her hair. Aelius couldn't look away, and luckily she didn't command him to this time. It had seemed a crime for her lush, glossy hair to be confined in the six tight braids that all brides wore. Her fingers moved quickly, slipping between the segments to unweave the braids. Her hair had caught his attention from his first brief glimpse of it at the dinner party beneath her modest palla. Now, he watched as the braids unraveled into an abundance of dark curls falling halfway down her back, a mesmerizing sight. He could have watched her all day.

Finally, she left the dressing table and climbed into bed next to him. She pulled the covers up to her chin and rolled over, facing away from him. "Blow out the lamp."

He reached for the lamp on the bedside table and extinguished it. Darkness engulfed the room. He stretched out in bed, and waited for sleep to come. The sound of her breathing, light and rhythmic, filled his ears.

Somehow, he was married. To a senator's daughter, no less. That was the part he was supposed to care about, the part that should win him the election. But at this moment, lying in bed with her after their wedding, it wasn't the senator's daughter who occupied his thoughts. Instead, it was the erudite, prickly, beautiful woman with glossy hair and an elusive, possibly mythical, smile. Somehow, that woman had just become his wife.

CHAPTER 9

IN THE DAYS AFTER the wedding, Crispina spent most of her time with Gaia. Aelius was rarely at home, so they only saw each other in the evenings. Crispina set up a little library in one of the spare bedrooms. She commissioned a carpenter to install shelves and purchased more scrolls to fill them with, everything from a treatise on new architecture styles to a history of Alexander's foray into India. She'd even managed to find some writings from Judaea, though her Aramaic was rusty. Gaia made no complaint when Crispina spent the whole day sequestered in her library reading.

Crispina aimed to resume her visits to her students on the Aventine as quickly as possible, but didn't want to push her luck too soon. She waited a week, then tried to feel out how accommodating Gaia would be of any ventures outside the house. "I plan to visit my friend Horatia tomorrow," she said one day at lunch.

Gaia glanced up from her food. "How nice. Was she at the wedding?"

Crispina shook her head. "Her husband was, but she was close to giving birth. Her husband sent a message yesterday to say the child had come." That much, at least, was true, and Crispina did plan to pay a visit to Horatia. She and Decius had been blessed with another healthy son.

"Well, I'm sure she'll appreciate your visit."

"She lives quite close, so I plan to walk there." Crispina watched Gaia's face, curious if she would insist she take an escort.

Gaia shrugged. "Exercise is most beneficial, as long as the weather is nice."

Crispina's heart leaped. *Freedom, at last.*

She spent the rest of the day preparing the items she would need to take to her pupils: a basket of wax tablets and styluses for writing, a few basic scrolls for the children to practice reading, some food for the children and their families, and her disguise, the garb of a priestess. Or at least garb that looked enough like a priestess no one would bother her. There were so many tiny cults in the city, each with its own ministry, that it was easy enough to impersonate a nondescript priestess without raising anyone's suspicions.

The next morning, she gathered up her basket and left the house. No one stopped her or insisted she take an escort. A broad smile spread across her face as she emerged into the sunlit street. She took a deep breath, savoring her freedom—only to regret it as the stench of horse droppings hit her nose.

Crispina headed down the street and ducked into an alley a few houses over. There, she retrieved a long, shapeless gown of undyed linen from her basket and pulled it over her head. It fell to her ankles, covering her dress beneath. She twisted off her wedding ring and hung it on a cord around her neck, tucked out of sight beneath the gown. Then, she removed her green palla and replaced it with a long veil of the same undyed linen fabric as the tunic. She pinned and tucked it in a way that covered all of her hair, and pulled it around her face and shoulders like a cloak. Priestesses were notoriously modest, so the more fabric covering her, the better.

Once disguised, she resumed walking, head bowed in an affectation of religious humility. Aelius lived in a different neighborhood than her parents or Memmius, so she had less distance to travel to the block on the Aventine where she conducted her lessons. Would the children even remember her? Would they blame her for her months-long absence?

The buildings changed as she crossed into the neighborhood where her students lived, becoming darker, dirtier, some with smoke-damaged walls and terraces precariously supported on decaying beams. She passed the blackened hull of a burned-out apartment building. Fire was all too common in these crowded areas. The smell of dung and rotting fish wafted over her. The Aventine bordered the river, where all sorts of refuse was dumped, and the stench was always stifling.

She ducked into the courtyard of the apartment building where she usually taught. Her gaze flicked around. It was just as she remembered: dingy and in disrepair. A lone slave swept leaves from one corner of the courtyard with listless strokes of a broom.

A movement beneath a rickety-looking table caught her attention. She squinted into the shadows, and then smiled as a boy of eight with dirt-smudged cheeks crawled out. "Hello, Silus."

He chewed on his fingernail, surveying her with an appraising gaze. "Did you bring anything to eat?"

She proffered her basket, piled high with figs, sweet cakes, and rounds of cheese, the best Gaia's kitchen could spare. "I always do, don't I?"

His eyes lit up. "She's back!" he shouted.

A moment later, five more children materialized from doors, behind stacks of barrels, and hurtled down the stairs that led to the second level of the apartment complex. "Careful!" Crispina warned as one tall boy vaulted down the last few stairs and skidded to a halt in front of her.

Twelve grasping hands extended toward her. Crispina dutifully handed out the goods in her basket. "Remember, save some to share with your families."

The tall boy, Sextus, shoved a little girl aside to push to the front of the crowd and tried to reach into her basket to grab a handful of figs. Crispina jerked the basket out of his way and fixed him with a sharp look. "Apologize to your sister."

It had taken a while to master the withering glare and icy tone necessary to discipline these children, but she hadn't lost her touch. Sextus quailed and mumbled an apology to his little sister.

"Junia, do you accept his apology?" Crispina asked the girl.

She glared at her brother and tipped her chin up, as if debating withholding acceptance, but nodded. Crispina gave them each a handful of figs.

Crispina glanced over the children. She usually had seven regulars. Some other children would filter in and out each week. "Silus, where is your sister?" At fourteen, Silus's sister Marcia was one of the older members of their little school.

"Married," Silus said through a mouthful of cheese.

Crispina winced. "I see." She had been hoping to have more time. Marcia had only just memorized the alphabet and begun to read simple words. Crispina knew that unlike the boys, a girl's future only extended to being a wife and mother, but she had hoped if Marcia received a solid education, she could in turn teach her own children. "Well, please give her my best wishes the next time you see her."

"Won't see her," Silus said, stuffing another piece of cheese into his mouth. "Went to live in Ostia."

"I see," Crispina murmured again. Marriage on its own was trying enough for a young woman, and to leave behind everything one knew for a new city with a strange husband must be devastating. If Marcia had been better schooled in reading and writing, she could have sent letters to her family. But now, she would be almost completely isolated. Crispina hoped Marcia would find happiness with her new husband, but this development only further strengthened her belief in this mission.

Crispina set aside her worries about Marcia and focused on her current pupils. She passed out the wax tablets and styluses and quizzed the children on their letters. Most of them had forgotten much of what they'd learned in Crispina's absence, which galled her. Sextus confused P and D, and Junia kept writing her M's with an extra peak. Hopefully, marriage to Aelius would allow Crispina to resume a more regular schedule.

When the children started to lose focus, Crispina allowed them to draw whatever they wished on their tablets, and when that exercise had run its course, she packed everything up, distributed the remaining food, and bid them goodbye with a promise to be back next week.

She walked to Horatia's house with a bounce in her step. She always felt rejuvenated after one of her lessons. It coupled the thrill of doing something wrong and slightly dangerous with the certainty she was improving the lives of these children. They had been born into poverty, but if they learned reading, writing, and basic math, they could achieve a future that contained more than manual labor. Maybe one day, one of her pupils could even run for political office like Aelius. They already had a leg up, as they'd been born free.

In an alley near Horatia's house, she paused to strip off her priestess garb and put her wedding ring back on. Horatia knew of her exploits, but Decius didn't, and she didn't want to cause any gossip that might get back to Aelius. For all his talk of offering her freedom, there was no way he'd look past his wife holding lessons in a slum. Her Aventine venture had to remain a secret, as it always had been.

Once restored to her normal appearance, she knocked on Horatia's door. A slave let her in and escorted her to the atrium, where Horatia reclined on a couch in the sunlight, a tiny baby asleep in her arms.

Horatia shot her a glowing smile and held a finger to her lips. "He's just fallen asleep."

Crispina sat on the couch next to her and peered at the baby's face. The sight of the newborn stirred a tense feeling of jealousy inside her—not of the child himself, but that Horatia was so easily able to do what Crispina couldn't. She pushed the feeling aside, determined to be happy for her friend. "He's very precious. Do you have a name picked out?"

Horatia nodded. "But of course I can't tell you until the ceremony in a few days." Newborn boys were officially named on the ninth day after their birth. "Do you want to hold him?"

"No, thank you. I won't risk disturbing him." Being around Horatia's older son, especially in infancy, had made her question if she actually wanted a child or just wanted to prove that she could have one. The constant shrieking and squalling set her teeth on edge, and she had never found babies to be as adorable as their mothers seemed to. Even now, gazing at the infant clasped in Horatia's arms, she felt no urge to hold one of her own.

"Now tell me everything," Horatia said. "How is married life?"

Crispina shrugged. "Pleasant enough so far. I was able to go visit the children today. I just came from there, in fact. Marcia got married and went to live in Ostia."

Horatia frowned. At first, Crispina thought she was frowning at Marcia's fate until her next words. "Are you sure it's wise to keep up with that?"

"This was the whole reason I married Aelius in the first place," Crispina said. "I wanted freedom to resume my lessons. Which used to be *our* lessons." Until Horatia had gotten pregnant for the first time, teaching the children had been their joint secret. But once Horatia became a mother, her passion had faded.

"I suppose it would be different if you had children of your own to look after. What if Aelius finds out? A politician's wife can't be grubbing about in a slum. It could embarrass him."

"I don't intend for him to find out." Irritation sharpened her voice. It was true, Crispina had more time on her hands without children to look after, but even if she was blessed with a child, she would never abandon her students.

"He might divorce you if he does find out."

"We agreed not to separate until after the election at the earliest. A divorce for any reason would draw too much attention."

"How romantic," Horatia muttered.

"This marriage is not about romance," Crispina snapped. "Not all of us have the luxury of a fawning husband who grants every whim."

Horatia narrowed her eyes. "I suppose I can't blame you for being jealous."

Crispina bit her lip on another sharp remark. She didn't want to quarrel with her best friend, especially not days after Horatia had given birth. Her problems weren't Horatia's fault, so she forced a neutral expression and changed the subject to ask about the arrangements for the baby's naming ceremony.

CHAPTER 10

T HAT EVENING, CRISPINA SAT and brushed out her hair at the dressing table in their bedroom. At home, a slave would do this for her, but she'd been trying to minimize her requests to Aelius's slaves since her marriage, and she hadn't brought any from her parents' house. Had Gaia once brushed out her mistress's hair?

The thought made her uncomfortable, but before she could dwell on it, Aelius entered. He hadn't been home for dinner, so Crispina guessed he'd been with Catullus or another friend.

He sat and unlaced his sandals. "Good evening. How was your day?"

He always insisted on making conversation during their evenings in the bedroom together. Crispina wanted to tell him not to bother with the effort, but it did make the nights less awkward. "Fine," she said. "I visited Horatia and her new baby."

"Boy or girl?"

"Boy."

He kicked his sandals off. "Do you find it uncomfortable to be around babies?"

Her hand stilled, the brush pausing halfway through her length of hair. The directness of the question surprised her. She thought they had a tacit agreement not to discuss anything so…fraught.

She resumed brushing. She could ignore the question. But as she considered it, the weight of her feelings pressed heavy on her chest. Usually Horatia was the one she confided things she couldn't tell anyone else. But she couldn't talk to Horatia about this.

"I don't know," she murmured. "I felt jealous, certainly, that she can do something I can't. The same way I imagine you felt jealous of those who won the election that you lost."

His face contracted in a momentary expression that almost looked like pain. *Interesting.* His former loss pained him. She expected any man would be galled or embarrassed at a public defeat, but Aelius seemed to feel it more deeply. Which explained why he was willing to go to such great lengths to avoid another loss.

"But I'm not certain I would actually enjoy having children," she continued. "They are loud, dirty, and demanding." Even her students exhausted her as much as she enjoyed them. "Maybe it's not just a physical ability I lack. The deficiency seems to extend to my nature as well. I just wasn't meant to be a mother."

"Perhaps it's your mind's way of reckoning with whatever has prevented you from conceiving," Aelius said quietly. "I wonder, if you were presented with a child somehow, you might feel differently."

"Well, I won't be, so it doesn't signify." She set her brush down, eager to change the subject. "How was your day?"

He rose and went to the basin to splash water on his face. "Catullus is helping me to ferret out the names of men who might be running in the tribune election. It's many months off, but the sooner I figure out who my opponents are, the sooner I can determine their weaknesses and how to defeat them."

"Such ruthlessness." She tried to imbue her voice with a dry apathy, but something in his drive for success appealed to her. Her father had inherited his membership in the senatorial class, and Memmius had been born into enough money and privilege he'd never had to strive for anything. "Am I to have another Sulla on my hands?"

A grin lightened his face. "Perhaps Sulla just needed a wife to keep him in line. I bet a woman with a good head on her shoulders could have kept him from marching on Rome."

"Well, he had four, so they evidently didn't do a good job." The famous dictator had even divorced his third wife for infertility. At least Crispina knew she was not the only woman to be humiliated like that.

"Four wives?" Aelius let out a long breath. "I've got some catching up to do."

Crispina rolled her eyes and got into bed. Aelius blew out the lamps and joined her a moment later, keeping carefully to his side of the bed. He had a peculiar way of plumping his pillow that had at first irked her, but now, after a week of marriage, the sequence of *thump-thumps* were becoming more familiar than annoying. She could almost predict their rhythm, like anticipating the next verse of a song.

Don't get too comfortable. This marriage would end, and she'd have to get used to sleeping alone once more.

Crispina woke in darkness with a growling stomach. She sighed, willing herself to go back to sleep, but her stomach wouldn't stop whining. At this rate, she'd wake Aelius.

She gritted her teeth and swung her legs out of the cozy bed, wincing as her feet landed on the chill stone floor. She eased the door open and tiptoed out of the room. One good thing about this house being so small was that she had less distance to travel to the kitchen.

She passed through the narrow hallway that opened onto the peristyle, the small private garden at the back of the house. At this hour, it was lit only by moonlight. As she crossed through the garden, a noise made her stop short. At first she thought it was just a slave snoring, as the slaves slept wherever they could find space to lay a blanket, but it was an irregular sniffling noise, not the rhythmic sound of snoring.

A tiny sob sounded, coming from the corner of the garden. Crispina debated pretending not to have heard it. She was not skilled at comforting people, and certainly had no experience comforting slaves.

But Aelius treated his people well, and she sensed he would want to know if one of them was unhappy.

Crispina cleared her throat. "I can hear you." Her voice echoed in the darkness.

There was a rustling, shuffling sound, and a shadowy figure uncurled itself from behind a bush. Crispina recognized Cassandra, the brown-haired young woman who helped in the kitchen.

Cassandra twisted her hands before her. "F-forgive me, mistress." Tears shone on her cheeks in the dim moonlight. "I didn't mean to disturb you."

Crispina stepped nearer to her, keeping her voice low so as not to wake anyone else. "You're upset. Tell me why."

Cassandra shook her head. "It's nothing, mistress. Please, may I fetch you anything?"

"I rose to get a bite to eat, but now I wish to know why you were crying." Her words sounded much too peremptory. If she really did want to help Cassandra, ordering her to spill her secrets was not going to get her very far. She strove to soften her tone, speaking as she would to a pupil she wanted to encourage. "My husband would want to know if there was anything wrong."

"The master is a kind man," Cassandra murmured. "There's no need to burden him with my troubles."

Cassandra's hand went to her stomach in an unconscious, momentary caress. Crispina nearly missed the gesture, but her eyes caught the movement of Cassandra's pale hand in the darkness. She drew in a breath, putting together the pieces. She had seen that gesture dozens of times from Horatia during both of her pregnancies. Between that and Cassandra's tears ...

"You're with child," Crispina said.

Cassandra flinched and took a quick step back, nearly stumbling into the bush. "Yes, mistress." Her voice trembled.

"Why not say so? A child is a happy thing." Crispina forced a smile. First Horatia, now her husband's slave. As if she needed another reminder she was a failure.

Cassandra swallowed hard. "Forgive me, mistress. I was afraid. I-I know of your...struggles."

The crying was starting to make sense. "You thought I would be angry?"

Cassandra nodded jerkily. "I feared you would s-sell me. Once I got too big to hide it."

"You know Aelius would never permit that." Her words came out too coolly. She took a breath and tried to sound kinder. "Would you tell me who the father is so we may congratulate him?"

A pained look came into Cassandra's eyes. "I…"

Crispina thought through the male slaves in the household. Cassandra seemed to be on friendly terms with everyone, but Crispina had no idea who she might have a special fondness for. "Is it Malchio? Ajax?"

Cassandra shook her head.

"Hector?"

"No, mistress." Cassandra bit her lip.

Crispina hadn't yet learned the names of all the slaves, so she had no more options to put forth. "Won't you tell me? It must be someone in the household."

Cassandra remained tight-lipped and silent. A horrible possibility hit Crispina, and a heavy stone of dread settled in her stomach. Her throat tightened, but she managed to get the words out. "Is it Aelius?"

He had promised fidelity to her, yes, but Cassandra must be months along. It could have happened before the wedding, before they'd even met.

A shocked noise burst from Cassandra. "No, mistress! The master would never…and I would never…it's not him, mistress."

The vehemence of her denial assuaged Crispina's anxiety, and she let out a relieved breath. "I see." Aelius did not seem like someone who would force his attentions on one of his slaves, and she was comforted she hadn't been completely wrong about him.

"It's someone from another household, mistress," Cassandra confessed. More tears sprang to her eyes. "I-I fear..." Her words broke off in a sob.

"Has this man mistreated you?" Crispina asked. Because slaves were considered property, Aelius would be entitled to demand financial satisfaction from anyone who had harmed one of his people.

Cassandra shook her head. "I love him." Her face crumpled, and she pressed a hand over her mouth to muffle another sob.

"And you're sad because you're parted from him?"

Cassandra wiped her eyes and took a deep, shaky breath. "I learned today that his master, Epidius Verus, means to s-sell him. He's young and strong, and I'm afraid he'll get sold off to a mine and I'll never see him again." She bowed her head, wrapping her arms around herself as if to hold in all her grief.

Crispina eyed her uncertainly. Surely she should offer some comfort, but the thought sent a prickle of unease over her skin. Consoling someone felt like attempting to speak a language she hadn't studied. Times like these made her grateful, in a twisted way, that she wasn't a mother. She would certainly fail at providing the sort of solace and warmth a child required.

But maybe instead of comfort, she could help solve Cassandra's problem. "Why is he to be sold? Has he displeased his master in some way?" People did not sell their hardworking slaves for no reason.

"He wouldn't tell me," Cassandra said. "Said it was better for me not to know. But as far as I know, he's never done anything to displease. He doesn't deserve this, mistress."

"It does seem like an injustice," Crispina said. She'd been brought up to regard slaves as invisible, interchangeable, but meeting Aelius and Gaia had changed her view. The thought of Aelius's father reappeared in her mind. What if Gaia had once been as grief-stricken and helpless as Cassandra now looked? Would anyone have come to her aid?

"Do you know when this sale is to happen?" Crispina asked.

"Tomorrow, mistress," Cassandra said, her voice breaking. "I said my goodbyes today. I told him I'd name the child after him if it's a boy. Taurus."

"If it's to happen tomorrow, then we must act quickly." Crispina beckoned Cassandra to follow her. "Come, let's consult with Aelius."

"But it's the middle of the night, mistress! He's asleep!"

Crispina shrugged. "Then we'll just have to wake him." In truth, she wasn't sure if Aelius would be irked to be awoken in the dead of night to advise on how best to reunite his slave with her lover, but Crispina could weather his annoyance.

She strode back to her bedroom, Cassandra trailing behind her. Upon entering the darkened room, she asked Cassandra to light a lamp and went to Aelius's side of the bed. Crispina allowed herself a moment to glance down at him, his expressive face relaxed in sleep but still supremely handsome. Then, she put a hand on his shoulder and gently shook him.

She nearly had to pummel him to wake him up. Cassandra, twisting her fingers until her knuckles went white, seemed to be on the verge of passing out from the horror of waking the master.

"Aelius!" Crispina hissed. "Wake up!"

Finally, Aelius's hazel eyes blinked open. "What's wrong?" he grumbled, hauling himself into a sitting position.

"I need to discuss something with you," Crispina said.

"And it couldn't wait until morning?"

"No." She glanced back toward Cassandra, hovering near the door as if debating whether to flee into the hallway.

Aelius followed her gaze. "Is everything all right?"

Crispina hesitated for a moment. She should have thought more carefully about how to present this to him. This was the first time she would ask a favor of him, and she feared she was not off to a good start after rousing him in the middle of the night.

"Cassandra is pregnant," she announced, deciding to get straight to the point. "And the father of her child, whom she loves, is about to be sold off tomorrow to a mine or somewhere horrible."

Aelius's eyebrows shot up. "I see."

"I would like for us to purchase him," Crispina continued. "I know you don't need another slave, and it may be an unnecessary expense, but you can use the money from my dowry, and—"

"There's no further discussion needed." Aelius swung his legs out of the bed and rose to stand before her.

Crispina broke off. Her gaze snapped to his face, shadowy in the insubstantial lamplight. She didn't know him well enough yet to read his expression. Was he about to refuse, or...

He addressed Cassandra, still lurking in the back of the room. "In the morning, give Ajax the name of your beloved's current master. I'll send him with six hundred denarii to make an offer of purchase. It's a better price than he'll get from a dealer."

"Oh, sir," Cassandra whispered. "Thank you, from the bottom of my heart." She hid her face in her hands as another wave of tears overtook her. Crispina hoped they were happy tears this time.

Aelius crossed to Cassandra and folded her into a gentle embrace. She sagged into his arms, alternately sobbing and gasping thanks. He murmured soothing words into her ear and patted her back with a soft touch. Crispina felt a twinge of embarrassment at the effortless way Aelius comforted the young woman. She had been unable to summon that much warmth to offer Cassandra.

But at least she had solved Cassandra's problem, and the lovers would be reunited in short order.

Cassandra calmed and withdrew from Aelius's embrace. She wiped her eyes with the back of her hand. "I had planned to name the child after his father, if it's a boy. But now, I think I should name him after you, sir, for a boy, or you, mistress, for a girl. If you would permit it."

Aelius smiled down at her. "We would be honored. Now, I think you should try to get some rest."

"Of course, sir." She bowed formally to him and Crispina, and left the room.

Aelius turned to Crispina, his brow furrowing in an expression she couldn't place.

She lifted her chin, meeting his eyes. "I'm sorry for waking you, but I thought you would want to know of the situation."

"You were right." His gaze grew faraway, and he glanced at the door through which Cassandra had left. "I often wondered if my mother was once in Cassandra's position." An edge of vulnerability roughened his voice.

Crispina sensed he was confessing something hidden, something he'd never spoken about to anyone before. She took a moment before replying, wanting to take the appropriate care with her words, as if handling a glass cup that had been blown too thin. "Do you mean…your father…?"

"I have never brought myself to ask her," Aelius said. "And she has never volunteered it."

"Even as a child, you never asked?"

He shook his head, gaze downcast.

Crispina absorbed this in silence. She couldn't imagine having the self-control to avoid such a crucial question. A new layer of respect for him settled atop the foundation of regard that had already been built.

Aelius continued, "In truth, I think I never asked because I knew the answer." His jaw tightened, and he sat on the bed with his back to her, shoulders tense. "My mother spent a great deal of time behind closed doors with our master. I never asked her because I couldn't bear knowing for certain every time she looked at me, she would see a ghost of violence that had been done to her."

Crispina recalled Horatia's questions about Aelius's father, the hypothesis he could have been the son of their former master…and the grim reality of what Gaia might have been forced to endure. Her heart twisted, and she felt an urge to go to Aelius, attempt to comfort him despite her ineptitude, but a deep guilt held her back. After all, she'd been aware her father and ex-husband had taken liberties with their slaves and she'd turned a blind eye to it. She'd never found it as abhorrent as it seemed now. Her past nonchalance left a bitter taste in her mouth.

"I'm sorry." Her words came out in an unsteady murmur. "Your mother loves you very much. Anyone can see that."

"I know. That's why I promised myself I would never ask her to tell me. That part of our lives is behind us. I don't need to know who my father is." He turned toward her and gave her a wry smile. "That must sound so strange to you, who can trace your lineage back to the founding of the city."

Admiration bloomed in her chest. All her life, she'd been raised to think that family and ancestry were everything. The patrician class to which Crispina belonged traced their lineage back to the first hundred senators chosen by Romulus at the city's founding. Crispina had always been taught that being a member of such a family was the highest possible honor, and maintaining the purity of their bloodlines was of the utmost importance.

In her lessons, she had been forced to memorize her family's genealogy going back centuries. Yet Aelius was striving for success without even knowing for sure who his father was.

"I suppose you're a direct descendent of Romulus?" Aelius continued, joking.

"No, but my father will tie himself in knots to claim ancestry from Aeneas," Crispina said.

His mouth curved in a warm smile, then opened in a yawn. "May we return to bed?"

Crispina nodded. She blew out the lamp and slid into her side of the bed. Aelius said nothing further, and soon the deep, even sound of his breathing filled the room.

She envied his ability to return to sleep. Her mind was still too active, coming to terms with the feeling of something shifting, changing, remolding between them. Now, they were no longer just two people being cordial to each other for the sake of a marriage. They were co-conspirators in this scheme to reunite Cassandra with her lover. *Partners*. The seed of something new was growing, and Crispina wondered if she'd be able to uproot it when the time came.

CHAPTER 11

B Y THE NEXT AFTERNOON, Ajax had succeeded in bringing home Cassandra's lover, Taurus. Aelius did not relish purchasing another slave, but in this situation, it was the right thing to do.

Crispina and his mother joined him in the atrium to greet the new member of their household. Taurus, a freckle-faced young man clothed in a plain linen tunic, fell to his knees before Aelius and grasped his hand to kiss it in a formal gesture of supplication and gratitude. "Thank you, sir, for your generosity and kindness."

Aelius helped him to his feet. "You are very welcome here."

Taurus bowed to Crispina and Gaia in turn, then retreated to clasp Cassandra's hand, casting her a look of naked adoration. She smiled up at him.

"I wondered if you might tell us any more about the circumstances that led to your departure from your former master," Aelius said. "Cassandra wasn't able to give us the full story."

Taurus shifted from foot to foot. "I'm very sorry, sir, but I can't say. But I will swear on the life of my unborn child I did no wrong."

That was rather mysterious, but Aelius assumed the young man had a good reason for holding his tongue, so he let it be. "Very well. Cassandra can show you around, and you can settle in."

Cassandra and Taurus bowed to them once more, then left the atrium.

Gaia looked at Crispina with an approving gaze. "You did very well, dear."

A flush brightened Crispina's pale cheeks. "Thank you."

His mother went to go work on some weaving, and Crispina accompanied her to help. Aelius stared after his wife for a moment. She had impressed him last night. Ladies of her station were raised to barely consider slaves as human, yet she'd gone out of her way to help Cassandra. Especially with a pregnancy involved: Aelius could easily imagine that another woman with Crispina's challenges would have turned spiteful and jealous. Perhaps there was more to his new wife than her chilly exterior suggested. Perhaps they were better suited than he could ever have expected.

Later that day, Aelius ran his gaze down the list of names he and Catullus had compiled. The poet sat across from him in Aelius's study, stretching his legs to rest his feet on the corner of Aelius's desk.

Aelius shot him a disapproving glance, but said nothing. He could tolerate Catullus's informal habits as his connections had been invaluable in uncovering the names of men who would likely stand for the tribune election.

Aelius chewed his lip as he returned his attention to the names, scribed in black ink on papyrus. "I know of many of these men. They have influence and supporters. I can't hope to beat them." Aelius grabbed a pen and placed a dot next to each opponent who was all but certain to win a seat. His anxiety grew as he counted them. Nine men with nearly definite victories. There were ten tribune seats up for election, so that left only one spot.

Three names remained on the list which were unfamiliar to him. "Cornelius Zeno?"

Catullus shrugged. "Haven't heard of him, so that means he's unremarkable. Therefore you have a shot at beating him."

Aelius underlined the name and glanced at the next one. "Servius Domitius Cotta?"

"Gambling debts. Lots of them."

Aelius considered. "I could threaten to expose his financial irresponsibility." He underlined Cotta's name.

Catullus nodded. "Indeed. Who is next?"

"Publius Veturius Rufus. Do you know him?"

Catullus straightened up. "That one is interesting."

"I doubt that bodes well for me," Aelius muttered.

"The Veturius family is newly wealthy, and obscenely so. His father was a baker who won the contract to supply bread to the army."

Aelius's stomach dropped. "So Rufus can buy as many votes as he need. I can't compete with that." He put a dot next to the name, his stomach sinking. That made ten candidates nearly certain of victory, which accounted for all of the seats.

Catullus leaned forward, planting his forearms on the desk. "You forget. If there's one thing patricians hate more than an upstart freedman, it's new money. It upsets the social order and threatens the dignity of their ancient families. Rufus can try to buy votes, but if you also make an appeal to the patricians who control those votes, coupled with your new father-in-law's influence, I would bet my toga they'll choose you over him."

Aelius twirled the pen between his fingers. "You think so?"

Catullus grabbed the list and skimmed it. "Defeating Rufus is your best chance to win a seat. Focus on winning support away from him, and you might do it."

It made sense, and Aelius nodded slowly. He opened his mouth to ask how exactly he was meant to go about that, but a knock came at the door. "Yes?" he called.

Ajax entered, bearing a folded letter. "This came for you, sir."

Aelius took the letter. "Thank you." He broke the wax seal. He knew few people, so he rarely received letters, and he read the missive with interest. "Crispina and I are invited to dinner tomorrow at the house of someone I don't know." He handed the note to Catullus.

It must have been one of Crispina's acquaintances. He had never received a dinner invitation before. Already, his marriage was paying off.

Catullus read the invitation. "The Larcius family. This is good. The wife is a terrible gossip, so she invites a wide variety of people to her dinners to try to gather as much gossip as possible. There will be senators there as well as wealthy plebeian merchants, no doubt. I imagine she wants a look at Crispina's new freedman husband."

Though the prospect of being a spectacle was not appealing, the dinner would still be an excellent opportunity to start building connections and making friends. He grabbed a blank wax tablet and jotted a reply to accept the invitation on behalf of himself and his wife.

Crispina tucked herself close to Aelius's side as they entered the overdecorated dining room of the Larcius family. Usually social situations inspired nothing but apathy in her, but it was her first outing with Aelius since their wedding, and nerves tumbled in her stomach.

The two of them made quite the pair, after all: a patrician divorcée and a freedman turned aspiring politician. Though Crispina had only become an object of interest in the months since her divorce, Aelius likely had years of practice dealing with stares and muttered comments.

The guests hadn't been seated yet and milled around the room chatting with each other. But the conversation paused and everyone turned to stare once Crispina and Aelius crossed the threshold.

The hostess, Ulpia, sailed forward out of the crowd. Red carnelian glimmered at her ears and around her neck, clashing horribly with her orange gown. "Crispina, my dear, how I've missed you!"

Crispina did not smile, but allowed Ulpia to kiss her on both cheeks. Ulpia had been instrumental in spreading rumors about Crispina's infertility and failing marriage across the city, and Crispina hated her for it. "Thank you for inviting us. Please meet my husband, Aelius Herminius."

Ulpia turned to Aelius. Her smile faltered. She extended a hand in greeting, then snatched it back as if she didn't want him to touch her.

Crispina bristled. She opened her mouth, ready to chastise the horrible woman for her rudeness, but the gentle pressure of Aelius's hand on her arm held her back.

Aelius, charming as ever, smiled at Ulpia. "Thank you very much for the invitation to your beautiful home. I particularly admired the roses in your atrium. Such large blooms. My mother would love to know the name of your gardener. She's been struggling to get ours to bloom."

"Oh." Ulpia's brow wrinkled, disarmed by Aelius's compliments. "Yes, I suppose I could send my horticulturist to her with some advice."

Aelius inclined his head. "That would be most generous."

Some other guests entered, and Ulpia excused herself to greet them. Crispina glared at her orange-swathed back. "I hope she chokes on her wine."

"Then my mother shall never get her gardening advice." His tone was casual, his bearing relaxed. Nothing about him indicated any notice of the woman's rudeness.

"Your mother doesn't need gardening advice," Crispina said. "Her flowers are lovely."

"Yes, but people like it when you ask them for help. It makes them feel useful and important."

Crispina let out a tight breath. Aelius was used to this treatment, and he'd evidently figured out how to navigate it.

Someone cleared their throat behind them, and Crispina turned to see a slim man smartly dressed in a green toga with an embroidered border. He spoke in clipped tones, addressing her husband. "Our hostess tells me you are Aelius Herminius." Rings bedecked his slender fingers, the gold matching the color of his hair.

Aelius nodded. "I am, sir. And you are?"

"Publius Veturius Rufus." He jerked his head in a stiff nod. He stood closer to Crispina's height than Aelius's, and the tense posture of his neck and shoulders made it seem like he resented every degree he had to raise his chin to meet Aelius's eyes.

The name meant nothing to Crispina, but Aelius's eyebrows lifted and he stepped closer. "How interesting to make your acquaintance. I imagine we shall be seeing much of each other over the coming months."

Crispina edged forward. "And why is that?" It was rude to interfere in her husband's conversation, especially when she hadn't been formally introduced to Rufus, but she hated standing by and listening to something she only half-understood.

Rufus cast her a disinterested glance, tinged with irritation at her interruption. She sensed his disposition was closer to Memmius's than her current husband's. Memmius would have ignored her for a week if she'd behaved like this in his presence.

"We are both to stand for the tribune election," Aelius said. "Rufus, please meet my wife, Crispina."

Rufus's head twitched in the barest nod before he returned his attention to Aelius. "You stood for the last election, correct?"

Aelius's expression grew taut. "I was not successful, but I hope the experience will serve me well."

A thin smile appeared on Rufus's face. "I expect it will. If you should find yourself in a similar position this year, I hope you will not take it too hard. May I introduce my friend, Trebonianus?" He waved to a man around Aelius's age a few feet away, who came over to greet them.

A strange quiver rippled up Aelius's spine. The man Rufus was introducing, Trebonianus, stopped short and stared at Aelius, his mouth falling open for an instant before he clamped it shut.

Crispina's gaze flicked between the three men. She was missing something, and she didn't like to miss things.

"Forgive me, have you met?" Rufus said as the other two men stared at each other. A sly smirk played around his thin lips.

Aelius snapped himself out of whatever had overtaken him and smiled. Crispina knew him well enough by now to detect the hardness that lingered behind his eyes, the tension in his bearing. "We have. How nice to see you again, Trebonianus. It's been a while."

He nodded to Trebonianus, who only stammered. Aelius took Crispina's hand. "Excuse us, I've just seen some oysters circulating over there, and my wife is uncommonly fond of them." He steered Crispina away.

"Who was that?" she murmured once they were out of earshot.

Aelius headed for an empty corner of the room, where they slipped behind a large potted plant. "Trebonianus is the son of my former master."

Crispina drew in a sharp breath. "Rufus…he…"

"He must have known I'd be in attendance, that we're running in the same election, and discovered my history with the Trebonianus family."

The pieces clicked into place in Crispina's mind. "He invited Trebonianus here to humiliate you."

"I imagine so, yes."

Anger unfurled in Crispina's chest like a sail catching wind. "That detestable man. How dare he? He must answer for this insult." She took a step out of their shelter behind the plant. She wanted to find the biggest pitcher of wine she could and dump it all over Rufus's head. It would cause a scene, and thanks to their hostess's gift for gossip, the anecdote would be all over the city by tomorrow. Everyone would know what Rufus had done, how disgustingly he had behaved. Her own reputation would suffer, but it was in tatters anyway.

Aelius's hand closed around her wrist. "Don't," he murmured.

"You can't let him get away with this!"

"Causing a scene is exactly what he wants," Aelius said.

Crispina ground her teeth. "Are you *sure* I can't throw a jug of wine in his face?"

A hint of a smile twitched at his lips. "You do have a predilection for dousing men who displease you, don't you?"

She rolled her eyes. "Then let's leave. I can feign a headache."

Aelius shook his head. "We'll stay and behave as if nothing is amiss. Come, people are sitting for dinner."

With a tight sigh, Crispina allowed Aelius to lead her over to one of the low couches bordering the dining table. The rage still boiling in her chest surprised her. But Aelius was her husband now, and an insult to him was an insult to her.

Luckily, Rufus and Trebonianus sat across the room from them. With effort, Crispina kept her gaze focused on Aelius and their closer dinner companions. Aelius wasn't hard to watch. His face was so expressive, whether in attentive, quiet contemplation of what someone else was saying, or moving and changing as he spoke. He was charming and affable without being too familiar. Even if someone displayed initial hesitation to speak to him,

Aelius easily won them over in a matter of words. Crispina only wondered how he would transform friends into votes.

When the dinner was over, they returned home. Crispina collapsed gratefully into the chair at her dressing table. Her head was still ringing from the constant noise and music.

Aelius began disentangling himself from his toga. "I'm going to invite Rufus to debate together in the Forum. I must show him that whatever tactics he thinks he can use to discredit me won't work."

Crispina's anger had cooled but not faded, and it flared again at the reminder. "What if he brings Trebonianus again?"

"He won't. I could tell Trebonianus didn't know I'd be there. He'll be irked with Rufus for surprising him like that, no doubt."

"I'm sorry you had to sit there across from a man who used to own you."

"His father owned me," Aelius corrected. "Trebonianus and I were nearly the same age." A crooked smile crossed his face. "I was jealous of the education he was receiving, so I used to empty his tutor's inkwells into the garden plants. Took a surprisingly long time to be caught, and I still think the punishment was worth it. They were starting to think the house was possessed of a spirit that hated ink." He chuckled ruefully.

The stark reminder of the difference in their upbringings made Crispina's cheeks heat with a peculiar mix of embarrassment and anger. As a child and young woman, she had felt stifled, trapped, but it was nothing compared to what Aelius had endured. He'd lived a life that hadn't truly been his own. She started to understand why he was so determined to win respect from the society that disdained him for the offense of having been enslaved.

"Promise me you will beat Rufus," Crispina said.

"That is the idea, yes."

Crispina plucked the pins from her hair. "You must prepare for this debate. How do you plan to convince people to vote for you? What do you offer them?"

Aelius watched her as he always did when she was taking down her hair. She wasn't sure what he found so fascinating about her hair, but it seemed a harmless enough fixation, so she allowed him to look. "The usual. Increasing the grain dole, land for veterans. The same things every politician runs on."

She worked a comb through the knots that had arisen in her hair. "The state can't afford to increase the grain dole, and land is already given to veterans."

He shrugged. "More land, then. I'll promise whatever it takes to win."

She set down the comb and turned to face him. His indifference irked her. "Is winning all you care about? What about after the election?"

"I told you, I want to be consul. The tribune position is only a stepping stone."

Her fingers curled around the ivory comb, the tines digging into her palm. "But as tribune, you have a year to pass bills and enact policies that could truly help the people. The tribune's powers are unique. You can veto a consul! And yet you don't care about anything but winning?"

"I care."

"You care about yourself. About winning. About gaining power and influence for yourself." Maybe he was more like other

men than she'd realized: selfish, small-minded, hungry for power at the expense of all else.

His eyes flashed. "The things I care about won't get me
elected."

"Such as?"

He occupied himself with folding his toga for several long
moments. "It hardly matters, as it will never come to pass. But
if I win the tribuneship, I would put forth a bill banning the
sale of pregnant slaves, so fathers can't be separated from their
children. And another to waive the inheritance tax on men who
free their slaves in their will."

Crispina stared at him. Of course, it made perfect sense that
he would care about the rights and treatment of slaves. And he
was right that no one would vote for him if they thought he was
going to espouse such radical policies. The uprising of Spartacus
was barely a decade past, still too fresh in everyone's minds.

"I admire that," she said quietly.

"You do?"

She nodded. "But I would urge you to reconsider your second
point. If a man frees fifty slaves when he dies, then his son
will just buy fifty more. It would only increase the demand for
slaves."

He sat on the bed. "That never occurred to me."

"Instead, I would propose some sort of tax break or incentive
for rural landowners to employ laborers on their farms. The
majority of slaves in the Republic are located on Italian farms, I
believe, because they are cheaper than paying free laborers. But
if there was a benefit to employing men other than slaves—say,
a tax reduction that increased with the proportion of free men

employed—the demand for slaves would decline. And people would vote for it if they thought it would save them money."

Aelius's mouth dropped open. "By the gods, you should be running for office."

His compliment made her blush, and she fixed her attention on brushing her hair once more. Their discussion made her wonder if she should tell him about her lessons with the children. Maybe he wouldn't be as horrified as she had imagined.

No, she decided. It was one thing to discuss legislation and improvements in the abstract. It was quite another for a politician's wife to run a secret school, directly consorting with the poor. If there was even a slight chance Aelius would react badly to it, she couldn't risk telling him. In the interest of her students, her lessons would have to remain a secret if she wanted them to continue.

CHAPTER 12

NEXT WEEK, CRISPINA WALKED through the streets on her way home from a lesson with the children. She smiled, their antics still fresh in her mind. Junia's handwriting was improving, and Sextus had gotten every letter right when she quizzed him.

A voice caught her attention as she crossed the edge of the Forum. She stopped short and looked around. A crowd had gathered in the middle of the Forum. Two men stood atop a raised platform, both dressed in the chalk-whitened toga of political candidates. One was Rufus, and the other was her husband.

She'd known today was the day of their debate, but she hadn't realized the time would coincide with her return from her lesson. She eased into the shadows of a nearby building and watched.

Aelius cut a fine figure up there; the bright white toga set off his golden skin, whereas it made Rufus's fairer skin look sallow. Aelius's voice carried across the crowd with ease. He seemed to have mastered the art of speaking loudly and clearly without shouting, as some orators resorted to.

A flare of something like pride warmed her chest, a similar feeling as when Sextus had gotten all of his letters right. How strange, to be proud of one's husband.

Rufus was speaking now. "The tribuneship is meant to advance the interests of the people, is it not?" The crowd murmured and nodded in agreement. "Yet, for all my opponent's humble origins—which we all know of, and which I hardly need mention—he's gone and married a daughter of one of the oldest families in Rome."

Crispina rolled her eyes at the exaggeration. Her family was well-respected, but they were hardly the Julii.

Rufus continued. "Clearly, my opponent is trying to set himself up as some sort of aristocrat. A bold strategy for someone born even lower than myself, the son of a baker!" He gave a self-deprecating laugh.

Crispina ground her teeth. Rufus was not going to let anyone forget Aelius's origins, even as he simultaneously accused him of being a social climber.

Aelius stepped forward. "It's true, my father-in-law is a senator." Smoothly, he ignored the jab at his birth, as if he hadn't even heard it. "But fostering influence with the senatorial class is hardly a bad thing. We all know how much power they wield. If we truly want to protect the people of Rome from abuses of power by those born into privilege, we must work together with those who hold that power." His tone was measured, reasonable, but forcefulness hummed behind every word.

Some shouts of agreement sounded from the crowd, but Rufus didn't give up. "So you admit that your marriage is founded on political gain."

"I did not—" Aelius started, but Rufus kept talking.

"You married your wife for her father's sake. Why not just marry him instead?" A crude joke, but the crowd laughed.

Aelius's face tightened, but he issued an easy reply. "Alas, the gentleman is already wed."

A few more sniggers sounded from the crowd.

Rufus let the laughter die down. "Yes, and I suppose he wouldn't have been nearly as fun on your wedding night."

Another burst of laughter erupted from the audience. Crispina chewed her lip, hoping Aelius would turn the subject back to something safer. Rufus's glib words didn't bother her, but she didn't want prurient jokes to overtake the purpose of the debate.

Aelius's hand was clenched into a fist, but he somehow managed to maintain his relaxed tone. "Have a care, that is my wife you're talking about."

Don't let him get to you, Crispina willed. *Laugh it off and move on to something else.*

Rufus ignored the warning, playing to the crowd. "Yes, your wife. The infamous Crispina. How much did her father pay to get her off his hands? We all know how she was cast off by her previous husband for—" His words broke off in a strangled cry. In a blur of movement, Aelius seized the smaller man by the front of his tunic and snarled something into his ear.

Crispina pressed a hand to her mouth. Rufus's face reddened. He got an arm up and landed a punch to Aelius's jaw. The crowd roared in delight. Aelius released Rufus and stumbled back. Crispina sent up a brief, desperate prayer that this scuffle would be the end of it, but a moment later, the men dove for each other. They dragged each other down the steps off the platform. The crowd surged to surround the fight.

Crispina took an anxious step forward, but forced herself to stop. She was of no use here. Her chest tightened in helpless anxiety. Aelius was taller, but Rufus was quick and vicious. Both men had served in the army, as military service was required before running for office; both knew how to fight, and likely how to kill.

The crowd egged them on, some shouting Aelius's name, others encouraging Rufus. If there was one thing Romans loved, it was a good brawl.

Finally, some more level-headed members of the audience intervened to separate the men. Over the heads of the crowd, Crispina caught a glimpse of the two, bloodied but both upright, white togas dirty and dangling from their shoulders in disarray. *Praise Juno, he's not badly injured.*

Rufus spat in Aelius's direction and made a rude hand gesture. Aelius lunged for him once more, but someone held him back. The crowd filtered between them as a barrier. Rufus moved to leave, and Aelius did the same. It seemed to be over.

Crispina turned and ran. She had to get home before Aelius did. Firstly, to conceal where she'd been, and secondly, so she could prepare hot water and bandages to tend his injuries.

She paused in an alley across from their house to rip off her priestess disguise, then shoved the fabric into her basket. She left the basket in the alley—she could come back for it later—and ran to the house. She banged on the front door, and when it opened, burst inside. "Gaia!" she called.

Gaia emerged into the atrium. "What's wrong? Are you all right?"

Crispina tried to catch her breath. "Don't ask me how I know this, but Aelius was just involved in a brawl. He should be home shortly. He'll need looking after."

Some women would have shrieked at the thought of their son being injured. Others, like Crispina's mother, would have demanded to know how she knew that and wouldn't have done anything useful until she gave an answer. But Gaia merely nodded. "I see." She summoned Malchio, issued a quick order, and Malchio hurried to the kitchen to prepare hot water and bandages.

Gaia turned back to Crispina. "How did you come to know this?"

Crispina hesitated. "I was returning from Horatia's house…a brawl broke out at Aelius's debate in the Forum."

"I didn't realize Horatia lived near the Forum."

"Er, I took a detour, as it was such a nice day."

"And you were not able to find Aelius and bring him home yourself?"

Crispina winced. Now Gaia thought she had abandoned Aelius to a street fight. "I was frightened to get caught up in it."

"Was he badly hurt?"

"I don't think so."

Gaia let out a sigh. "Well, I suppose all that matters is that he's safe and will be home soon."

The front door opened, and a moment later Aelius emerged into the atrium. He was limping, and blood splattered his face, arms, and toga, crimson against the white fabric. Gaia gasped and ran to him.

He raised a hand. "I'm fine, Mama."

"You are clearly not." She glared at him. "By the gods, what happened to you?"

"Some remarks were made. It escalated to violence."

"Remarks? About what?"

"Nothing of consequence." Aelius dabbed the side of his hand beneath his bleeding nose.

"It must have been of consequence to provoke violence," Gaia said. "You're not given to brawling in the streets."

"It was the usual," Aelius said. "Disparaging my birth, that sort of thing."

Crispina swallowed, trying to keep her face neutral. She knew exactly what had provoked Aelius. He had been defending her, not himself.

Gaia grabbed his arm and pulled him toward his bedroom, where the slaves had filled a metal tub with water. A smaller vat of steaming water rested next to it, and a pile of bandages sat on the dressing table.

Crispina followed. She lingered on the threshold, not sure what to do. She had no experience caring for a battered and bloodied husband, and she hoped Gaia would take charge of the situation.

Instead, Gaia gave her a gentle push into the room. "I will leave him in your hands." Before Crispina could protest, Gaia slipped away and shut the door behind her.

Aelius unwound his toga with a grimace. Crispina knew she should help him, but she couldn't seem to figure out what to do. His tunic would have to come off next, and that would leave him naked.

Naked. A shiver ran through her.

"This was all prepared very quickly," Aelius said, breaking through her trepidation about his naked body. "And Mama did not seem surprised."

Crispina answered the unspoken question. "I was returning from Horatia's house when I heard a commotion in the streets. I figured out what had happened, and ran home to warn Gaia." The lie came out easily.

"I see."

"Are you badly hurt?"

He shook his head. Then, he tucked his hand into the neckline of his tunic and pulled it off so quickly Crispina didn't have time to turn away. His body—all lean angles and warm golden skin—filled her vision. Heat rushed into her cheeks, and her mouth became parched.

He dropped the tunic onto the floor in a pile with his toga and stepped into the bath. Crispina finally found the wherewithal to avert her gaze. She stared resolutely at the chest of drawers on the other side of the room. The image of his body didn't leave her. It was impressed into her mind like a seal into warm wax.

Water splashed as he sank into the tub. "You can look at me, you know," he said. "I am your husband, after all."

She dared a quick glance. His lower half was submerged beneath the water, to her mingled relief and disappointment. But his upper half—gleaming shoulders, muscled chest, the beginnings of a flat stomach—was all too visible. She had barely ever seen a naked man in the flesh, despite her three years of marriage. Memmius had always come to her in the dark, and she was certain that even if every lamp had been lit, he would have looked nothing like Aelius.

"Shall I leave you to bathe?" She prayed he wanted solitude.

"I believe you're meant to dote on me." He stretched a hand toward the vat of hot water and the stack of bandages. "Besides, I can't reach."

"Our agreement said nothing about doting," she muttered, but she fetched the hot water and bandages. She dampened a cloth and handed it to him. He passed it over his face, wincing as it brushed his split lip.

"I wasn't entirely truthful with my mother about why the fight started," he said in a low voice as he rubbed the blood from his cheek.

I know.

"The disparaging remarks were not about me, but you." He tilted his face up to meet her gaze. "Rufus said things…about you. I know it was foolish of me to rise to him, but I couldn't let it stand."

Crispina took a step closer, until her hand brushed the edge of the tub. "You don't have to defend me."

His damp hand covered hers. "You are my wife. For as long as we are married, I will defend you."

Her throat tightened. He had to know what his actions today meant for his political ambitions. Despite loving a good brawl, Romans didn't want to vote for a candidate who brawled in the Forum. He had risked everything to stop someone from speaking ill of her. Her knees weakened, but she parlayed the movement into a graceful kneeling, a hand on the side of the tub for support.

Crispina took the wet cloth from him and ran it over his shoulders, where some dirt lingered. The cloth slipped, and her fingers brushed warm skin. Her breath caught. The cloth tumbled into the water, but she didn't retrieve it. The barest touch of her hand on his body seemed to siphon warmth into her. It flowed from her hand, down her arm, blossoming in her chest and pooling low in her belly.

The delicious warmth spurred her hand to move, to seek more. Her fingers skimmed up his shoulder to brush his throat. He turned his head toward her, his eyes closed. Before she could reason herself out of it, she leaned forward and pressed her lips to his.

Water surged and splashed in the tub as his hands found her shoulders, pulling her closer. One dripping hand slid into her hair. This kiss was nothing like the momentary dry peck they'd shared at their wedding. This was fire and heat, longing and desire.

Aelius flinched as her cheek brushed his injured nose. The movement brought her back to her senses, and she pulled away. Legs shaking, she scrambled to her feet. Aelius stared at her, his eyes hot and dark.

"I…I…" She struggled to summon some dignity. "I will leave you to bathe in peace." Then she ran for the door and closed it behind her.

Crispina leaned against the wall in the empty corridor. She raised a hand to her lips, still warm and sensitized from his mouth. *Gods, what was that?*

"Mistress? Are you well?" Malchio had appeared in the corridor, carrying a pitcher and a stack of fresh cloths. "I brought some more hot water." He moved toward the door.

Crispina straightened up hurriedly. "He's…he's naked!" The words burst from her mouth before she could realize how ridiculous they sounded.

Malchio gave her a strange look. "I imagine so, mistress. May I go in?"

She flushed and moved away from the door. "Of course."

Malchio entered, leaving her alone once more. She tried to shake off her discomfiture. She couldn't go down this road. Kissing led to sex, and sex led to obligation and disappointment.

She remembered the dread that used to fill her as each night with Memmius approached. He had never been cruel or intentionally hurt her, but she had learned all she needed to know about the marriage bed. Her relationship with Aelius was on her own terms, and she wouldn't give that up. It didn't matter that kissing him set her aflame and cast her mind into wanton disarray. She had insisted on a chaste marriage for a reason, and one foolish kiss couldn't make her forget that.

CHAPTER 13

AELIUS'S NOSE AND LIP throbbed the next day, and a black eye had blossomed. The heat of his fury yesterday still surprised him. He hadn't gotten into a fight since his days in the army. He'd made a firm practice of letting insults and snide comments roll off his back like rain on polished marble. But once Crispina's name had come out of Rufus's mouth, all his carefully honed self-control had snapped.

And somehow, the aftermath of his brawl had induced his wife to kiss him.

He shook his head in disbelief as he sat in his study glancing over some correspondence. He and Crispina were supposed to attend a dinner party tomorrow, but the host wrote to suggest it may be better if they remain home, as Aelius surely needed to recover after the unfortunate incident in the Forum.

Aelius grimaced. No doubt the first of many invitations that would be rescinded or simply never arrive. How badly had yesterday's impulsive violence damaged his prospects?

Very, a disagreeable voice in his head answered. *Attacking your political opponent is not going to endear you to anyone.*

His mind turned to something more pleasant: the feel of Crispina's fingers on his skin, the warm press of her mouth, the silk of her hair against his palm.

Why did she have to go and do that? He was better off not knowing what it was like to kiss her. The brief taste left him hungry for more, but she'd made it clear nothing of the sort would happen. First, she'd fled from the bedroom as if he'd sprouted horns. Then last night, she had retired early and barricaded her half of the bed with strategically placed pillows. The message was clear: the kiss was a one-time anomaly, a mistake that would not be repeated.

Maybe he should get into another brawl. Something about it must have aroused her, and his political prospects were likely already damaged beyond repair. Maybe a career of street fights was the best he could hope for.

A shadow fell across his desk, and he glanced up to see Catullus, entering without invitation.

The poet's eyes widened, flitting from Aelius's face to his bandaged knuckles. "Infernal Dis, it's true." He dropped into a chair. "The whole city is talking about it. I thought the gossip had to be an exaggeration."

Aelius groaned. "How bad is it?"

Catullus hesitated, and Aelius's stomach dropped.

"Bad," Catullus finally said. "But there is a bright side."

Aelius leaned forward. He had hoped Catullus might see some way to get him out of the mess he'd created. "Yes?"

"As much as you've damaged your own reputation, Rufus has suffered equally. Because while no one wants to vote for a man who punches his rivals, Rufus crossed a line by insulting a respectable wife."

"So we're both doomed," Aelius muttered.

"It seems that way, yes."

Aelius sat back in his chair and let out a sigh of defeat. Marrying Crispina was supposed to help him win the election, not destroy his chances. But barely a month into their marriage, everything was ruined.

"You did succeed in making quite the impression," Catullus said, his tone much too jaunty. "Everyone knows your name now. I even heard some gladiators are going to dress up in white togas and reenact your fight in the arena."

"Lovely." Aelius couldn't hide the bitterness from his voice.

Catullus rose. "I'll leave you to your wallowing. You know where to find me if I can do anything to help." He left.

Aelius slumped in his chair. Hopelessness crashed over him like a wave hitting sand. Was he really doomed to another defeat?

A vision tugged at his chest, of being confirmed as consul before the senate ten years from now. Abandoning his goal would leave him with nothing. He thirsted to succeed, to win, to prove himself. He couldn't let this one disaster break him.

He rose and paced the small study. There had to be a way to fix this. His mind ran back over the conversation with Catullus. *The whole city is talking about it…Everyone knows your name now…*

Maybe he could turn his ill-gotten notoriety to his advantage. An idea sparked. He turned it over in his mind. It was distasteful, yes, and it would require Crispina's support, which she might withhold.

But it was all he had. Before he could reason himself out of it, he grabbed a blank piece of papyrus and started writing.

The reply to Aelius's letter came in the evening. He read it over, then took it into his bedroom. Crispina was already in bed reading, her hair in a thick braid over her shoulder.

"What are you reading?" he asked. Best to get her in a good mood before asking for her help.

"Catullus left some poems for me when he was here earlier."

Aelius frowned. "I know the sort of filth he writes. He should not be giving that sort of thing to another man's wife." Catullus's penchant for flirtation knew no bounds.

Crispina flipped one piece of papyrus to the back of the sheaf. "It's not like that. He asked for my help. He knows I have an ear for poetic meter." Her eyes skimmed over the poem in front of her. "He keeps using dactyls where there should be spondees, and there are extra feet all over the place." She pursed her lips. "Really, he should be ashamed to call himself a poet."

None of this made any sense to Aelius, but that didn't lessen his admiration. Crispina could discuss history, debate politics, and critique poetry. He would have to get Catullus to teach him some basic concepts of poetry so he could hold his own with her in discussion.

He placed the letter on a table. "I have a favor to ask."

She glanced up from her reading. "Yes?"

He hesitated. This was the first time he would explicitly ask anything of her, and he had a feeling she wasn't going to like it. And when Crispina didn't like something, she made her displeasure clear.

"You must know this incident"—he gestured to his bruised face— "has severely damaged my hopes of winning the election."

She looked away and nodded, her expression inscrutable.

"There is a way to fix things. I have written to Rufus."

She straightened up. "Why?"

"He knows as well as I do that we have both doomed ourselves. I—"

"This is his fault, not yours," Crispina snapped. "He was the one spewing insults."

"I shouldn't have laid hands on him," Aelius said. "No matter how much he deserved it."

Crispina's lips tightened, but she offered no retort.

"As I was saying, I have written to Rufus. Suggesting we do something to restore both our reputations. Specifically, a mutual public apology. If the whole city is talking about our fight, they'll be paying attention if we are seen to be civil to each other."

Crispina returned her gaze to the poetry, her brow furrowing as she considered. He wondered if she would poke apart this proposal as she had his political ideas. But soon, she nodded. "It could work. But what does this have to do with me?"

"Rufus's insult was against you," Aelius said. "The people do not take kindly to slandering a respected wife. Thus, I would like you to come with me and allow Rufus to apologize to you."

She frowned. "Why should I forgive a man who insulted me before the whole city?"

"You don't have to forgive him," Aelius said. "Just be seen to accept his apology."

She glared at him, jaw tense. "I don't like being made into a spectacle."

"Neither do I." He crossed around the bed to stand before her. She gazed up at him, and suddenly he was back in the bathtub, her perfumed scent surrounding him, his hands twined with the silk of her hair.

He cleared his throat. Now was not the time to lose himself in fantasies. "Will you do this for me?"

She glowered down at the poetry for a moment. "Will it help you beat him?"

"I think so." As things stood now, neither he nor Rufus had any shot at winning one of the ten tribune seats.

"Then yes, I suppose." She set her jaw, distaste written all over her face. "When is it to happen?"

Relief and surprise mingled at her acquiescence. He had worried she wouldn't cooperate. After all, accepting an apology from someone who insulted her had not been stipulated in their agreement. "Next week. Once our faces heal and we become more presentable."

"Good. I'll need time to practice looking forgiving." She turned back to her reading, and Aelius undressed for bed.

On the day of the apology, Crispina wore her brightest clothing, a stola of scarlet topped with an orange palla. She loaded her fingers, wrists, and ears with gold jewelry. If she was going to make a spectacle of herself, she might as well give the people something to look at.

Catullus had helped spread rumors around the city that a reconciliation might be forthcoming. People eyed her and Aelius as they walked to the Forum. It was high noon, when the maximum number of people were out and about.

Rufus appeared in the Forum exactly as they'd agreed. He must have had a similar idea as Crispina, looking to draw as much visual attention to himself as possible. Four attendants flanked him, dressed in matching red tunics. Rufus wore a blue tunic edged with gold embroidery. A cluster of gold rings and bracelets adorned his hands and arms. Aelius's only ornament was the silver wristband that covered his brand.

They approached as if meeting by chance and stood an arm's length apart. Bruises still shadowed Rufus's face, more visible on his fair skin than Aelius's swarthier complexion. Crispina felt a thrill of satisfaction at the sight of his injuries.

"Rufus." Aelius inclined his head.

People stopped and stared.

"Aelius. Crispina." Rufus glanced around, as if ascertaining whether enough people had taken notice. He spoke louder than necessary for a private conversation. "How nice it is to see you both. Allow me to be the first to apologize for our disagreement last week. I should not have behaved in such a manner."

"I believe it is my wife who requires an apology, not me," Aelius said.

Rufus turned to Crispina. "Lady, my sincerest apologies for any offense I caused you."

Crispina did not grace him with a smile. "I am sure it will not happen again."

Aelius nudged her. Crispina's teeth clenched, but she forced herself to relax. *You're doing this for Aelius. So he can beat this insufferable man.* She extended her hand. Rufus took it and bent over it with a light, formal kiss.

"And I must apologize as well," Aelius said. "I should have settled our disagreement with words rather than fists." He raised his voice slightly. "After all, we are both working toward the same cause, the good of Rome, and I hope our interactions will be more collegial from this day forward."

"Indeed." They nodded to each other once more, and then it was over. Rufus continued on his way, and Aelius took Crispina's arm and walked through the crowd of people that had assembled. Everyone was staring at them, eyes alight with interest, some whispering behind their hands.

"Did I perform to your satisfaction?" Crispina murmured.

"It might have been more convincing if you had smiled."

"I don't smile at men who insult me. No matter if they apologize." Even the gesture of offering her hand to Rufus rankled. She would sooner have slapped him.

"You've never smiled at me, and I've never insulted you."

She glanced at him. "I didn't know you were keeping track."

He shrugged. "It's the sort of thing one notices after a month of marriage."

"I—" Crispina cut herself off. She'd been about to apologize, but she owed him no apology. She hadn't done anything wrong. Their marriage wasn't about affection or companionship, so her lack of smiles shouldn't matter.

Nevertheless, his observation stung. Was she really so cold that she'd never smiled at him? She didn't dislike him. She'd been proud of him when he'd debated Rufus in the Forum, before the fight broke out. She'd even kissed him.

She could have allowed herself to soften, assure him she hadn't meant to be so cold.

But softening would mean opening her heart, and that would make their inevitable divorce more difficult than it had to be. So she tugged her palla around her shoulders, raised her chin, and said nothing.

CHAPTER 14

T HE APOLOGY WORKED, AND soon invitations came trick-
ling back, to Aelius's relief. Over the next month, he
and Crispina settled into a routine: days occupied separately,
evenings either dining with his mother at home or attending a
social engagement, nights spent next to each other in a silent,
kissless bed.

Crispina seemed content, if not deliriously happy, which
suited him well enough. She and his mother interviewed
painters and artisans for some improvements to the house.
They occasionally asked his opinion on a certain fresco design
or mosaic style, and he tried to pick whichever option he
thought they were angling for.

After the incident with Rufus resolved, a renewed hope flared
that he actually had a shot at winning the election. It was still early
days. With the election months away, his actions were focused on
making friends rather than securing votes, but the former pursuit
progressed well. Each dinner party resulted in new connections,
which led to more invitations. Sometimes they even were asked
to two parties on the same evening, and flitted from one to the
other like bees between flowers. He knew Crispina did not enjoy
the endless evenings of eating and making conversation and

would prefer to be in bed reading history or critiquing another batch of Catullus's poetry, but she never complained.

On one such evening, Crispina sat beside him as he reclined on a dining couch at a large house on the Palatine Hill. Conversation had turned to his altercation with Rufus, as it often did these days. For better or for worse, the incident had made him famous, and everyone had an opinion on it.

"Personally, I don't think you should have apologized," one man said. "It showed weakness."

Another man on the opposite side of the table sniffed. "Laying hands on him was unforgivable in the first place. To be frank, I'm surprised he hasn't sued you for assault. The last thing this city needs is more violence, not with a civil war less than twenty years past." His voice lowered, and his mouth twisted into a sneer. "Though I suppose we can hardly expect better, when power is offered to those not born to it."

Aelius wasn't sure if he was supposed to have heard that last snide remark, so he decided to ignore it. Beside him, Crispina stiffened. He put a hand on her arm, worried she would summon a sharp retort that would offend their companions.

But when she spoke, her voice was as sweet as the honeyed dates piled before them. "Forgive me if I misunderstand, sir, but are you suggesting you would *not* have defended your wife against a public insult?"

The man's face reddened and he cleared his throat. "Of course I did not mean that. But there are other ways to settle a dispute. Civilized ways."

One of the other men's wives leaned forward. "Well, I thought it was gallant." She shot Aelius a dazzling smile. "I think we should elect men who respect a woman's honor just as much as their own, and are willing to fight for it."

Several other wives nodded in agreement.

Aelius returned the lady's smile. "Thank you, lady."

The conversation turned to other things. He leaned close to Crispina. "Thank you," he murmured. She had effortlessly turned the conversation in his favor without causing offense or ruffling any feathers.

She acknowledged him with a slight tilt of her head.

After the food had been served, a painted ceramic bowl was passed around, heaped with a fine whitish powder. Most of the guests took a pinch and sprinkled it into their wine goblets. Aelius frowned when it reached him. "Do you know what this is?" he asked Crispina in a low voice.

She took the bowl and bent her head to sniff. "I believe it's blue lotus, dried and crushed."

"For what purpose?"

It was hard to see in the lamplight, but a flush seemed to rise in her cheeks. "It induces a feeling of peace and tranquility. And…is generally used to increase libido."

"And you know this how?"

Now she was definitely blushing. She passed the bowl to the next person without taking any. "I think we should leave."

Aelius glanced around the room. Husbands and wives were inching closer to each other. Not necessarily each husband to his own wife, either. *Ah.*

Crispina rose and slipped toward the door, and Aelius followed.

They climbed into their litter waiting outside, which set off toward home. "I didn't realize it was going to be one of *those* parties," Crispina said, her fair skin still reddened. The blush turned her ivory complexion to rose, making her look even more beautiful.

"Have you been to one of *those* parties before?" Despite himself, his interest was piqued at the thought of Crispina indulging in the sort of debauchery they'd left behind.

She gave him a sharp look. "No. But Horatia has imparted some stories." She said nothing further.

There was a time when he would have seriously considered staying at such a party. But now, the thought of returning home with Crispina to an evening of quiet conversation in their cozy bedroom held far more appeal than anonymous lust.

But his relationship with Crispina hadn't been entirely free of lust, had it? The specter of the fiery, impulsive kiss in the bathtub rose in his mind. He had wanted her since he first laid eyes on her, and it seemed that part of her, even if a deeply buried part, wanted him too.

If she did desire him, then there was no reason to keep up their celibate arrangement. It all became enticingly simple in his mind. Why shouldn't two married people who desired each other act on that desire?

"Have you ever used that substance before?" Aelius asked as they returned to their bedroom.

Crispina sat at her dressing table and sifted her fingers through her hair, removing the silver pins and length of thread that held her braided bun in place. "Yes," she admitted.

"You have?" His voice rose in surprise.

She shot him an icy glare, as if regretting her honesty. "Only once. I thought it would help things between me and Memmius.

But it only gave me a terrible headache." One of the silver pins slipped from her fingers and clattered to the floor.

Aelius bent to pick it up and laid it on her dressing table. "May I help you?" He rested a hand on the thick braid that had been released from its coil at the back of her head.

"If you wish." She reached for a cloth and dampened it with oil from a small vial, then scrubbed it over her face to remove the light layer of makeup.

Bolstered by her accession, he untied the thin leather cord binding the end of the braid, then sank his fingers into her locks, disentangling the three parts. Her hair was warm silk against his palms, the feel of it somehow innocuous and wanton at the same time.

"So you would never want to try it again, the blue lotus?" His voice came out in a gravelly rumble.

"With you? I wouldn't need it with you," she said swiftly, then stiffened, her fingers curling around the oil-soaked cloth in her hand. Her next words were spoken in a clipped, austere tone. "Because of course the terms of our marriage did not extend to such things."

I wouldn't need it with you. His pulse leaped. He saw straight through her flimsy attempt to disguise her true meaning, and he wouldn't let her get away with it. "We left room to renegotiate." He combed his fingers slowly through her beautiful hair, continuing to draw the plaits loose.

"On the condition that you would seduce me. And no seduction has taken place."

"I disagree."

She turned toward him, dark eyebrows arched. "Oh?"

"You kissed me that day in the bath. It stands to reason that I must have seduced you somehow, even if I don't quite understand how."

"I see." She met his gaze. "So because of one ill-considered kiss, you now believe you have earned the right to avail yourself of your husbandly privileges?"

He shook his head and removed his hands from her hair. "Not at all. I claim no rights over you. But I think there is room in our marriage to find some pleasure with each other. You were married before. You must remember the pleasures of the marriage bed."

Her face twisted, and she barked a humorless laugh. "I know less than you might think of the marriage bed, but one thing I do know is there is no pleasure to be found there."

He frowned. "What do you mean?"

She looked away, but he caught a trace of embarrassment in her face, a vulnerability he hadn't expected. The pieces came together in his mind like repairing a shattered vase. "Was your husband cruel to you?"

She shook her head. "Never." Her voice lowered, and she spoke so quietly he could barely hear her, as if each word was a struggle. "But he only came to me in the dark. It was quick. Unpleasant. I hardly even know what a man looks like."

Anger tightened his chest at the thought of Crispina being treated as anything less than a goddess. "Not all cruelty is violent. Depriving one's wife of affection and treating her only as a broodmare is cruel. Is that why you stipulated our marriage be chaste? You were afraid I would be like that with you?"

She shrugged. "What reason did I have to think otherwise?"

He knelt next to her chair. "If I could offer you something different…" He placed a tentative hand on her knee, ready to move it if he felt her tense. "Would you agree?"

She gazed down at him. He sensed her weighing things out in her astute mind. Would she trust him enough to explore this with him?

She shifted, and he thought she meant to move away from him, but instead she placed her hand on top of his. She spoke hesitantly. "I suppose…there are certain things I should like to learn. Purely from an educational perspective. There's only so much books can teach, after all."

His heart sped up, racing as it did after running laps at the gymnasium. "Such as?"

She glanced at him, then looked away, her brow wrinkling. "I…" She bit her lip. "I don't think I can say it."

"You're going to have to."

She chewed on her lip. He could sense her struggling between embarrassment and desire, the urge to retain her cool composure and the longing to let it melt. *Trust me,* he silently urged.

"I…" She cleared her throat and spoke in a small voice. "I would like to see you."

His pulse spiked, his blood heating as molten desire unfurled inside him. "See me?"

"I told you, I hardly know what a man looks like." She stared down at her knees, her cheeks reddening to that beautiful rosy hue. "I want to see…all of you."

Her words cast his mind into chaos, but he managed to summon a careless grin. "You're in luck, as I'm an excellent specimen."

A hint of her usual haughtiness sparked in her gaze. "Perhaps I should be the judge of that."

"Indeed." He rose to his feet and tucked a hand into the neckline of his tunic. In one fluid motion, he stripped it off.

CHAPTER 15

CRISPINA STARED AS AELIUS tossed his tunic to the ground. Her face burned, but she refused to allow herself to look away as she had when he was in the bath. She valued knowledge and learning, after all. This was just one more thing for her to learn about.

But it was impossible to maintain that academic mindset when confronted with Aelius's lithe, golden-skinned body. Her mouth went dry as her eyes skimmed from his chest down his stomach to his hips…and lingered on his cock.

She had seen them before on statues, of course, but this one was much more intriguing. It was already swelling and she hadn't even touched him yet. A wave of dizziness passed over her, and she realized she'd forgotten to breathe.

Once her legs felt steady, she stood and approached him, needing to get closer. Maybe he wouldn't look as good up close. Maybe he would have some imperfection that would shatter the illusion of his beauty.

But once she stood within arm's length of him, he only became more compelling. There were imperfections: a mole on the left side of his collarbone, a thin scar across his shoulder, a light fur of hair that covered his muscled chest. But they merely made him seem real, a man of flesh and blood who was somehow, in this moment, all hers.

"Do you like what you see?" His voice was a quiet rumble. He stood calmly, no trace of modesty or embarrassment.

She envied his composure. She felt utterly discomfited, and she wasn't even the naked one. "I refuse to say anything that would further inflate your ego."

He reached for her hand and placed it on his chest. She closed her eyes for a moment at the warm, solid feel of him. Something smooth and metal brushed her hand. He was still wearing the silver armband which covered the brand on his wrist.

With gentle fingers, she grasped the edge of the armband to slide it from his wrist. He flinched back, pulling his arm from her grip.

"I'm sorry…" she faltered.

He let out a breath and shook his head. "It's nothing." He pulled the armband off and tossed it to the floor.

She knew he was self-conscious about his brand and what it represented, and his vulnerability in fully baring himself to her touched her heart. This was no longer just about seeing a naked man. Something deeper was brewing between them, the bubbles just barely breaking the surface.

She touched his chest again, first one hand, then another. Her hands roamed over his shoulders, pulling him closer. He felt so *good* to touch—like running her hands over a newly acquired book she was longing to read.

When her fingers brushed his throat, he cupped her face in his hands and bent to kiss her. His mouth was gentle on hers, almost hesitant, but the stiffness between his legs left no question of his desire. A thrill shot through her as he drew her closer. Was she really doing this—embracing a naked man, who somehow happened to be her husband?

A surge of boldness overtook her. She dropped her hand lower and took hold of him. He broke off from their kiss with a sharp gasp, which lengthened into a moan as she stroked him.

"I do know some things," she murmured, satisfied at his reaction.

"I can see that," he said, his voice strained.

Still stroking him, she drew back to put some distance between them so she could examine how her hand looked wrapped around him.

His breathing roughened. "Bed," he gasped. She refused to release him as they stumbled over to the bed, keeping firm hold of his cock. He collapsed onto the mattress on his back, and Crispina perched on her knees at his side. In this position, she could look her fill at his entire body, could watch how his chest rose and fell with increasing speed, how his stomach muscles contracted and released as her hand moved over him, how his cock twitched as she stroked him.

"Am I doing it right?" she asked.

He reached down and placed his hand over hers, adjusting her grip and tweaking her rhythm.

"Gods below, that's good," he breathed when she got it.

"Tell me what it feels like."

His eyes were closed, his brow furrowed as if concentrating hard to summon words. "Your hand is so warm. Soft and tight at the same time. It feels incredible."

Heat blossomed in her core as her arm worked up and down. She experimented with slowing down, grazing her fingertips over him until he groaned with frustration. When he begged her not to stop, she relented and kept up a steady rhythm.

"I want to watch you come," she murmured. She had never actually seen it happen, and she sensed it would be quite educational.

"Fuck, Crispina," Aelius gasped. "When you talk like that—" The words turned into a strangled groan. His hips bucked into her hand, and shudders wracked his body as a silvery liquid exploded over her fingers.

His body went limp, his chest heaving. Crispina examined the fluid on her hand. So that was what Memmius was doing inside of her all those times. *Educational, indeed.* She rose from the bed, fetched a cloth and cleaned off her hand, then returned to sit beside him. His breathing had slowed, and he opened his eyes, his features relaxed in an expression of exhausted bliss.

She wasn't quite sure what to say. "You, er…I suppose you enjoyed that?"

He let out a breathless chuckle. "Did you?"

She gave a shy nod. *Enjoyed* was an understatement. Working Aelius with her hand like that, watching him lose himself to pleasure—it caused a tingling heat to creep over her skin, and she wanted more. She just didn't know exactly what.

Aelius pulled himself into a sitting position with a sigh of effort. He touched her cheek, gazed into her eyes. "Thank you," he murmured, then pulled her close to kiss her.

Her heat flared like sparks catching fresh tinder. It roared into a full blaze as his hand slid down to cup her breast. His fingers were gentle, almost reverent. She let out a soft moan against his neck as his thumb swiped across her nipple.

"Take off your dress." The words hovered between a request and command.

Crispina hesitated, wondering how far to let this go. She had already satisfied him, what more could he want?

"Why?"

"Because I've longed to see your body since the first moment I ever saw you. Because even a glimpse of your bare shoulder makes me ache." He brushed his lips across her collarbone. "Because I want to pleasure you until you forget your own name."

Her breath caught. She stole a glance at his cock, which had now softened. Whatever he had in mind, it seemed unlikely to include that.

And she desperately wanted to find out what he had in mind, so she struggled out of her dress. He helped her tug the fabric over her head, then tossed it in a ball onto the floor.

Cool air rushed over her skin. She watched Aelius's face, searching for any hint of displeasure or disappointment. She found only rapture in his gaze.

"You're a fucking goddess." His voice, usually so smooth and charming, turned rough and hungry as he gazed at her.

He grazed a fingertip over her nipple so lightly it felt like the brush of a feather. She leaned into him, needing more. He squeezed harder, then gently laid her back on the bed. His hand covered one breast, his mouth the other one. Her back arched at the feeling of his fingers and tongue sliding over her nipples. His other hand slid down her stomach, caressing the curve of her hip, then lingered on her thigh.

She sensed what he was waiting for and parted her legs just a bit. His hand slipped between them, fingers heading straight for the spot where all her desire centered.

"Oh!" Heat flared at his touch. She grabbed his shoulders, overcome by the rush of sensation.

He paused. "Did I hurt you?"

She shook her head. "I...it..." Her mind couldn't seem to form words.

He let out a low chuckle. He stroked her in a gentle, firm motion. "What does it feel like?"

She dug her nails into his shoulders, needing something to anchor herself in the sea of pleasure. "I-I can't think."

"I'm making you feel so amazing you can't think?" A roguish grin lit his face, and his fingers moved faster.

"Arrogant ass," she gasped.

"I won't tolerate insults while I'm in the midst of pleasuring you, so if you want to talk, you're going to have to say something useful." He withdrew his hand. Her body immediately ached with need at the absence of his touch. He leaned in to speak close to her ear, his breath tickling her hair. "I want you to..." He deliberated for a moment, until a wicked gleam lit his hazel eyes. "Recite the *Iliad*. I know you know it."

"What? That's ridiculous."

His fingers drew tantalizing circles on the inside of her thigh. "That's my price. I want to hear your voice, stammering and breathless, until you forget the words altogether."

Her cheeks burned. This was humiliating, and she should put a stop to it at once, but her body was still crying out for his touch, and playing along seemed the easiest way to get him to put his hands back. "All right," she muttered.

He slid his hand between her legs.

"Sing, muse, of the wrath of—"

He pulled his hand away, frowning at her like a displeased teacher. "In Greek, Crispina."

She rolled her eyes but obeyed, reciting the words she'd memorized as a child. Aelius touched her as she spoke, his fingers rekindling delicious pleasure between her legs. Any time she paused for more than a breath, he stopped touching her, so she had to keep the words coming. As her pleasure mounted, she spoke quicker and quicker—butchering the poetic meter. Achilles' wrath and the might of Greek armies had never seemed so sensual.

The words became garbled and unintelligible, but she kept talking. At one point, she forgot the next line, so she started over from the beginning. Aelius didn't seem to notice; he didn't even know Greek, after all. His focus remained intent, the circular movements of his fingers steady and firm.

The poetry became nothing but gasps and moans as her yearning rose higher and higher. Finally, the pleasure crested in a hot, rolling wave that racked her body in spasms that felt endless.

The sensation left her in a rush, and she collapsed back onto the bed, finally silent. Aelius grinned at her, looking much too pleased with himself. He lay next to her and wrapped an arm around her shoulders. She turned onto her side, seeking the brush of his warm skin on hers.

He skimmed a hand down her back, then settled his hand in the curve of her waist. She nestled her head into his chest. Being held in a naked man's arms, while just as naked herself, was novel, but somehow the way Aelius held her felt familiar, as if they'd been doing this every night since their wedding. The sense that she belonged here soothed her breathing into a slow rhythm, and she allowed it to lull her to sleep.

CHAPTER 16

CRISPINA WOKE TO AN unusual coolness across her chest. She opened her eyes. Her skin was bare, the blanket bunched around her waist. Memories of last night flooded back. *Aelius. Naked. Gods, the* Iliad. Heat rushed to her cheeks.

She glanced over at Aelius. During the night, they had returned to their usual sleeping arrangements, each person neatly contained in their own half of the bed.

Crispina hesitated, then inched closer. His warmth beckoned her, an inexorable pull that induced her to lay her head on his shoulder and stretch a tentative hand across his chest. Her body relaxed into his, like putting on a pair of well-fitting shoes.

He stirred. Not wanting to wake him, Crispina moved away, but his arm curled out to hold her to him. He mumbled something in her ear, but his voice was too heavy with sleep to make it out. His intentions became clearer when his lips found her neck and his hand her breast. She arched into his touch, an echo of the desire she'd felt last night suffusing her.

He rolled on top of her, his weight pressing her into the bed. The night's rest had certainly restored him, and she felt stiffness bumping at her hip.

"I want you," he growled in her ear, his voice scratchy but clearer now.

Though she only wanted to surrender to the pleasure she now knew he could give her, her body tensed. She put a hand on his chest. "I…I don't think…" She tried to find the words to articulate the reason why she didn't want to give in.

Aelius moved off of her, giving her a questioning look.

She glanced away, unable to meet his gaze. "I enjoyed what we did last night," she said. "But I don't wish to…to…"

"You don't wish to do it again?"

She shook her head hastily. "I do. But nothing…further." Sex led to disappointment and resentment, and she couldn't bear that from him.

He gave a slow nod and mercifully didn't press for further explanation. They dressed in silence. After breakfast, Aelius disappeared into his study, and Crispina left the house to meet Horatia at the baths. It was one of the days reserved for women to bathe, and Horatia was apparently desperate to get out of the house now she'd had the baby.

"Do *not* look at me," Horatia snapped as they shed their clothes in the warm changing room. "I grow more hideous with each child."

Crispina focused on removing her own clothing. "I'm sure nothing of the sort is true."

Horatia wrapped a towel around herself and sat on a bench while Crispina finished changing. "You must cherish all of *that*." She gestured to Crispina's body. "At least you will never have to see it stretched and distorted by some ungrateful little creature."

"Mm." Crispina tucked a towel beneath her arms, pulling it tight around her chest. "Let's go." They proceeded into a hot, darkened room containing a circular pool. Steam rose off the surface of the water. Hushed voices from two other women sounded from the opposite side of the pool.

Crispina and Horatia shed their towels, laying them on benches at the perimeter of the room, and stepped into the warm water. Crispina kept her eyes carefully averted from Horatia's body until her friend was submerged up to her neck. Crispina sank into the water with a sigh. Its warmth reminded her of Aelius's hands on her last night. She rested her back against the edge of the pool and leaned her head on the stone rim with a smile.

Water rippled as Horatia swam near. "Was I presumptuous with my comment earlier?"

Crispina opened her eyes. "Pardon?"

"You're glowing. Is there some news?"

"Oh." Crispina shook her head. "Not that sort of news. But…" She moved closer to Horatia and lowered her voice. "There were some developments last night."

Horatia's eyebrows lifted, her eyes sparking with interest. "Do tell."

Crispina provided a rough outline of what had and hadn't taken place last night. She left out their debasement of Homer's poetry; she feared she would forever associate the destruction of Troy with Aelius's nimble fingers.

Horatia looked befuddled. "But why on earth wouldn't you let him bed you, if he was that good already?"

Crispina blushed. Her mind turned to the tangle of reasons why she had pushed Aelius away this morning. "I know it seems silly. But I couldn't help feeling that if we were to lie together and I didn't conceive, he would truly realize how broken I am. He would resent me." She had spent years seeing the disdain and bitterness on Memmius's face every time he looked at her. She couldn't suffer that from Aelius, not even in their temporary marriage.

"But he knows already."

"It's one thing to know, intellectually, that something is amiss. It's another to lie with a woman time after time with no result. It's easier this way. Safer." There was another reason lingering in the back of her mind she didn't dare speak aloud, a tiny seed of hope that she couldn't help clinging to. Maybe, just maybe, if she were to lie with Aelius, a child would result. Maybe the problem wasn't hers, but her former husband's.

But she had been disappointed too many times, and she couldn't bear it again. For as long as she kept Aelius at arm's length, she could keep that little spark of hope alive. But once it was extinguished, she would have nothing. Even though she didn't long for a child, something in her still yearned to prove she could do it, this basic thing that every other woman seemed to be able to achieve without even trying.

"I suppose I can understand," Horatia said. "In any case, there are plenty of things you can do to enjoy each other."

Crispina found herself eager to absorb Horatia's knowledge of these matters. "Such as?"

Horatia cast a quick glance around the room and dropped her voice to a whisper. "Use your mouth on him."

"My…my mouth?" The idea was indecent, shocking—and intriguing.

Horatia nodded.

"How exactly does that work?"

Horatia grinned and made a few illustrative gestures with her hand and mouth.

Crispina flushed even hotter. "And Decius allows this?" She had trouble imagining Horatia's staid, soft-spoken husband permitting something so lewd.

"He loves it, and I'm sure your husband will as well," Horatia said with a knowing grin. She giggled. "Your cheeks are so red, my dear!"

"It's the steam," Crispina muttered, and changed the subject.

Reclining in bed, Aelius stole a surreptitious glance at Crispina as she combed out her hair in the evening. Memories of last night had tormented him all day: the taste of her skin, the grip of her hand on his cock, the way her voice became high and desperate as her pleasure increased…

But this morning she had set a boundary. He didn't fully understand her reasoning, but he knew better than to pry. Instead, he would leave it up to her to guide any further intimacy between them.

If there was to be any.

Crispina rose from her dressing table. Out of habit, he turned his head away, knowing she was about to remove her dress.

"Don't." Her voice made his gaze snap back to her.

With deliberate movements, she tucked her fingers beneath the shoulders of her dress and slipped it off her arms. The fabric pooled at her feet.

Aelius sat up, swinging his legs to the edge of the bed. His gaze ran over her curves. His mouth went dry at the sight of her, his pulse spiking. She walked toward him, an alluring sway to her hips that made his cock stir.

He stood to meet her as she approached the bed.

"Take that off," she murmured.

He yanked his tunic over his head faster than ever before, fumbling in his urgency, and dropped it to the floor. Her gaze ran over him. A small smile curved her lips. Finally, she was smiling for him.

Apparently his naked body was the key to her smiles, which he tried not to feel too smug about.

He lifted a hand to caress her lips. "You're smiling."

"So I am." Her tongue flicked out to taste the tips of his fingers. A stab of heat pulsed in his groin, and he pulled her to him. Their lips met in a slow, tantalizing kiss. His arms dropped lower, hands circling around her body to grasp her plush bottom. She let out a little gasp that made his cock throb.

He drew her toward the bed. With gentle pressure on his shoulders, she pushed him down to sit on the edge of the bed. Then, as he stared in disbelief, she dropped to her knees between his legs, took hold of his cock, and lowered her mouth onto it.

A shudder racked his body at the feel of her hot, wet mouth. The mouth that had, moments ago, smiled for him for the first time. "Wh-what in the underworld are you doing?"

She pulled her lips off him, which made another shiver run through him, and glanced up at him with dark eyes. "Horatia told me about it. I thought it sounded like fun." She took him into her mouth once more.

"F-fun," he gasped. Her tongue slid up and down, teasing and exploring. He reached out and gently twined a hand in her hair, feeling the silken waves sliding through his fingers. She took him deeper, tugging a groan from his lips. His grip on her hair tightened for a moment before he forced himself to release her, afraid of causing pain. He clenched his hands into fists at his side as her mouth worked him. Her movements became more confident, the rhythm steadier.

He didn't want this to end, but with the way she was using her tongue… "Crispina," he grunted. "I'm going to—"

"Do it," she ordered, her voice sultry and commanding at the same time. "I want to feel you spill in my mouth."

There was no possible way to withstand hearing those words from her lips, lips which were currently pleasuring him to within an inch of his life. The erotic rapture mounted in a hot, rolling wave, and Aelius abandoned himself to it.

CHAPTER 17

CRISPINA CROUCHED IN THE dirt, gathering wax tablets and stacking them into her basket. The tablets were filled with clumsy letters etched by her students, and each one made her smile. She moved fast, anticipation filling her at the prospect of returning home to a companionable afternoon with Gaia and an evening of pleasure with Aelius.

There was no dinner party tonight, so they would have the night all to themselves. The past month had been full of exploration and learning. They had discovered more pleasure than she thought possible, especially given the boundary she'd established.

Most of her students had already departed after the lesson concluded, but one boy remained, hunched over his tablet. Crispina surveyed him. He wasn't one of her regulars, and she suspected he had only shown up after hearing rumors of free food. He hadn't said a word throughout the lesson. He appeared to be about seven years old, with skinny limbs poking out of his threadbare, dirty tunic. He was currently occupied in stabbing his tablet with the stylus over and over again, chipping away at the layer of wax.

Crispina cleared her throat. "May I have that back?"

He glanced up at her with disinterest, then returned his attention to the destruction of the tablet.

"Excuse me." She adopted the cool, steely tone she used when reprimanding the students. "It's polite to reply when someone asks you a question. I'm taking this away from you if you're going to destroy it." She reached for the tablet.

He jerked it away, but she managed to grab a corner. They engaged in a brief, ignominious tug-of-war. Crispina had to exert all of her strength to yank the tablet away from the child. She stowed it safely in her basket. "And the stylus?" She held out a hand, palm up.

The boy heaved a sullen sigh and placed the stylus into her hand.

"Thank you. Now, where are your parents? Do you live nearby?"

He shrugged.

She reverted to something simpler. "What is your name?"

He lifted his chin. "Quintus Fabius Maximus."

"That is *not* your name." That was the name of the famous general who had faced off against Hannibal a century and a half ago.

He glared at her. "Yes, it is."

She narrowed her eyes. "I suppose I can call you Quintus."

He shook his head. "Maximus," he insisted.

Maximus was a ridiculous name for a seven-year-old. "I'm not calling you that. Will you tell me where you live?" She tried for an encouraging smile. "I can walk you home."

He toyed with a pebble in the dirt. "Not s'posed to go home."

Crispina frowned. "What do you mean?"

Another shrug. "Ain't enough food."

"Isn't," Crispina corrected automatically, but her heart tightened at his words. Someone here would know where the boy lived. She could take him home and speak to his mother, perhaps offer some assistance. "Come with me. We'll sort this out."

She reached for his dirty hand, but he shied away, fixing her with a stubborn glower. "Not unless you call me Maximus."

Crispina let out a tight sigh. She had better things to do than argue with a child about the grandiose name he'd appropriated for himself. "How about Max?" she offered. The abbreviated name sounded slightly less ostentatious.

He considered for a moment, then nodded. She grabbed his hand and led him toward the block of apartments that surrounded the courtyard.

Crispina knocked on door after door, asking those who answered if they knew Max or his parents. Most either shrugged and shut the door in her face, or surveyed her with blank looks and shook their head.

One young woman, a baby at her hip, gave Max a long look. Crispina's interest piqued, hoping she would have something helpful to say. But the young woman only sighed. "With respect, lady, some children are better off away from home." She withdrew into her home and shut the door.

Crispina contemplated her words. Maybe the boy had been forced out by his parents, deemed too much of a burden to feed and clothe, or maybe he'd escaped an unhappy home. Perhaps striving to return him to his home would only bring misery down upon him.

She glanced up at the sky. The afternoon had waned, and the sun was dipping toward the horizon, casting long shadows over the courtyard. Crispina needed to get home before dark. Which meant she had to figure out what to do about Max.

"When is the last time you were home?" she asked.

"Couple days."

"And where have you been staying since then?" Maybe he had found a temple or somewhere to take him in, give him a safe place to sleep.

"Down by the river."

Decidedly not safe, then. Crispina put her hands on her hips and gazed up at the sky, as if the gods might reveal an answer written in the clouds. If she brought Max home, she would have to tell Aelius how she'd found him. He would insist she stop her lessons. Aelius might be generally tolerant, but there was no way he would think it suitable for a prospective tribune's wife to be skulking around a slum.

Or, she would have to lie to her husband, spin up some other story about how she came upon Max. And would Aelius even agree to let a strange child stay in his house?

She would face that battle when she came to it. She let out a sigh of resignation. "All right. You're coming with me."

He looked up at her with a suspicious frown. "You can't order me around."

"Maybe not, but I can offer you good food and a warm bed. Is that inducement enough?"

He narrowed his eyes at her. "You got any more of those cakes?" He nodded toward her basket.

"The kitchen is full of them."

Anticipation lit his face, and he allowed her to lead him from the courtyard.

CHAPTER 18

CRISPINA SPENT THE WALK home thinking up a plausible story. She would have to lie to Gaia too, which pained her. At least Gaia was undoubtedly kind-hearted enough to take the boy in, and hopefully she could convince Aelius if he balked.

She drew Max to a halt in a side street a block from home. She handed him the basket. "Hold this a moment." She unpinned the linen covering from her hair and removed the long shapeless tunic that covered her usual dress. She folded the garments and stowed them in the basket.

Max watched her. "You ain't a real priestess?"

"Aren't," she corrected. "And no. It's…a disguise." She hesitated. How best to make sure the boy didn't give her away?

She crouched down so her face was at his level. "You must promise not to say anything about my lessons, do you understand? It's a secret. If my husband finds out, you'll end up back on the streets." *And possibly me with you.* "And there will be no more cakes."

He nodded slowly.

"Do you swear?"

He made a fist and pressed it to his chest. "On all the cakes in the world," he said solemnly.

She bit back a smile. "Very well, then. Let's go."

They crossed the short distance to the house. Crispina dropped Max's hand once they crossed the threshold. Ajax let them in and raised his eyebrows at Max, but said nothing. Crispina handed her basket to him. "Put this in my library, please."

Ajax nodded and disappeared.

"This way," Crispina said to Max, beckoning him into the atrium. He craned his head up, gawking at the columns that surrounded the pool.

Gaia sat on a bench on the other side of the space, taking advantage of the late afternoon sunlight to work on some mending. She set it aside and rose to her feet when Crispina entered, her face brightening in her customary smile.

Her smile faltered when her gaze landed on Max. "We have a guest, I see?" She came around the pool toward them.

Crispina took a deep breath, summoning the story she had concocted. "This is Max. I ran across him at the market. He's been abandoned by his family, and I couldn't leave him there. I was hoping he could stay with us for a while. Until we sort things out." At least most of that was true.

Max cast her a critical glance, but kept silent as promised.

Gaia gave Max a warm smile. "Hello, Max. What an interesting name."

He stared up at her, mouth falling open. It seemed Gaia's beauty could entrance a male of any age.

Crispina nudged him. "Don't be rude. Say hello."

He mumbled something that might have been a greeting.

Crispina turned back to Gaia. "Aelius isn't home?"

Gaia shook her head. "He'll be back for dinner."

"Do you think he'll…" She didn't want to raise the possibility that Aelius might not let Max stay, not when the boy
could hear it.

Gaia seemed to understand. "He may take some convincing,
which I trust you can manage. In the meantime, I believe
someone could use a bath." She raised an eyebrow at Max's
dirty face and threadbare clothes. "Come along, young man."
She held out a hand. Max latched onto it and trotted after her
toward one of the spare bedrooms.

Crispina followed. She felt a small flare of relief. If Gaia
liked the boy, Aelius would be hard-pressed to throw him
out. She knew Aelius valued his mother's opinion over nearly
everything else, and she hoped it would be enough in this
case.

Getting Max into the tub took both wrestling and cajoling,
but once he felt the warmth of the water, he suffered Crispina
and Gaia to scrub him clean. His skinny body was peppered
with scrapes and bruises. He must have gotten into some
scuffles while living on the streets. His back bore different
marks, faded and thin, as if inflicted by a switch or strap.
Crispina drew in a breath. No wonder he wasn't eager to go
home. By the tightness of Gaia's lips, Crispina knew she had
noticed the marks too, but she said nothing.

After the bath, they dried Max and dressed him in one of
Aelius's tunics. Even the short tunic reached to the boy's ankles,
and the neckline kept slipping off his shoulders. Crispina made a

mental note to send someone to Horatia's later to see if she had any spare child-sized tunics to lend.

Crispina surveyed Max uncertainly as he munched on a plate of figs and grapes on a bench in the atrium, a bribe for the successful completion of the bath. She glanced at Gaia, who was drying her arms. "What exactly does one do with a child?" She knew they had to be kept busy somehow, but she was utterly at a loss for how to pass the time until dinner.

Gaia set aside the towel. "Boys this age are full of energy. They need ways to expend it." She beckoned to Max, who had finished his fruit. "Max, I want you to see how many times you can run around the atrium. I'll give you a honeyed date for each lap you complete. Agreed?"

He nodded and took off, sprinting down the side of the atrium. Crispina watched him, a smile growing. His energy, despite the rough few days he must have had, was infectious.

"Was Aelius like this at his age?"

Gaia's eyes tracked Max as he rounded the corner and ran down the other side of the room. "He was mischievous, yes, always getting into trouble. Little things, like stealing snacks from the kitchen or dousing another child in the atrium pool. He was smart enough to avoid getting in serious trouble. He knew there was always a chance we could be separated." Gaia spoke of her past calmly, with no shame or anger.

Crispina's stomach tightened. "I'm sorry for all you've suffered."

Gaia cast her a glance. "Everyone has their own suffering. Even someone like you, born into privilege and luxury. You have known hardship and pain, if I'm not mistaken."

Gaia was being too generous in comparing her past to Crispina's. Crispina said nothing, watching Max complete another lap. His pace was flagging, and when he reached the spot where they stood, he stumbled to a halt and threw himself to the ground, lying on his back and breathing hard. "Three," he gasped. "You owe me three dates."

Gaia smiled. "Well done. You'll have them at dinner."

A noise sounded from the entrance: the front door opening. Crispina flinched. Aelius was home. She cast Gaia a panicked glance, but Gaia looked as calm as ever.

Aelius entered the atrium. "Good evening—" His words broke off when he saw Max, lying on the flagstones.

The boy scrambled to his feet and fixed Aelius with a wary glare.

Aelius glanced from Max to Crispina to Gaia. "Why is there a strange child in my house?"

Crispina stepped forward. "I, er..." Her tongue was tied in knots. Lying to his face was harder than she imagined. She decided to skip the lie. "His name is Max. Or at least, that's what we've agreed to call him. He has nowhere to go. I thought perhaps we could take him in for a while."

Aelius frowned. "Is he some relation of yours?"

Crispina shook her head. "No. I, er, I encountered him in the city today. He was lost, abandoned. Hungry. I brought him home. I didn't know what else to do." She let out a breath. None of her words were technically false.

His frown deepened, his face acquiring a look of stern bewilderment. "So you brought a street rat into our house?"

Gaia cleared her throat. "There's no need for rudeness." She nudged Max on the shoulder. "Why don't you take another lap around the room?"

Max huffed and broke into a jog.

Aelius's expression hadn't lightened. "There are thousands of hungry, homeless children in Rome. Please tell me you have a better reason for bringing this one home."

"It was the right thing to do." Crispina met his gaze, refusing to quail before him though she knew she had overstepped. As master of the house, he had ultimate authority over everyone and everything under this roof. Now, tall and glowering, he looked every inch the threatening paterfamilias. But she would make him see that she was right.

Aelius turned to his mother. "And you are in favor of this?"

Gaia opened her mouth to reply, but at that moment Max rounded the corner nearest to them. He overshot the turn and careened into a pedestal holding a painted vase on the edge of the room. The pedestal rocked. The vase toppled.

Crispina leaped toward it, but too late. With a deafening crash, the vase shattered on the stone floor.

Max leaped back. "Juno's cunt!"

"Max!" Crispina's voice rose to a shriek. Such language was appalling, even more so coming from a child. "That language will not be tolerated!"

"Now look what he's done!" Aelius exploded.

Max hid behind Gaia, who had blanched at his exclamation but allowed him to use her as a shield.

"It's just a vase, Aelius," Crispina said.

"It was an antique," Aelius snapped. "An expensive antique, inherited from my stepfather."

Crispina pressed her lips together. Aelius had never shown any particular interest in art objects before. He was seizing on this to stoke the flames of his displeasure.

"Clearly, we need to talk. In private." Aelius strode toward his study.

Crispina cast a helpless glance at Gaia before hurrying to follow him.

Once in his study, he pulled the door shut hard behind her. Crispina took a deep breath. "I know this is all rather a surprise. Believe me, I did not expect to be returning with a child today, but—"

"Then why did you?" Aelius demanded.

"I told you, I couldn't leave him. He needed help. I tried to find his family, but I couldn't, and even if I did, he said they forced him to leave. And I don't think it was a happy home." She stared at him. Here was the face, the body she'd gotten to know so well by now. She knew the freckles on his chest, the spot on his neck that made him shudder when she kissed it. She knew what his face looked like when he was lost in ecstasy.

Now, that face was stern, frowning, displeased. He folded his arms in front of him. Lamplight glinted off his silver armband. "I did not realize you were desperate enough for a child that you would snatch one off the streets."

Crispina's teeth ground together. His words stabbed at the tender part of her heart that was starting to belong to him, but she summoned a façade of coldness to dull the pain. "I did not realize you were selfish enough to deny shelter to a helpless child."

"I haven't denied anything. I suppose the boy can help in the kitchens or run errands. As I did at his age."

"If he stays, he will be treated as a guest." Crispina took a step closer, fists clenching at her sides. "I know you suffered greatly as a child, but you never had to worry about going hungry or sleeping outside."

Aelius's face looked like it had been iced over. "Don't compare that child to me. I lived every day fearing I'd be separated from my mother."

"At least you have a mother who loves you. Max has no one. I thought you cared about those who are vulnerable and powerless. You seek to represent the people as tribune. Now is your chance to care for one of them."

"That child is a freeborn Roman citizen," Aelius hissed. "No matter his disadvantages, he has something I will never have, no matter how high I rise." His hand went to his silver armband, fingers wrapping around it. "If word gets out that I've taken a foul-mouthed, unkempt brat into my house, it will draw attention. And that kind of attention is the last thing I need. The patricians I'll need to court don't want to support a candidate who fills his house with grubby children. It's just not done, Crispina."

"Is the welfare of a child not worth risking your political success?"

"Nothing is worth that."

Crispina folded her arms across her chest and fixed him with her steeliest glare. "Are you going to throw him out, then?"

Aelius glowered at the floor, a muscle in his jaw pulsing.

"Think very carefully," Crispina murmured. "If he goes, I go."

Aelius's head snapped up. They shared a long gaze. Then, he pushed past her, flung open the door, and thrust himself through it. He called for his cloak. A moment later, the front door opened and closed.

Crispina let out a long breath. At least he hadn't insisted Max leave.

She left the study and returned to where Gaia and Max waited in the atrium. She cast Gaia a rueful look. "Aelius left." A humiliating thing to admit to her mother-in-law.

Gaia nodded calmly. "We heard. He will return."

Max looked up at her, his brow creased and his jaw set. A hint of apprehension darkened his gaze. He must have heard enough to understand Aelius didn't want him here.

Crispina summoned a smile and held out a hand to him. "Dinner should be ready by now. And I believe we owe you some honeyed dates?"

"You ain't throwing me out, then?"

"Aren't. And no." *At least, not tonight.* "Are you hungry?"

He nodded eagerly and grasped her hand.

CHAPTER 19

Aelius stared at the dinner laid out before him on Catullus's dining table. He hadn't known where else to go but Catullus's house, and his friend had welcomed him immediately.

Catullus listened with the appropriate shock at the story of what Crispina had done. Aelius rubbed his temples when he finished the tale. What was she thinking, bringing that boy home? It was inconceivable. The child could rob them all blind. He'd already destroyed one expensive vase.

"What do I do?" Aelius asked, a question for himself as much as for Catullus.

Catullus delicately picked a fish bone from the filet before him. "Either the child stays, or he leaves. If he leaves, Crispina made it clear she would leave as well. And I don't think you want to risk that sort of scandal."

"Having the child stay attracts gossip on its own," Aelius countered.

"You keep claiming that is the reason why you are so averse to the child, but I wonder…" Catullus gave him an intense, searching stare. "I have never known you to become this perturbed by something."

Aelius glanced away. Catullus's gaze was like a too-scratchy tunic. He wanted to shrug it off and escape from it.

"I think you are jealous of the boy," Catullus murmured into his wine cup.

Aelius barked a laugh. "Jealous! How do you figure?"

"Firstly, I imagine there is some jealousy at the attentions of your wife. Crispina has put someone else over you, after all. She threatens to leave you if you do not let the boy stay."

Her ultimatum had rankled, it was true, especially as they had just started to grow close to each other. But Aelius kept silent, unwilling to admit there might be a seed of truth in what Catullus said.

"Secondly, I presume, based on your history, you would envy a young boy who has been plucked from hardship and disadvantage, carried into a life of privilege and luxury. A life that could erase his humble origins. Why him and not you?"

Aelius took a sharp breath. His hand went to his silver wristband. Suddenly, the unreasonable frustration that filled him when he looked at Max made sense.

"So was I right?" Catullus asked.

"Maybe," Aelius muttered. This was one of those uncanny insights that must make Catullus such a good poet. Regret filled him at the harsh words he'd spewed at his wife. "I suppose I should go apologize to Crispina."

"Grovel a bit," Catullus advised. "You know she appreciates a good grovel."

Aelius groaned and rose to his feet. "Thank you for dinner."

"Good luck. If she's barred the door, you can sleep here."

Aelius grimaced and left.

He returned home before full darkness had fallen and went to the dining room first. It was empty but for Cassandra clearing away the dinner plates. Her belly was now clearly round with child. She nodded to him when he poked his head into the room. "Good evening, sir."

"Have they gone to bed?"

"I believe they are putting the boy to bed in one of the spare bedrooms, sir." Her nose wrinkled. The whole household must be wondering what their mistress was thinking, bringing home a child off the streets.

"Thank you." He left. At the other end of the hall, light spilled from a door left ajar, and his mother's voice sounded from within. Aelius approached. He lurked outside, not sure if his intrusion would be welcomed. The sliver of open door revealed the boy sitting in bed, pillows mounded behind his head. Gaia fussed over him, straightening the blankets and plumping the pillows. A shadow moved beyond his view, which must be Crispina, standing off to the side.

"Now, are you comfortable?" Gaia asked.

Max nodded, then yawned. Gaia smiled, patting his hair. "You've had a long day, haven't you? Good night, my dear." She leaned down and kissed his forehead.

Jealousy twisted inside Aelius, and he had to look away. He retreated to his own bedroom. He was being ridiculous. There was no sense in being jealous of a child, even if Aelius had never had such a nice bedroom as a child and had been relegated to sleeping on a pallet beneath a kitchen table.

He was not that child anymore. He had a home all his own, a name, a family. A future that was his to mold. He had achieved a great deal, and he could afford to give a little to a child in need.

Crispina entered the bedroom a moment later. She drew to a halt when her gaze found him. "You're back." Her voice was wary, uncertain.

"I dined with Catullus. How is the boy?"

"Nearly ate us out of house and home. He will sleep well tonight." She hesitated. "He is sorry for breaking the vase."

"I don't care about the vase." He crossed the room to take her hands. "Crispina, I'm sorry for how I acted. I was rude, and selfish, and wrong. The boy will stay, for as long as you wish him to." He wanted to ask what that meant—a week, a month, longer?—but held off.

Her features softened, her fingers twining with his. "What led to this change of heart?"

"Catullus," he admitted. "He pointed out that I may have been acting so horribly out of jealousy."

"Jealousy? Of a homeless child abandoned by his family?"

His armband felt heavy on his wrist. "Of a child lifted from hardship and offered all these comforts."

Chagrin flickered across her face. "I'm sorry. I know I came on too strong, I should have thought…"

"You did exactly as you should have." He pulled her against him. The warmth of her body soothed the last traces of his bad temper. "I didn't like fighting with you."

She leaned her head against his shoulder. "Nor I you."

"I suppose I owe the boy—Max—an apology as well."

She nodded. "But that can wait until tomorrow." She tilted her face up. His arms tightened around her, and he closed his eyes as his mouth met hers.

Crispina woke with Aelius's naked body curled around hers, as had become their routine of late. She smiled and relaxed into his warmth.

But something was not routine. It itched at her for a moment until she remembered. She jolted upright, the movement jerking Aelius awake. *The boy. Max. Here.*

Would he have woken already? What did children do in the mornings? He would need to be fed, she was fairly certain of that. She swung her legs out of bed and fetched a dress from her wardrobe.

Aelius stirred with a groan. "It's early."

"I want to check on Max." She threw the dress on and brushed her hair, yanking the comb through the tangles that had arisen overnight.

His eyes opened fully. "I'll come with you. I should introduce myself properly to our guest."

Her chest warmed with gratitude that he now accepted Max's presence. She knew they needed to have another conversation about what the future held: would Max stay permanently? Would they try to find his family? What happened when they divorced? But for now, this was enough.

They went to the door of the spare bedroom. Crispina knocked gently. "Max? Are you awake?"

No response. She pushed the door open gently. "Max?"

The room was empty, the covers on the bed rumpled. She drew in a sharp breath. "Where is he?" Had he run away, disappeared somewhere? Her heart sped up. He had seemed fine last night, but she would never forgive herself if her fight with Aelius had scared the boy into thinking he was not welcome.

"Perhaps he woke early and went to the kitchen to find some food." Aelius started down the corridor, then paused in front of the door to his mother's room. He tipped his ear to the door, then beckoned Crispina closer.

She joined him. From inside Gaia's room, she heard Gaia's laugh mixed with the sound of Max chattering about something to do with horses. Relief flowed through her.

She tapped on the door. "Gaia? It's Crispina and Aelius. We were looking for Max."

"Come in," Gaia called. "He's here."

Crispina eased open the door. Gaia was sitting up in bed with Max beside her. "I hope he's not bothering you."

"Not at all. Apparently our guest is afraid of the dark and found it more comfortable to spend the night with me than alone."

"Oh." It hadn't even occurred to her that he might be afraid of the dark. She should have asked, or offered to leave a lamp lit. She really was ill-suited to taking care of a child. But perhaps this was just one more thing for her to learn. "Well, thank you. Max, are you hungry?"

"Starved." He gave her an accusatory look, as if she hadn't fed him triple helpings of dinner last night.

"Come along, then. We can see to breakfast."

Max hopped off the bed and sprinted to the room's threshold, but stopped short when he caught sight of Aelius in the corridor. He stared up at Aelius warily, hugging his arms around his thin body.

Aelius crouched down to put his face level with Max's, speaking in that smooth voice that never failed to win people over. "I wanted to introduce myself properly, Max. I'm Aelius, Crispina's husband. I'm very sorry for our argument yesterday. I should have welcomed you into our home straightaway."

Max narrowed his eyes. "I ain't afraid of you."

"Am not," Crispina said through a smile.

"Good," Aelius said. "I'm not afraid of you either, but perhaps I would be if I were an antique vase." He leaned toward Max, his voice dropping to a conspiratorial whisper. "I *am* afraid of her, though." His chin jerked toward Crispina. "Just a bit. So you must do exactly as she says when she is looking after you. Or else you may find yourself turned into a frog."

Crispina put her hands on her hips. "Please don't put ideas in his head."

Max surveyed her. "She ain't scary. When she—"

"Isn't," Crispina corrected firmly, cutting off the rest of Max's words. She was afraid he was going to forget his promise from yesterday and mention something about her lessons. "Come along. Breakfast awaits." She held out a hand.

Max eyed her hand for a long moment, then took it. "I wouldn't mind being a frog. Just so you know."

Crispina cast a dry glance back at a grinning Aelius. "I'll keep that in mind."

By the end of her first day with Max, Crispina wanted only to sink into a large tub of hot water in a dark, silent room.

"Are all children like this?" she asked Gaia as Max cavorted around the atrium, chasing a leather ball.

Gaia smiled indulgently. "He is rather energetic, isn't he?"

They had removed everything breakable from the near vicinity, but Max had still managed to topple a stone planter, spilling dirt onto the tile floor. Even with Gaia's help, it seemed a Herculean task to come up with enough activities to occupy the child for the day. Children, it seemed, couldn't be left to their own devices. They had to be entertained, and it was exhausting.

They had set him to shelling peas in the kitchen for a while, turning it into a challenge to see who could shell the most in the shortest time. After that, Crispina had managed to get him to sit still for half an hour for another reading lesson, but he seemed more interested in scraping all the wax off the tablet than reading the letters she scratched out for him.

There had been a brief moment of quiet after lunch when he had been content to sit and watch Gaia weave, but soon he'd regained his energy and challenged himself to see if he could throw the ball far enough to land on the other side of the atrium pool. That activity was what had topped the planter.

He needed other children to play with. Unfortunately, none of the slaves had children. Crispina planned to visit Horatia tomorrow and ask her if she would allow Max to visit Paullus, as the boys were close enough to the same age.

A noise sounded from the front door, and Aelius emerged into the atrium toting an oddly-shaped bag over his shoulder. "Hello, ladies." He greeted Crispina with a kiss and smiled at Gaia. "I've brought gifts for our young guest." He waved Max over and set down his bag.

Max approached, clutching the ball in both hands. His eyes widened as Aelius removed four wooden ships from the bag, each a different size and shape. They even had sails of fine white linen.

Aelius laid them out in a row. "I thought we could try to sail them on the pool. Which do you like best?"

Max immediately jumped toward the biggest, a red-painted naval trireme with two sails. Aelius selected a smaller vessel modeled after a pleasure yacht one might sail at Baiae. "Shall we try them?"

Crispina retreated to the other side of the pool, leaning against a column to watch them. Gaia disappeared to check on dinner, and likely to steal some quiet time. Crispina could have done the same, but she couldn't stop smiling at the sight of Aelius and Max.

They launched all four boats into the pool. One sprang a leak and sank immediately. Another became overbalanced by its mast and toppled over. Aelius's pleasure yacht and Max's trireme remained afloat. Max jumped up and down in excitement. He leaned forward, blowing air into the sails to send the boat halfway across the pool.

Aelius's yacht soon overtook the trireme, by virtue of Aelius's larger lungs. Max stuck his arms into the water and stirred up waves. Crispina wasn't sure if he was trying to sink Aelius's boat or induce his own to travel faster.

But the boats were stuck in the middle of the pool, too far away for the sails to work. Max's shoulders slumped. "They're stuck!" he complained.

Aelius nudged him. "All is not lost." He gave Crispina a significant look. "I sense the presence of a sea goddess who may take mercy on our vessels."

Crispina rolled her eyes but approached the pool from the opposite side. The boats had drifted a bit, so if she knelt and stretched as far as she could, her fingertips could brush each. She arched an eyebrow at Aelius, then flicked the sail of his yacht, causing the boat to capsize.

Aelius let out an outraged shout. "That's not fair!"

Crispina shrugged. She hooked a finger onto the edge of Max's boat and drew it gently toward her. "The goddess is fickle."

Max let out a gleeful shout as his boat bumped against the other side of the pool. "I won!" He raced around the pool to retrieve his dripping boat from the water, holding it reverently.

"Through treachery," Aelius grumbled.

"I'm sure the goddess will be on your side another time," Crispina said. "Max, go put that in your room before dinner."

As soon as Max vanished, Aelius wrapped a firm arm around Crispina's waist, drawing her close. "I rather like my fickle goddess."

Heat rushed through her at his embrace. "Perhaps she will not be so capricious if worshipped properly."

"Mm." He lowered his head to brush her cheek with his lips. "I am prepared to worship. And make a *very* large offering." His hand squeezed her bottom, sparking another jolt of desire that tightened in her core.

She wanted nothing more than to abandon dinner and retreat to their bedroom, but Max reappeared. Aelius jumped away from her, affecting a casual posture.

Max frowned at her. "You're all red."

"That's very rude," Crispina said, hoping the sharpness in her voice would hide her embarrassment. "Run along to dinner."

He trotted toward the dining room. Crispina turned to shoot Aelius an apologetic smile, then followed.

CHAPTER 20

T HE NEXT DAY, CRISPINA left Max in Gaia's care and paid a visit to Horatia. She relayed the real story of how she'd ended up with Max, the argument with Aelius, and their reconciliation. Horatia listened with wide eyes.

"So, I came to ask if you have any tunics Max might borrow until we can make some things for him," Crispina finished. "And I thought Max might enjoy meeting Paullus. He needs a friend, and they could play together. May I bring him over? Or would you prefer to visit?" Horatia had not visited Crispina since before her marriage, which Crispina had attributed to the recent birth of her baby.

"I'll send someone with some spare tunics straightaway," Horatia said. "But for the other matter, well…" She fiddled with a carnelian ring on her left hand. "I'm not sure they'd get along."

"They're children. Children play together, don't they?"

"You said yourself the child was unruly and foul-mouthed. I worry about the influence he'll have on my Paullus."

Crispina raised an eyebrow. "Max may have absorbed some undesirable habits from his upbringing, but he's a good boy. Your son's influence would only help him develop more genteel behavior."

Horatia chewed her lip. "Is Aelius going to adopt him?"

The unexpected question threw Crispina. "I-I don't know." She hadn't thought that far ahead. Would Aelius do that?

Horatia shifted on the couch. "I realize you're not a mother, so it's difficult for you to understand these things."

"What things?" Horatia's air of superiority rankled, but Crispina strove for equanimity. She had already recognized she knew very little about caring for a child, so maybe Horatia's experience would be helpful.

"Well, as a mother, I must put my child's happiness above all else, even helping a friend."

"How is meeting Max detrimental to Paullus's happiness?" A defensive edge sharpened Crispina's voice.

"It's nothing personal, of course. I'm sure he's a delightful boy. But Paullus is of an age where his friendships matter to his future success. He must be associating with future senators and consuls. Not..." Her words trailed off.

Crispina bristled. "Not what?"

"Not a vagrant who's become your latest project," Horatia snapped.

Crispina's nails dug into her palms. Horatia could be haughty and vain sometimes, but she hadn't thought her friend's worse traits would extend to depriving a child of a playmate. Anger bubbled inside her, and the words came as fast and sharp as arrows. "Paullus would be lucky to befriend Max. You've changed, Horatia. Once we used to hold those lessons together. But now all you care about is—"

"Yes, I've changed," Horatia interjected. "Those visits were a novelty. A distraction. Now, I'm a wife and a mother. I have to worry about my own children and their future. Not some vagrant whose parents can't be bothered to provide for him. And I can see that marriage has changed you as well. I can't imagine you'd pursue something so obviously unsuitable without the influence of your freedman husband."

Crispina narrowed her eyes. "Is that why you haven't once invited me and Aelius to dine with you since we've been married? Or visited me at home?"

Horatia blinked. "I see you all the time."

"But you've never met Aelius. You've never stepped foot in our house." She hadn't allowed herself to acknowledge how impolite Horatia had been until now, but the realization crashed over her in a disquieting wave. "You think he's beneath you."

Horatia's face flushed. "Is that such a surprise? He's a *freedman*, Crispina."

"He is my husband." Crispina surged to her feet. "Am I beneath you too?"

"Of course not!" Horatia protested. "You're, well…one of us."

One of us. All her life, Crispina had been raised to believe that family, ancestry determined everything. It put power at the fingertips of a select few, and everyone else was supposed to be content with their lot. Her lessons had challenged those beliefs in a small way, yes, but Aelius was the one who had truly shattered all of her illusions.

"If you don't want him," Crispina said, "then you can't have me either. We are bound together."

"Bound together?" Horatia let out a disbelieving laugh. "You never talked this way when you were married to Memmius. Don't tell me you're actually falling for a freedman."

"What if I am?" Crispina shot back. The words came out before she could think them through. Their meaning hit her with a rush of dizziness.

Somehow, inexplicably, she was falling in love with her husband.

"You know he's going to divorce you," Horatia said. "I thought that was always the plan."

Crispina cleared her throat. *It is.* "We have nothing left to discuss." Without another word, she left the room and strode through the house until she reached the front door. A slave opened it for her and stood aside.

She paused before the open door, wondering if Horatia would run after her and apologize. But the house was silent, so she nodded to the slave and left.

She took the long way home, hoping the walk would boil off some of her anger. It didn't. When she arrived home, she went straight to the library and slammed the door behind her. She could hear Max and Gaia laughing somewhere in the house, but she didn't want to see them, didn't want to have to explain why she was angry. Max might not understand, but it would hurt Gaia to know that Crispina's friend didn't think Aelius was good enough to associate with.

Crispina paced the small library in a tight circle. She wished there was something in here she could throw, smash. She eyed a tempting inkwell, but that would only make a mess.

She had never argued with Horatia before, not like this. Her friend could often be snobbish and haughty, but it had never bothered Crispina so much.

You just took the side of a man you've known for mere months over the best friend you've grown up with. But somehow, Aelius had slipped into her heart without her notice. His side was the one she wanted to be on, no matter the cost.

A knock came at the door to the library. "Crispina?"

Aelius. She frowned. She hadn't expected to see him until evening. "Yes?"

"Are you hungry? I decided to come back for lunch. Thought you could use the company."

She felt a flare of appreciation beneath her anger. Aelius rarely returned home for lunch, and he must be doing it now because of Max. "Thank you. I'll be out in a few minutes."

He paused. "Can I come in?"

She didn't want him to know about her argument with Horatia, but if she refused to see him, he would know something was wrong anyway. She sighed. "Yes."

He opened the door, entered, and closed it behind him. "You look upset."

Her lips tightened. He'd gotten to know her too well. *Might as well come out with it.* "I went to see Horatia to tell her about Max. She doesn't want him to associate with her son."

His eyes darkened. "On what grounds?"

"Apparently her son needs friends of a higher caliber. Max will be a bad influence." Bitterness tainted her words. "I think I may not see her again. She said certain things that will be hard to forgive." *About you both.*

Aelius nodded slowly. "I'm sorry. I know you're close."

"But there was one thing she mentioned that I hadn't thought of. She asked if..." Crispina hesitated. It felt much too soon to bring this up. "She asked if you might adopt Max. One day. If he were to stay here."

Aelius was silent, his face unreadable.

"I understand if you wouldn't," Crispina said hurriedly. "I'd never ask it of you, I know it's a big—"

"I might," Aelius said quietly.

Crispina stared at him. "Really?"

"One day, if his family doesn't make themselves known, I might." A tentative smile crept over his face. "I would have had nothing if my stepfather hadn't adopted me. I wouldn't have been able to run for office. A name is the greatest gift anyone has ever given me. If I could give that to someone else, why wouldn't I?"

Her eyes prickled. "I…that's…" She couldn't summon the proper words to express the warmth that was suffusing her, a different kind of heat from her anger.

Aelius stepped toward her and clasped her shoulders, then drew her in to embrace her. His hand came up to cradle the back of her head, pressing her gently to his chest. "Of all the things I never expected from our marriage," he murmured against her cheek, "a child was at the top of the list."

Her throat tightened, and she was glad she could hide her face in his chest. She took a deep, shuddering breath to compose herself, then pulled back. "Time for lunch?"

He smiled down at her, and dipped his head to kiss her on the forehead. "Time for lunch."

CHAPTER 21

ELIUS'S WORDS LINGERED IN Crispina's mind for the rest of the day. *Of all the things I never expected from our marriage, a child was at the top of the list.* Sitting next to him at dinner, while he tried to dissuade Max from tossing nuts into his goblet, she thought back to their first meeting, when she'd found him arrogant and thoughtless.

Now, he had somehow become her family. Even as they had grown closer over the past weeks, she'd still been keeping her distance, knowing their marriage would end. Aelius needed an heir, and until today, Crispina believed another woman would have to give that to him.

But nothing was certain anymore. If Aelius adopted Max, could she have a life with him?

She glanced over at her husband. He had given up trying to get Max to stop throwing nuts and now they were both trying to see if they could land a nut in Gaia's goblet across the table. Gaia cast her eyes skyward and covered her goblet with a napkin.

Crispina could imagine no place she'd rather be, no people she'd rather be with. She wanted Aelius, wanted a life with him, wanted to be standing at his side when he won this election and all the ones to come, wanted to grow old with him. An image rose in her mind: ten years from now, Aelius being confirmed as consul before the senate, herself at his side as he achieved his great, improbable dream.

Her eyes moistened, and she turned her face quickly toward her plate. Gods, what was wrong with her?

She focused on Aelius once more, on his nimble fingers as he launched a nut across the table. She knew those hands almost better than her own these days. Another thought intruded, one wholly inappropriate for the dinner table. Perhaps Max's arrival had inadvertently removed the last barrier between her and Aelius, the one thing she'd been holding back.

She reached for her wine, her throat suddenly parched. Yes, she wanted him…and tonight, maybe she would have him.

Aelius caught her staring at him and grinned at her. She returned the smile, suddenly wishing they were at a loud, crowded dinner party so she could lean over and whisper something enticing in his ear.

But Max and Gaia were their only companions, so she held back until the meal was finished, until she and Gaia put Max to bed, until she joined Aelius in their bedroom.

He reclined in bed, reading over a piece of papyrus.

"Reading anything good?" Crispina asked as she bent to take off her sandals.

"A list of influential patricians and notes on how to win over each of them. I already crossed off your father. I presume becoming his son-in-law is enough to gain the votes he controls."

"What will you promise the others, since you can no longer sell yourself into marriage for a handful of votes?"

Aelius glanced over the list. "One man has shipping interests, so I would promise to support a bill mandating harsher penalties for smuggling. This other man wants to build a temple, Catullus tells me, seemingly out of piety but no doubt so his own name will be plastered all over it. He will need the plebeian assembly's approval to consecrate the land. I can promise to help with that if elected."

"The city doesn't need another temple when the homes of its own citizens are crumbling," Crispina muttered. She thought of the slum where she'd found Max, the dilapidated apartment blocks at constant risk of fire or collapse.

Aelius sighed. "Believe me, I know. But I need to ensure enough support to win the election. Unless you have a better idea?"

Crispina folded her arms as she thought, momentarily allowing herself to be distracted from her aim tonight. "What if there's a compromise? Downgrade the temple to a shrine, and suggest the man use the remaining funds to rebuild areas of the city in disrepair. He would please the gods and the people at the same time."

Aelius gave a slow, approving nod. "You're right."

She shot him a smile, then pulled her dress over her head and tossed it away. Aelius sat up in bed. He had seen her body many times by now, but he always had the same stunned, worshipful expression on his face whenever she bared herself.

He patted the bed next to him. "Come to bed."

"I need to take down my hair." Still naked, she sat at her dressing table and removed the pins and thread holding her hairstyle in place. Now that the discussion of politics was done, her mind returned to what she wanted tonight.

It would be easy, not to mention pleasurable, to go along with the activities they always enjoyed. He wouldn't ask for more.

If she wanted this, she had to ask for it. Nerves tumbled in her stomach.

Aelius got out of bed and came to stand behind her. She stilled her hands and let him take over. He extracted the last few pins, then leaned over her to pick up the ivory comb from her dressing table. He ran it through her hair gently, reverently, to clear the tangles. Then, his fingers divided her hair into three parts. He braided it just as she liked, not too tight or too loose, and tied it with a thin leather cord. His hand swept from her hair to the front of her throat, gently tipping her head back. He bent and kissed her.

Her nervousness spiked as their lips met, but she allowed the pleasure of his touch to wash away her anxiety. She broke the kiss to stand and turn around. He kicked the chair out of the way and pulled her to him, his hands skimming down her back to grasp her bottom. His arousal, temptingly stiff, pushed against her hip through his tunic. She stroked it through the fabric, and he groaned in her ear.

He drew her toward the bed, and a moment later she was beneath him, his fingers delving between her legs.

"Aelius, I…" She swallowed hard. "I want you," she whispered.

He chuckled. "I'm yours." He lowered his head to kiss her shoulder.

"No, I, I…" She shivered as his lips tickled her skin. "I *want* you." She tried to imbue the words with more significance, but he merely looked at her with a raised eyebrow.

She tried again. "I want you...inside me." Her cheeks burned. Divine Juno, why did this have to be so difficult?

"As you command." He slid a gentle finger inside her, followed by another.

She arched into him, her eyes fluttering closed as he filled her. "I didn't mean fingers," she managed amid a gasp of pleasure. He was going to make her spell it out, wasn't he?

He withdrew his hand. "Tell me what you meant." His voice sounded deeper, rougher than usual.

She struggled for words once more. "I think you know what I meant."

"I want to hear you say it. I *need* to hear you say it."

She kept her eyes closed. There was no way she could look at him now. "I want...your cock..." Her voice dropped to a pathetic mumble. "Inside me."

His breath caught. His lips brushed her neck. "And what do you want me to do with it?" he murmured against her skin.

Her eyes shot open. "I imagine that's perfectly clear. Surely you're not that dense." She managed to regain some sharpness to her voice.

His hand found her breast, thumb sliding over her nipple. "You know a great many words, Crispina. Use them."

"I fear I would rather recite Homer." Her voice became unsteady again, rendered breathless by his touch.

He let out a soft chuckle. His hand trailed down her stomach to tease between her legs. He stroked her slowly, maddeningly.

She groaned. Why did her husband have to be the sort of man who delighted in these evil games? Why couldn't he be the type who would fling her onto her back and take her as soon as he had the barest permission?

"All right," she finally gasped. "I want you to fuck me, Aelius. There. Are you happy now?"

"Blissfully. Just one more question."

"Aelius!"

He stopped touching her and sat up, taking the warmth of his body away from her. His face grew serious. "Why now? Why tonight, after all these months?"

Another question that would be painfully difficult to answer. Crispina sat up too. "This will sound strange, but I believe it's partly due to Max."

His eyebrows raised. "That beastly little scamp has made you want to lie with me?"

Crispina smiled. "In a strange way. I didn't want to lie with you at first because I was afraid of what would happen if I didn't conceive a child. I was holding onto a tiny, foolish hope that maybe it would be different with a different man. And I didn't want that hope to go away. Even though I've never longed for a baby, I just…wanted to know if I could do it. But now, with Max, I've realized we could be a family of sorts. So it doesn't matter if I can bear a child or not."

A relieved smile lit his face. "Was that what it was? I was afraid you didn't think I was good enough for you."

"You are the best I could ever hope for. More than I deserve." *And to Dis with what Horatia or anyone else thinks.*

He cupped her cheek, then his brow furrowed, and he hesitated for a moment. "I know our arrangement included talk of ending things after the election. But now…" He lowered his head to brush her forehead with a kiss. "I can't bear the thought of being parted from you."

Her heart felt as if it would burst. Warmth swelled within her, and she pulled him close. "Make me your wife, Aelius, truly. Forever. And *don't* make me do any more talking."

He let out a dark chuckle as he rolled on top of her. His weight pressed her into the bed. A memory flashed through Crispina's mind of the last time she had done this with Memmius. Her chest tightened, but she took a deep breath and ran a hand down Aelius's arm, feeling the light fur of hair that coated his lean muscles. His weight was grounding and comforting, not oppressive and stifling.

She braced her knees against his hips, opening herself to him. "Yes," she hissed as he eased himself inside her.

He worked himself into her with gentle, easy movements. When he finally sank all the way in, he let out a rough sigh, sensual tension etched in every line of his face.

Warm pleasure filled her. She hooked her calves over his legs, urging him deeper. He kept his arms braced on either side of her head to hold most of his weight off of her, and moved in slow, smooth strokes.

Too slow. She tangled a hand in his hair and pulled. "Harder." She needed more, needed to feel him in every inch of her body.

He obliged with a groan, setting a hard, fast rhythm that made undignified sounds burst from her mouth with every thrust. She clung to him, digging her nails into his back and shoulders as the pleasure grew nearly unbearable.

He lowered his chest onto her, finally letting her take his full weight. The change in position, while slight, tweaked something between them. The pleasure swelled and burst. Shudders wracked her body, and she writhed beneath him, hips bucking as if she'd throw him off.

But he kept her pinioned beneath him, a hand gripping her hip to keep him deep inside her. She reveled in his iron grasp as pulsing, sparkling waves of pleasure coursed through her.

Aelius slammed into her one final time with a grunted curse. Then his body went limp, and he collapsed onto her, chest heaving. Crispina stroked the back of his head. He raised his head enough to kiss her forehead, then rolled off her, freeing her from his weight. "My wife," he whispered with a lazy, exhausted smile.

Crispina snuggled into his chest, heedless of the sweat that coated them both. "Always."

CHAPTER 22

C RISPINA SMILED TO HERSELF as she knelt in the dirt to gather the writing materials from today's lesson. Max was off in another corner of the courtyard tossing a ball with the rest of her students.

Her smiles came easier nowadays. Five months of blissful coupling with Aelius had that effect, apparently. Their marriage was now eight months old in total, and now only five weeks remained until the election.

A chilly winter had passed, during which Cassandra gave birth to a healthy baby girl. Taurus was a doting father, and the couple named their daughter Aelia Crispina.

Little Aelia was the only baby who would grace their home for now. A familiar ache brewed low in Crispina's stomach as she reached for the last wax tablet. She sighed. Her courses would arrive in the next day or two, no doubt. Right on schedule. Over the past five months since she'd been lying with Aelius, she had slowly abandoned her hope of conceiving a child. The disappointment lessened each month. Now, she barely spared it a thought.

The only true dark spot in her happiness was her falling out with Horatia, but even that couldn't dull her joy. Horatia had sent her a letter about a week after their fight with a detailed apology. Upon reading it, Crispina felt a momentary tug toward forgiveness, but cast the letter aside without replying. She had Aelius, Max, and Gaia now. She didn't need her old snobbish friend, apology or no.

Crispina stacked the wax tablets in her basket, then counted the styluses. One was missing. She glanced up to scan the ground for it—and her gaze lit on a pair of feet wearing sandals of tooled leather. Her head jerked up to see the hem of a blue-dyed tunic, embroidered with silver thread. Much too fine for this neighborhood.

She looked up even further to find a man's narrow face staring down at her. Sunlight turned his blond hair to flashes of gold.

Crispina scrambled to her feet. "Rufus," she gasped. What was Publius Veturius Rufus doing here, of all places?

Her husband's opponent lowered his head in a stiff nod. "Crispina."

Two hulking men flanked Rufus, each twice his size and wearing matching gray tunics. The courtyard had gone silent. Crispina glanced around. The children had vanished. Except Max, who was staring at the four of them with his small fists clenched.

Crispina's mouth went dry. Danger hummed in the air, but she couldn't think what this all was about. She thought back to the last time she'd seen Rufus, when accepting his insincere apology in the Forum, and summoned the cool demeanor she'd affected then. "Are you lost, Rufus? I'd be happy to escort you home. Oh, forgive me, perhaps you're visiting family here."

His pale cheeks flushed. It was too easy to antagonize him by reminding him of his humble roots as the son of a baker. "Alas, lady, neither of your conjectures are correct. I came to see you."

"How…" She swallowed hard. *How did you find me here?*

"I've been having you followed for the last month. Your husband too, but I'm afraid he never goes anywhere interesting. Not like you."

Crispina's breath stopped for a moment, but she raised her chin. "What do you want, Rufus?"

"Merely to warn you." His voice warmed with sickly concern. "This is a dangerous neighborhood. I'm sure your husband would not want to hear that you put yourself at risk."

Out of the corner of her eye, Crispina noticed Max had inched closer, until he hovered about six feet from them. She willed him to stay quiet. Whatever this was, she didn't want him to get in the middle of it.

The threat was clear behind Rufus's words. Whatever he wanted, if she didn't give it to him, he would tell Aelius, and perhaps others, of her activities. Which meant she had to bluff.

She coated her words in ice. "I have no secrets from my husband. He knows of my little project here, and I have his full support."

Rufus raised a golden eyebrow but said nothing.

"I appreciate your concern, Rufus, but I must return home before twilight." She took a step toward her basket, lying on the ground to her side.

Rufus's hand flashed out and closed around her wrist. As soon as he touched her, Max let out a yell and barreled toward him, aiming a vicious kick into Rufus's shin. Rufus stumbled back with a grunt of pain and a curse.

Before Crispina could react, one of Rufus's burly minions stepped forward and swatted Max upside the head. The boy tumbled to the dirt.

Rage engulfed Crispina's mind like a flame to oil. She launched herself forward, ready to bludgeon the thug to death with her fists, but he caught her easily and pinned her against the wooden beam which held up the second story balcony. His forearm pressed into her throat.

"How dare you," she wheezed. She scratched at his arm, but he seemed to be made of stone.

"Enough." Rufus's cool voice cut through the air.

The lackey released her. She bent over, hands on her knees, trying to steady her breathing. Max had disappeared. She hoped he'd stay hidden this time.

"Your little pet needs better training," Rufus said.

"He's not a pet," Crispina snarled. "He's…" She stopped herself. She'd been about to say *He's my son.* "Tell me what you want from me so I can tell you to shove it up your blond ass." The time for icy composure was past. Now, fire brewed in her veins, and she wanted to incinerate Rufus where he stood.

He ignored the insult. "The election is but five weeks away. Every vote is critical. I would like to know whom your husband is meeting with and what he is up to, from now through the morning of the election."

"You should know that for yourself if you're having him followed."

"Ah, but I want to know in *advance*."

Her jaw clenched as she realized his aim. If Rufus figured out who Aelius was planning to meet with, he could get to them first and secure their votes for himself. Her mind whirled. Knowledge of this nature could make or break the election.

"I see," she murmured. "You must really be afraid that Aelius will beat you, if you've resorted to stalking and blackmailing his wife."

Rufus's eyes darkened. "I take no chances."

She tried for another bluff. "My husband does not discuss his affairs with me. I know nothing of whom he meets with."

"Even if that were true, which I doubt, I trust your wifely wiles will serve you well. Unless you're frigid as well as barren?"

Crispina drew in a sharp breath. "Watch your tongue, sir." She struggled to gather herself, to think logically. "If I go along with your scheme, Aelius will lose. If I refuse, you will no doubt spread rumors of my unusual activities here on the Aventine, which will likely cost him the election as well. My answer is clear. I will not betray my husband."

Aelius would be furious with her in either case. It would shatter the fledgling trust they had built and put their future together at risk. But that was a problem for another moment.

Rufus smiled thinly. "But what about your little stray? You seem very fond of him." The look in his eyes was knowing, dangerous…and it sent a chill down her spine.

"If you or your cronies lay another finger on Max—"

Rufus shook his head. "Nothing so crude. But I have contacts in this neighborhood, and ones like it. We can sniff out his family. I expect they'd be overjoyed to have their son back."

"They abandoned him," Crispina said. "They couldn't take care of him."

"Well, that is easily solved. If I located his parents, or someone willing to swear he belonged to them, I would of course offer a hefty stipend to provide for his welfare."

His words tightened an iron strap around her chest, stealing her breath. He was talking about taking Max away from her. She had no legal claim on him. There was nothing she could do about it if his real parents, or someone willing to swear to be his real parents, came forward. She recalled the marks on Max's back the first time she had bathed him. She couldn't risk him being given back to people who would mistreat him.

She drew a shaky breath. "Are you really so desperate to win you would take a child from a safe, loving home?"

"Yes," Rufus said without pause. "I will expect a note from you in two days, Crispina. Containing the names of people Aelius intends to meet with over the coming week. If I receive nothing from you, I will start making inquiries about your boy's family."

He didn't wait for a reply, but turned and left the courtyard, his henchmen following.

Crispina leaned against the wooden beam, shaking all over. What was she going to do?

Movement flickered in the corner of her vision, and she turned to see Max extricating himself from behind a barrel. He ran toward her. She dropped to her knees and caught him in a swift hug. "Are you all right?"

His skinny body shook against her. "I'm s-s-sorry." He was crying, she realized, which made her eyes burn with tears of her own.

She choked back a sob and stroked his hair. "It's all right."

"I t-t-tried to help you b-but—"

"Max." The sternness in her voice made his tearstained face jerk up to look at her. "You did nothing wrong, do you understand me?" Except trying to attack Rufus, but it was too late to chide him for that.

He gave a slow nod.

"Good." She gently took his chin and moved his face from side to side. A red mark glowed on his cheek where Rufus's minion had struck him, and she hoped it wouldn't bruise. "Did you hear anything of what I was discussing with those men?" She prayed he hadn't heard Rufus's threats.

He shook his head and wiped his nose on his arm.

Crispina grimaced, wishing she had a handkerchief. "We merely had a small misunderstanding, but it's sorted now. Everything will be all right."

He gave her a narrow-eyed look, and she could tell he didn't quite believe her, but he didn't argue.

"But it will worry Aelius greatly if he hears what happened, so we mustn't mention it." She needed time to figure out what to do before Aelius found out about any of this.

"You have a lot of secrets," Max muttered.

"Yes." The weight of her secrets pressed down on her, but she straightened her shoulders and rose to her feet. "After the election, we'll tell him everything. About these lessons, and what happened today. I promise." Once this was over, even if Rufus won, she could face the consequences of her deceptions.

He raised his chin. "All right. But I want to stop and get savillum on the way home."

The honey-sweetened cheesecake was Max's favorite thing to get from the food stalls that lined the streets. He seemed to know she would refuse him nothing after what had just happened. "Today, you can have as much savillum as you want."

A toothy grin lit his face. "Quick, let's go before they run out!"

Crispina hefted her basket and followed him from the courtyard.

That evening, Crispina sat at her dressing table and buried her face in her hands, finally letting herself feel the stress and exhaustion of the day. She had put on a brave face at dinner. The savillum had put Max in an excellent mood, and he was his normal rambunctious, jovial self at dinner.

The bedroom door opened, and Crispina straightened up quickly as Aelius entered. He glanced over her, brow furrowing. "Are you well, Crispina? You didn't eat much at dinner."

"My courses are upon me, I fear." At least that much was true.

"Ah." He nodded knowingly, by now familiar with the fatigue that plagued her at this time of the month. "May I help you with your hair?"

"I'd rather do it myself." She needed a few minutes alone with her thoughts.

Aelius kicked off his sandals and stretched out in bed. Crispina took down her hair and slowly dragged a comb through it. Every instinct screamed at her to tell Aelius what had happened, to share her burden with him. But every time she tried to summon the words, Rufus's threat returned to her. If he didn't receive anything from her in two days, he would start trying to take Max away from them.

If she told Aelius about Rufus's threats, she would also have to tell him about her lessons and about how she had really found Max. She'd have to confess that she'd been lying to him for months. The trust between them would shatter.

Besides, Aelius and Rufus had already gotten into one brawl. If she told Aelius that Rufus and his cronies had laid hands on her and Max, she didn't want to imagine what his reaction would be. She wouldn't put it past him to get himself arrested and sued for assault.

She gave the comb a vicious yank as if the pain could punish her for what she was about to do. She glanced over at Aelius and took a deep breath. "Do you anticipate a busy week ahead?"

He folded his arms behind his head, his body lean and relaxed. "I plan to pay a visit to Flavius Libo on Thursday. If that goes well, I hope he can introduce me to Appius Salonius. Oh, and there's a dinner party at the Caepio house on Wednesday. I had hoped you would join me but I realize now you may be indisposed."

"Yes, likely." She committed the names to memory. "If the election were tomorrow, do you think you'd win?"

He shrugged. "Hard to say. The next five weeks will be critical. I need all the votes I can scrape together."

The knife inside her twisted. She was going to doom him, and if he found out, he would never want anything to do with her again. If she was lucky, he would settle for a quiet separation, not wanting the scandal of a divorce to tarnish his reputation. But his anger might be so great that he would want no further connection with her. She'd be twice divorced. Twice abandoned, twice humiliated.

She laid down the comb, braided her hair, then joined Aelius in bed. He reached for her, but she pulled away. "I'm very tired."

He kissed her on the forehead, murmured a good night, and blew out the lamp. Crispina laid next to him and stared up at the ceiling in darkness.

CHAPTER 23

ELIUS RAN THROUGH THE facts about the man he was going to meet as he strode through the streets. Flavius Libo was a friend of Crispina's father, which meant his support should be easy to come by. Like Aelius, he'd served in the army, so Aelius planned to drop the mention of his legion early on to establish camaraderie. They'd met at a dinner party a month ago, so they weren't total strangers, but Aelius didn't know the man well. He did know the man had a significant farming estate in central Italy, so Aelius planned to test out Crispina's idea about providing tax breaks to rural landowners for employing free rather than enslaved men.

Libo had suggested meeting at the baths, which suited Aelius. People tended to be more willing to grant favors when they were relaxed and soaking in a hot pool.

Aelius met Libo in the columned entrance to the baths. They clasped arms. "How nice to see you again," Aelius said to the stocky, gray-haired man. "I trust your family is well?" Libo had a wife and two children.

Libo nodded as they proceeded into the baths. "And how is your esteemed wife?"

"Crispina is very well." In fact, Crispina had been tired and withdrawn for the past few days, but that was to be expected during this time of the month. "I was speaking with her father the other day and he mentioned you served in the seventh legion. I was in the ninth myself."

Libo's face brightened. "Ah, a worthy cohort."

"The gods know I would have killed for luxuries like this during my service." Aelius gestured around at their lavish surroundings as they entered the changing rooms. "Even clean hot water felt like a luxury sometimes."

Libo chuckled. "The mud in Germania still haunts my dreams."

Aelius joined him in laughter, and soon they were swapping war stories as they sank into a steaming pool.

"Do you miss the army?" Libo asked, immersing himself up to his neck. "The discipline brings a certain peace, does it not?"

Aelius saw his opening to turn the conversation to the topic he really wanted to discuss. "I'm grateful for the things I learned, but I never wanted to be a career soldier. My true interest lies in politics."

Libo nodded. "Ah, yes, I hear you are mounting a campaign for tribune of the plebs, correct?"

"Indeed. My father-in-law suggested I might find an ally in you. No doubt there are certain things you would like to see passed in the Plebeian Assembly. If I were to become tribune, I would be happy to assist however possible. And I have some ideas that could benefit your interests."

"Yes…" Libo's voice took on a note of hesitation. He shifted on the underwater bench, stretching an arm along the edge of the pool. "This is rather awkward."

Aelius raised an eyebrow. "Have I overstepped?"

"Not at all. It's just that Publius Veturius Rufus paid me a visit yesterday and had a similar line of questioning."

"I see," Aelius murmured. Rufus had met with Libo only yesterday? It was to be expected they'd be chasing the same votes, especially this late in the campaign. But still, the coincidence rankled.

Libo was still talking. "...We have neighboring estates in Baiae, you see, so I have an acquaintance with the young man. He somehow became aware that my wife has been angling to renovate the villa, and recommended several builders and artisans who would offer favorable estimates. Alas, I gave my word I would lend him my support in the upcoming election."

So you exchanged your political support for a refurbished summer house. No doubt Rufus had paid off the craftsmen to supply Libo with their services at a reduced rate. "How convenient."

"If I may say, you and Rufus are very similar. You are both very driven, ambitious young men. I know you are competitors now, but if you both attain positions as two of the ten tribunes, as I hope you will, you could find strength in an alliance."

Aelius summoned his most charming smile to mask his disappointment. "I will keep that in mind." Mount Olympus would crumble before he would ally himself with Rufus.

Conversation turned to other things. When they had their fill of the baths, Aelius headed home. The interaction still bothered him—not just that Libo had chosen to support Rufus, but that Rufus had somehow managed to secure Libo's support a mere day before Aelius. *It's just a coincidence*, he told himself. But he hadn't even had a chance to make his case to Libo. What if it happened again? Time was running short.

At home, his mother was teaching Max how to weave in the atrium. Or attempting to teach him, by the look of the tangled threads hanging off the loom. "Good afternoon," she greeted him as she tugged a knot of yarn apart.

Max stuck his fingers between the loosely woven threads and grinned at him.

"Good afternoon," Aelius said. "Where is Crispina?"

"Her library," Gaia replied. "She said she had a headache, and someone was being rather loud." She gave Max an accusatory but good-natured frown.

Aelius nodded to them and went to the door of Crispina's library. He tapped on it. "Crispina? May I come in?"

At her acquiescence, he entered and closed the door behind him. Crispina was seated at her reading desk, glancing over a scroll before her.

"You shouldn't be reading if you have a headache," he said.

"It distracts me."

Aelius dropped into a chair opposite her. "Rufus got to Libo before me."

Her hand twitched where it held the scroll. "I'm sorry."

"It was more frustrating than it should have been," Aelius said. "I know it's only one person, but he controls at least a dozen votes." He sighed. "I worry…" He shook his head. *I worry I can't do it. I worry I'll lose again.* "If I am not victorious this time, I will not try again."

"You'll give up?"

"It's not giving up." His voice came out sharper than he intended. "I will have lost two elections in two years. I would be a fool not to take that as a sign. Mama didn't even want me to run this time. She wants a country estate, a quiet life. Would you like that? A little villa somewhere in the hills?"

She finally raised her gaze from the scroll for a moment before casting her eyes back down. "I could appreciate that."

Aelius allowed his gaze to run over her. She was so beautiful, even with the shadows that had darkened beneath her eyes in the past few days. "You still have your courses?"

She nodded.

Shame. He longed for the solace he could find in her touch, her warmth. She could make him forget the election, forget Rufus, forget even his own name.

But that was not an option at present, so he rose from his chair and paced. "Perhaps I have been depending too much on patricians who may be influenced one way or another with petty promises. There are still votes to be won from the people themselves. That's what I did in the last election. People voted for me, even though I was a nobody."

"Will you go knock on doors all over the city, then?"

"Something like that. A speech in the Forum, I think. Catullus can help spread the word. Given what happened the last time I spoke in the Forum, people will want to come. Perhaps Tuesday." The new idea bolstered him, chasing away the fear of defeat. He could already picture himself standing before a crowd. Snippets of rhetoric popped into his mind. He would craft a speech that would make people remember his name even without a fistfight.

An odd expression, like a grimace, flickered over Crispina's face. "I see."

"Why don't you retire?" he suggested. "You look weary. I can have dinner brought to you."

"I'm not an invalid." Her voice was tight. "But I would prefer to be left alone."

"Very well." He dared a quick kiss to her forehead, then withdrew to his own study to draft his speech.

After Aelius left, Crispina sank her head into her hands. She did have a headache, but it wasn't from her courses. It was from the constant, crushing guilt of betraying her husband.

It's for Max, she reminded herself, but that didn't make it any easier. She hadn't slept properly since the incident with Rufus. She lay awake at night, listening to Aelius's breathing, wondering when it would all come crashing down around her.

For the first time, she wished he was more like Memmius, who never spoke to her if he could help it. But Aelius trusted her enough to share his thoughts, his hopes, his plans. If he hadn't talked about his plan to give a speech in the Forum, then she would have nothing to give Rufus. But now she knew, and Rufus was expecting a note from her tomorrow.

With a heavy sigh, she pulled out a double-leafed wax tablet and rubbed away the existing words with the flat end of the stylus. Then she inscribed a brief note. *Tuesday. Speech in Forum.* She closed the cover, hiding the words from view, and secured a leather cord around it.

She tucked the tablet behind a stack of scrolls on one of her shelves, then tried to return to her reading, wondering if the guilt would ever leave her.

CHAPTER 24

ELIUS STRODE THROUGH THE streets on the way to the
Forum, his speech running through his head as he
walked. A crowd had already gathered, clustered around the
plinth where speakers stood. A rush of gratitude sped through
him. Catullus's efforts to get the word out about Aelius's
speech had evidently paid off.

But as he drew closer, he realized they weren't waiting for
him. They were already listening to someone.

Sunlight glanced off blond hair, and Aelius jerked to a halt.
Rufus, clad in the same bright white *toga candida* that Aelius
wore, paced the plinth, speaking and gesturing expansively.

Aelius bit his lip, fuming. Again, Rufus had bested him,
simply through timing. Another coincidence? A dark suspicion grew in his mind. Could Rufus have a way of knowing
Aelius's plans?

His thoughts went to Catullus once more. Maybe Catullus
had spoken to the wrong people. Maybe word of his plans
had gotten back to Rufus somehow. He would have to ask
Catullus to be more circumspect.

The only other person who knew so much was Crispina. But
she was the last person who would speak thoughtlessly, and since
her rift with Horatia, her time had been spent focusing on Max

rather than socializing, apart from the engagements they attended together.

He watched Rufus for a few more moments, observing how he engaged and played to the crowd. Rufus was a talented speaker, though his mannerisms were a little too extravagant for Aelius's tastes.

Aelius debated cutting his losses, leaving before anyone noticed him...but he had come to speak and be heard, and he wouldn't give up so easily. He shouldered his way through the crowd, pushing to the front with murmurs of apology to the people he displaced. Once people recognized him, they moved aside easily. No doubt they hoped for the excitement of another fistfight.

Rufus broke off in his speech when Aelius reached the front of the crowd. He gazed down at Aelius, a slight smile playing around his thin lips. He did not look surprised to see Aelius.

"Ah, what a coincidence to see my esteemed opponent here." Rufus's voice dripped with saccharine congeniality. "Would you care to join me? Perhaps the voters would appreciate another debate."

A few shouts of approval rang from the crowd. Aelius fumed internally, but found a smile, pretending as if he'd planned this all along. "Indeed." He climbed up onto the plinth.

"I was just discussing my plan to increase the land allotment given to veterans who have served more than twenty years in the army," Rufus said. "Surely, as a veteran yourself, you would support such a thing?"

Aelius took a deep breath to center himself. Now was his chance to show himself as an eloquent, thoughtful leader who would put the interests of the people first. "I support the current land grants for veterans. Every man who has risked his life for Rome and endured the hardships of military life deserves to retire and raise a family in peace on his own land." The crowd nodded and murmured. "But in terms of increasing the land grants, I believe there are better ways to allocate state funds. For example—"

"So you want to take land away from veterans," Rufus said, his voice ringing out over the Forum.

"No, hardly—" He wanted to put forth Crispina's idea about tax breaks for landowners who employed free laborers, but Rufus didn't relinquish the advantage. He kept talking, leaving Aelius on the back foot. Aelius attempted to jump in and steer the conversation, but Rufus had been in control since the beginning. Aelius managed to make a couple of good points, and earned himself some approving nods from the crowd, but most of the focus was on Rufus.

After, when the crowd had dispersed, Rufus turned to Aelius with a satisfied smirk. Aelius muttered a goodbye. These were not the sort of setbacks he wanted to be dealing with so close to the election. Votes were already slipping through his fingers like sand, and if Rufus kept getting the better of him like this, Aelius feared for the outcome of the election.

"Give my regards to your wife," Rufus said. His voice sounded oilier than usual. Something about the remark struck Aelius as odd, as Rufus had never mentioned Crispina in their prior meetings, except to insult her. But it was a normal, polite thing to say, so Aelius nodded in acknowledgement, then stepped off the plinth and headed home.

In darkness, Crispina rose from bed, her stomach in knots. Careful not to wake Aelius, she tiptoed to her dressing table to retrieve the shawl lying over the back of the chair. She wrapped it around her shoulders, then stole from the room.

She crept past the slaves slumbering in the corridors and slipped into Aelius's study. She hated that she had to sneak around like this in her own home, hated that she was going behind Aelius's back. But the election was now only three weeks away, and Rufus had demanded another note from her. Crispina had already sent him everything she knew about Aelius's plans through election day, hoping that would put him off, but he wanted more. Aelius had returned from the Forum yesterday tight-lipped and irritated, and he had refused to speak of anything to do with the election since. So she had to resort to subterfuge and theft.

She fumbled in the dark to light the oil lamp that rested on Aelius's desk. It sparked, casting a flickering glow over the papers and tablets. She rifled through them, trying to find something that would keep Rufus at bay.

Most of them were notes on speeches. She read them over with a pang. His ideas were good, and he was an eloquent speaker. He deserved to win. And he probably would be about to, if not for her interference.

Crispina kept shuffling through the papers, then finally found one with a list of names, some crossed off, some encircled. Others had notes next to them: *shipping venture, tenth legion, estate mortgaged.* These must be the men Aelius planned to meet with along with notes on how he would gain their favor.

She clutched the piece of papyrus and searched for a blank piece where she could transcribe the notes.

The sound of quiet footsteps made her freeze. She held her breath. It was likely just one of the slaves. Even so, she blew out the lamp in case they saw light from behind the door and decided to investigate.

The footsteps drew closer. Crispina's mind raced to conjure a plausible excuse for why she was rifling through her husband's papers in the middle of the night. She straightened her spine and threw back her shoulders, hoping to evoke the image of a haughty materfamilias.

The door creaked open. Her stomach plummeted. The tall, shadowed figure standing in the doorway wasn't a slave, but her husband.

CHAPTER 25

CRISPINA'S HEART THUDDED IN her chest. Her made-up excuses vanished, and she stammered. "I…just…"

Aelius stepped into the room. His brows drew together. "I know you haven't been feeling well, so when I woke and you were gone, I came to check on you. But what are you doing in here?"

She cleared her throat, which felt as dry as the papyrus she was gripping. "I…" Her gaze jumped frantically around the room, landing on an inkwell. "Needed ink."

His frown deepened. Her fingers twitched, and the papyrus crinkled. His gaze jumped to it. "What's that?"

Her legs were stiff, clumsy. She jerked back a step and bumped into the chair behind the desk. Her arm flung out to steady herself, and her fingers released the paper. It fluttered to the ground.

Aelius bent and picked it up. He read it over. "These are my notes." He lifted his gaze from the paper and stared at her hard. "What were you doing with them?"

She could see in his searching stare that he was starting to put the pieces together. Her knees weakened, and she slumped into the chair. It was over. "I did something terrible," she confessed, her voice small and pathetic. "But I had no choice."

"I don't understand."

A wave of remorse flooded her. She forced herself to meet his gaze. Suspicion and confusion mingled on his handsome face.

"Rufus blackmailed me into betraying you. I've been giving him information on your plans for the past two weeks." The words felt like shards of glass on her tongue.

Shock rippled over his features. He turned away, braced a fist against the wall. Tension filled every line of his body. Crispina bit her lip, waiting for an explosion.

"Why?" he murmured, face still hidden from her. "You must have had a good reason. Unless this has all been a lie, and you've hated me from the beginning. I did fear I would never be good enough for you."

"No!" She rose to her feet, wanting to go to him but afraid to touch him. "I don't hate you. I lo—" She broke off. It was almost too painful to admit now, when she was about to lose him, but she had to lay herself bare. She owed him that much. "I love you."

His head jerked toward her. "You have a funny way of showing it."

"I also love Max." Her voice grew stronger. "Rufus threatened him. I did what I did to keep…" She cleared her throat. "To keep our family together."

He raked a hand through his hair. "How could Rufus threaten Max? And why didn't you tell me?"

She took a deep breath. "There's something you don't know about me." She told him, in halting words, about her secret lessons. About how she had really discovered Max. About how Rufus had followed her and blackmailed her, threatened to take Max away from them.

Aelius paced while she talked, arms crossed tight over his chest. When she fell silent, he stopped and faced her. "How much does Rufus know?"

"Everything you've told me about your plans through the election," she admitted, the words sticking in her throat. "He was relentless."

Aelius absorbed this with a face like stone. "You have cost me this election. Do you understand that? I can't do *anything* if Rufus can anticipate my every move."

She swallowed hard. "There will be other elections."

Anger flashed in his eyes. "Yes, but if I want to become consul in ten years, I needed this election. I needed to win *this year*. And your foolishness has taken that from me."

"It wasn't foolishness," she snapped. "I was doing a good thing by teaching those children to read. Education is everything. You of all people should understand that."

"Cavorting around slums dressed as a priestess is not a fitting endeavor for a tribune's wife," he shot back.

"Well, I won't be a tribune's wife now, will I?" The retort snapped from her mouth like an arrow from a bow. Once, she had entertained a brief hope that Aelius would understand and appreciate the passion behind her lessons. But deep down, she'd known he would react like this. Despite fostering a few radical ideas, he wanted to be seen as respectable, genteel, to put as much distance from his inferior birth as possible. And a respectable, genteel man did not permit his wife to "cavort around slums," as he so eloquently put it.

His hands balled into fists. "Leaving that aside, why did you not tell me the moment Rufus approached you?"

"I feared if I told you Rufus had threatened me and Max, you'd drag him out of his house and beat him in the streets. Then you'd certainly not win the election, and you'd be arrested besides."

He took a deep, shuddering breath. "I might have done that," he admitted. "But you should have told me. Instead you lied to me. About many things."

Tears pricked her eyes. The shattering of his trust felt like a hand squeezing her lungs, depriving her of air. "I know."

"You should have told me about Rufus." His voice grew stronger, angrier. "Maybe we would still be in the same place, but we could have dealt with it together, like partners. But you chose to betray me."

A hot knife twisted in her stomach. She tried to mask her devastation with anger. "If I had been honest with you from the beginning about what I was doing with my pupils on the Aventine, would you have let me continue?"

He glared at her. "You know the answer to that."

"Then we are not partners. You promised me freedom, but you would have sought to control me, to tell me what I can and cannot do, where I can and cannot go. We never would have had Max."

"And Rufus would never have had fodder to blackmail you. I would be on the verge of winning a tribune seat."

"So that's more important to you than our family," she spat. "By the gods, you are selfish."

"This election is more important to me than anything!" he shouted. "It's the only reason I married you."

The vitriol in his voice burned her. She opened her mouth, but no words would come out.

A sound by the doorway made them both turn their heads. Gaia stood there, a shawl wrapped around her shoulders. "I heard shouting."

Crispina and Aelius exchanged a fraught glance. Then Aelius squared his shoulders. "There will be no more. We're done." He headed for the door and disappeared into the darkened house.

Gaia fixed her cool gaze on Crispina. "What happened?"

Crispina swallowed hard. Drawing breath pained her, as if she'd been punched in the stomach. "I must let Aelius tell you. If you hear it from me, you'll find some way to see my side of it. And I don't deserve your kindness or sympathy." Her nails dug into her palms, the pain a tiny echo of what was going on in her chest.

Gaia stepped forward and reached out a hand as if to rest it on Crispina's shoulder. Crispina flinched away from the warmth of her touch. She deserved no comfort. "Please, don't." Any sliver of kindness would make her crumble, and if she crumbled, there would be no putting herself back together again. She slipped past Gaia and stumbled from the room.

It was dangerous to be on the streets alone in the middle of the night, but Aelius couldn't return to the bedroom he shared with Crispina, couldn't spend one more moment in the house with her. He glanced around the empty streets, daring a brigand to jump him. He could use a good fight right about now.

He indulged himself with a fantasy of going to Rufus's house, breaking down the door, dragging Rufus from his bed and beat-

ing him to a bloody pulp. But Crispina was right, damn her to
Dis. That avenue would only lead to his arrest, and where would
that leave his mother?

Instead, he went to the only other place he could think of:
Catullus's house. Catullus was habitually late to bed and even later
to rise, so Aelius had a feeling he'd be up even at this time of night.

A yawning slave let him in, and moments later Catullus met
him in the atrium, a blanket wrapped around his bare shoulders.
A young man with tousled hair trailed him, fixing Aelius with an
annoyed stare.

Catullus showed no trace of irritation, even though Aelius had
evidently interrupted something. "What's amiss? Or is this a social
call? I suppose we could make room for one more." He gave a
jaunty grin, though his companion scowled.

"I'm sorry," Aelius said, unable to entertain his friend's jokes.
"It's Crispina. She has…" He struggled to find the words to
articulate what she had done. "She's ruined everything."

Catullus's brows drew together. He turned to the young man.
"Go back to bed, love. I need to speak with Aelius."

The man huffed but left them alone. Catullus beckoned Aelius
to follow him into his study, and directed the slave who'd let him
in to bring them wine.

"Talk," Catullus ordered as soon as the door of the study closed
behind them.

Aelius sat and dropped his head into his hands. His mind was
still swirling. Images from the past hour kept coming back to him.
Waking to find Crispina gone. Discovering her in his study. The
anguish on her face as she confessed. This all felt like a bad dream,
but one he would never wake from.

He relayed the broad strokes to Catullus. His friend listened in silence, fingers tapping gently on the corner of his desk. When Aelius finished, his fingers stilled. "Fuck," Catullus said. "That's bad."

Sometimes Catullus didn't need masterful poetry to perfectly capture a situation. "Yes. The worst part is, I want to admire her," Aelius said. "A woman like her, taking an interest in the education of children in a slum? But she kept it from me. She lied to me, and then she betrayed me. It's all over." Not just his chances in the election, but his marriage, the love that had been budding between them. His heart twisted with another anguished throb.

"What are you going to do?" Catullus asked.

Aelius heaved a sigh. "I don't think there is anything I can do. Rufus has beaten me. Only a fool doesn't know when to admit defeat. Perhaps I should do as my mother suggested before all this. Get a nice place in the country, try to be satisfied with a quiet life." Give up his dream of a consulship once and for all.

"And Crispina?"

Aelius's lips tightened. He hadn't wanted to think about this part. "I can't be with her after what she has done. We must divorce." The formalities would have to wait until after the election. He didn't want to alienate what little support he did have by divorcing his wife days before votes were cast. He would ask her to return to her parents' house tomorrow, though.

Catullus nodded slowly. "I'm sorry." He leaned forward to clasp Aelius's hand. "If it's any consolation, I do believe she acted out of desperation."

"She told me she loved me tonight. In the same breath as she confessed feeding information to Rufus." Her words echoed in his mind. *I love you.* Once, he would have rejoiced at that, would have felt like dancing through the streets. But tonight, he could only feel the cruelty of those words.

"Do you love her?"

Aelius lifted his wine cup and drank deeply. "I fear I do," he admitted as he set the cup down. The pain he felt upon learning she had lied to him told him he loved her. If he hadn't loved her, he would have felt angry, yes, but this deep, twisting ache inside him spoke of love. Only love could make the betrayal cut with this degree of agony. "I want to hate her. I want to curse her. But instead I love her, even though she's taken everything from me."

"Mm." Catullus sipped his wine. "I believe hate and love are closer than we realize. Right now you are filled with passion toward her, whether good or bad, but in time, the fire will fade, and you will feel nothing."

"Is that supposed to make me feel better?" Aelius muttered into his wine cup. Catullus merely offered a sympathetic grin and topped up his goblet.

CHAPTER 26

CRISPINA SPENT A SLEEPLESS night staring up at the ceiling, wondering how it had all gone so wrong. Aelius did not return from wherever he'd gone. An additional layer of guilt settled over her. Gaia would be worrying about her son, out overnight. One more thing to blame herself for.

Once the gray light of dawn peeked in, Crispina rose. She knew what she had to do. The quicker she got it over with, the better.

She asked Malchio and Taurus to drag her trunks out of storage, the same trunks that had carried her belongings here on her wedding day. Once the trunks arrived, she stared at them sitting open before her, the insides dark and cavernous, ready to swallow up the life she'd built for herself.

Then, she took a deep breath and began to pile her belongings into the trunks. Her mind went back to the day that Memmius had told her he was divorcing her and that she was to pack her things and go. She hadn't been shocked or dejected. Failure was humiliating, but there was also relief in ending a marriage that brought neither of them happiness.

Now, severing herself from Aelius was like cutting off a limb, every item placed into the trunks a slash of the knife. She packed her clothes, her jewelry, her cosmetics. Then she went to her library and surveyed the shelves full of scrolls. Most of these had been bought after marrying Aelius. She didn't have the space for them at her parents' house, so she would only be able to take a few.

She ran her fingers along the stacks of rustling papyrus. She chose old favorites, a selection of books from Homer along with a manuscript of Sappho. She piled them into her arms and turned to leave.

Aelius stood in the doorway, watching her. His golden skin had a grayish pallor, as if he hadn't slept, and he was wearing the same clothes as last night.

She drew in a sharp breath at the sight of him. "You're back."

He nodded slowly. His gaze rested on the scrolls in her arms. "You are...packing?"

A bolt of pain shot through her, but she strove not to crack. The best she could hope for now was to leave with dignity. There was honor in that, like a defeated general falling on his sword. "I assume that is what you want."

He didn't speak for a moment. A wild hope flailed within her that he would somehow have forgiven her, would ask her to stay...

But he nodded once more. "A quiet separation is best for now. I will initiate a divorce once the election is over."

"I understand."

He moved aside from the door to let her pass.

She paused as she crossed the threshold and looked up at him. "About Max. I will take him with me." She strove to imbue her voice with total certainty, as if there was no alternative, even though a wife had no rights to any children after a divorce, and Max wasn't even legally their child. "I brought him here, so he's my responsibility. And you've made it clear you value your political career above a family."

His lips tightened. "Do you think your parents will allow you to bring a strange child into their home?"

She flinched. She knew the answer to that, but she didn't want to admit it.

"Max must stay here," Aelius said. "My mother loves him, and he's comfortable here. It would be cruel to take him away."

But I love him too. She fought to maintain her composure, trying to think of what was best for Max. All of this grief and heartache had been for his sake. He was happy here, and deep down she knew her parents wouldn't welcome him. Better for him to remain here, where he was safe and loved.

She managed a jerky nod, and left the library. She brought the scrolls she'd been carrying back to the bedroom, and stopped short when she saw Gaia standing by her half-filled trunks.

"Crispina, what on earth is going on?" Gaia demanded, eyes wide.

The dull ache in Crispina's chest tore open again. The last thing she wanted was to confess to Gaia that she was breaking up their family. "I…I'm leaving."

Gaia's slender fingers clenched. "But why? I know you argued last night, but please, there's no need to leave."

"Aelius has asked me to leave." Crispina crossed to the trunks and laid the scrolls carefully atop a pile of folded clothing.

"But *why?*" Gaia demanded. "This is nonsense. You love each other. Anyone with eyes can see it."

"Yes." Crispina closed the lid of the trunk.

Gaia let out a frustrated sigh. "I am going to go wring a more satisfying explanation out of my son." She strode from the room, looking as angry as Crispina had ever seen her.

Crispina packed a few more items, then went to find Max. This would be painful, but she needed to say goodbye.

It was still earlier than they usually woke, so he might not be out of bed yet. She found him sitting on the floor of his room playing with some of the carved toys Aelius had bought him.

He glanced up at her. "Morning."

She entered the room and sat on his bed. Guilt and shame coiled inside her like a snake consuming her from within. She took a deep breath. "Max, I need to tell you something."

"We ain't out of cake, are we?"

"Aren't." She forced herself to say the next words. "I'm leaving."

He set down a toy elephant. "You're going on a trip? Can I come?"

"It's not like that. I'm leaving this house, forever."

His eyes narrowed. "Why?"

"Because…" Crispina bit her lip. "Aelius and I aren't going to be married anymore."

His forehead crinkled. "But you're in love." He grimaced in disgust.

Was it that obvious to everyone around them? Crispina herself had only figured it out last night. "I know."

"My parents hated each other and they still were married," Max said. "I didn't think it was allowed to not be married anymore."

"It's called a divorce." The word seemed to carry a dark cloud with it, settling over her in a noxious haze.

"Huh." He nudged the toy elephant. "But why do you have to leave? Why don't he leave?"

"*Doesn't.* Because this is Aelius's house. And Aelius has asked me to leave. That's how it works." She tried for a smile, but her mouth didn't seem to remember how to move that way. "Aelius and Gaia will take excellent care of you. You're happy here, aren't you?"

He nodded slowly. "But…I like it when *you're* here."

"I know." She wished Rufus's cronies had pummeled her into oblivion that day on the Aventine. That would have been less painful than this.

"W-will you come visit?" he asked in a small voice.

Crispina choked back a rush of tears. Her heart, already bruised and battered, splintered. She wanted to assure him that yes, of course, he could see her anytime he liked, but she knew that would be a lie. "I hope we'll see each other again." Her voice was hoarse and unsteady.

His mouth set in a stubborn, glum frown. With a sudden burst of fury, he grabbed his carved elephant and flung it across the room. It clattered against the wall. "It's not fair!" he shouted.

"Max…" She reached for him, trying to fold him into her arms, but he shoved her away and ran from the room.

An hour later, it was done. Max was in the kitchen being comforted by Gaia, Cassandra, and a supply of sweets. Crispina hadn't tried to go after him. She'd upset him enough already.

Her trunks sat in the vestibule by the front door. They would be sent over later. In the atrium, Crispina adjusted the drape of her palla. Taurus waited to escort her across the city. He eyed her with veiled curiosity. Crispina imagined the news, or at least some version of it, had filtered throughout the household by now. Everyone knew she had betrayed her husband.

"Crispina." Gaia emerged into the atrium. Her face was drawn, eyes wide. "Please don't do this." She grasped Crispina's hands desperately.

Crispina's throat tightened. "Aelius wishes me gone. Didn't he tell you what I did?"

"Yes, but I believe if you give it some time and talk, he will come around."

"You are too optimistic, Gaia." Crispina gently extricated her hands. "You know your son. He would do anything to win this election, and I've taken that from him. It's over."

Gaia gazed up at her. "All I want is for him to be happy. I never thought politics would make him happy. But he has found happiness with you. If he does lose this election, I hope he will realize there is more to life than ballot boxes and Forum speeches. He will need you."

"Well, he knows where to find me." She was looking at a long, lonely future as a twice divorced woman, forever ensconced in her parents' house. At least this time, she had the memory of what it was like to be loved. "Forgive me, Gaia, but I must go." She glanced around the atrium, wondering if Aelius would deign to see her off. He was probably in his study, the door just a few feet away.

"Tell Aelius I said goodbye," she murmured. Then she walked out the front door. Taurus followed behind her.

They crossed the city. Crispina took a deep breath when her parents' house came into view. She hadn't seen her parents since the wedding. Now, she was to show up on their doorstep, disgraced and abandoned for a second time.

The slave manning the front door let them in, not without a curious glance or two, then went to fetch Crispina's mother. Crispina dismissed Taurus, then waited in the atrium.

Fresh dread swirled in her stomach. She would have done anything to avoid this confrontation if it were possible. She braced herself for her parents' displeasure and pity.

Footsteps sounded, and Mother came into view, flanked by one of her maids. She frowned at the sight of Crispina. "Was I expecting you? It's rather early."

Crispina shook her head. "I'm afraid..." She swallowed hard, forcing herself to get the words out. "Aelius and I are separating. We plan to divorce after the election."

Mother's manicured eyebrows shot up. "Blessed Juno. You couldn't even please a freedman?"

Crispina flinched. "Don't talk about him that way."

"Well, it's what he is. Really, Crispina. Two divorces in as many years? It's just embarrassing at this point."

Crispina pushed past her. "Excuse me, I'd like to lie down." She left the atrium and went to her old room, dusty and stripped of belongings. At least the bed was still there, though no linens were on it. She sat heavily on the bare mattress, then buried her face in her hands and let the tears come.

CHAPTER 27

A ELIUS SAT IN THE atrium with his mother, staring dully at his untouched plate of breakfast. Crispina had left less than an hour ago. Already the house felt darker.

Gaia wasn't eating either. A heavy silence reigned between them. Aelius detected blame and sadness in his mother's downcast gaze and tense shoulders. He knew the loss of Crispina had hit her hard, and that she resented him for not being able to forgive.

He cut a fig into tiny slivers, the knife clicking against his plate. Once it had been thoroughly disemboweled, he cleared his throat and spoke. "I will make inquiries about a suitable property in the countryside we could let." The prospect of living out the rest of his days in quiet, comfortable obscurity was as unappealing as the mangled fig on the plate before him.

Gaia nodded in acceptance. "If that is what you wish."

"I thought that's what *you* wished." He couldn't keep the sharpness from his tone.

Her gaze flicked up, anger sparking in her dark eyes. "If you cared what I wished, you would not have sent her—"

Max, who had been hiding in the kitchen since Crispina left, trudged into the atrium, shoulders bowed and face glowering.

Gaia rose to her feet. "Max! Would you like some breakfast?"

Fists clenched, Max marched straight up to Aelius and kicked him hard in the shin. Before Aelius could do more than let out a shocked yelp, Max aimed another kick at him.

"This is your fault!" Max yelled. He landed a punch to Aelius's shoulder. "She's gone and it's all your fault! I *hate* you."

"Stop it!" Aelius ducked as Max launched another blow. He managed to grab the boy's arm. A brief scuffle ensued. Max was quick, vicious, and angry, but Aelius used his superior reach to grab Max by the neck of his tunic and hold him at arm's length.

Max twisted and pummeled Aelius's arm. "Let me go," he snarled.

"I will when you've calmed yourself."

Max glared at him, still trying to break free. Gaia watched the display with wide eyes, but did not intervene. She probably thought Aelius deserved a few more kicks.

"I can stay like this all day." Aelius affected a cool, disinterested tone, but winced as Max landed another punch to his forearm.

Finally, Max seemed to tire himself out. His shoulders slumped, and he stopped trying to hit Aelius. Aelius released him. Max dropped to the floor, curling into a tight ball, his head buried in his knees.

His narrow shoulders shook, and Aelius realized he was crying. Aelius's heart twisted. *This is your fault.* He cast a helpless glance at his mother. "Can't you do something?"

She shook her head. "This is your problem to solve." She rose and departed the atrium, leaving Aelius alone with Max.

Aelius knew many things, but how to comfort a crying child was not one of them, especially after that child had just attacked him. "Max?"

"G-go away," Max muttered, not raising his head.

"No." Aelius lowered himself to the floor to sit cross-legged next to Max. "I know you miss her. The gods know I do, too. But I swear to you, you will always have a home with us."

The weight of such a promise, made without thought or hesitation, settled over him. Just a few months ago, he hadn't even wanted Max in his house, and now he was promising him a home in perpetuity? He hadn't realized how deeply Max had worked his way into his heart.

Before Crispina, the only person he truly loved was his mother. It had been just the two of them for his whole life. Then Crispina came, and Max. His heart had stretched and expanded without him even recognizing it. And now, with Crispina gone, emptiness yawned inside him.

He put a hand on Max's shoulder. Max tensed, but didn't pull away. Aelius gently drew Max into his arms, cradling the boy against him.

Max allowed himself to be embraced, his body still shaking with sobs. His tears sliced something deep within Aelius. Despite every attempt at control, he found his throat tightening and his eyes burning. He blinked back a tear. Gods, he hadn't cried since he was a child.

Max sniffled. "I m-miss her."

"So do I." Aelius's voice came out thick and rough.

"Why did she have to leave?" Max raised his tearstained face. "Why did you make her leave?"

"I..." Aelius swallowed hard. How could he explain that Crispina had done something unforgivable? "We could not make each other happy."

"But you *were* happy." Max's voice took on an accusatory tone.

"Yes." *Or so I thought*. There was no resolution to be had with this line of questioning, so Aelius changed the subject. "After the election, we're going to leave Rome and move to the country. Have you ever been outside Rome?"

Max shook his head grudgingly.

"There will be hills and vineyards and rivers. Fresh air, plenty of space for you to run around. You could learn to ride a horse."

He perked up. "A horse? A big one?"

"The biggest one we can find. Would you like that?"

Max sighed. "Maybe." His tears had stopped, but his face still looked glum.

"Good." Aelius gently extricated Max from his lap, then rose to his feet and extended a hand to pull Max up. "Are you hungry? Perhaps we can discuss what you might name your horse over some food." He gestured to the barely-touched breakfast still laid out.

A shadow of a smile flitted across Max's face. Food was always a reliable enticement. He grasped Aelius's hand, and followed him to the breakfast table.

CHAPTER 28

Aelius Herminius to Publius Veturius Rufus:

No doubt you will be saddened to hear that Crispina and I separated last week, with plans for a divorce as soon as the election is concluded. I trust you will find no further use for your threats and blackmail, and that neither she nor I will have reason to hear from you again. I congratulate you on your imminent victory and wish you every success. I trust you will use your newfound power well.

AELIUS BLEW GENTLY OVER the letter, waiting for the ink to dry. Then, he folded it and sealed it with a glob of wax. Writing the letter galled him. He hated to admit defeat even though it was unavoidable. But at least now Rufus would know Crispina could no longer be his pawn, his spy.

He gave the letter to Malchio to deliver, then went to find Max. He discovered the boy in the kitchen, avidly watching Hector, the cook, disembowel a brace of pigeons.

"Can't I try?" Max asked with a plaintive pout as Hector's heavy cleaver sliced through a breastbone with a grating crunch.

"You'll botch it," Hector said gruffly. He glanced up at Aelius. "Sir? Looking for something?"

"Someone." Aelius gestured to Max. "I wanted to speak with you about something, Max."

"But I want to see the guts!" Max protested.

Hector nudged him with the handle of his cleaver. "I'll save them for you, and you can have a look later. Now run along."

Max trudged from the kitchen, following Aelius back to his study. Aelius seated himself behind the desk and gestured for Max to sit in front of it.

Max lowered himself into the chair gingerly, as if worried it would collapse under his slight weight. "Am I in trouble? I didn't do it, I swear by Juno's—"

Aelius held up a hand. He didn't want to know what "it" was. "You're not in trouble. I wanted to speak to you on a matter of importance." The idea had been percolating in his mind since Crispina had first mentioned it to him what seemed like a lifetime ago. Now, with his wife gone and his dreams of a political career dashed, it seemed the only thing he could do to bring some certainty to his life.

"I would like to adopt you," Aelius said. "Do you know what adoption means?"

Max shook his head.

"It's when someone becomes part of a family they weren't born into. I know it's a bit unusual, as your parents are still living, but given they've abandoned you, I believe I can make a case a magistrate will approve. You would be my son, legally and in the eyes of the gods. My heir. Would you like that?"

Max blinked slowly. "Would I have to change my name?"

"You would add my family name, Herminius, onto your own," Aelius said. "Maximus Herminius—it has a nice ring to it, doesn't it? But we'd still call you Max."

Max shrugged. "All right."

Aelius leaned forward. "I want you to understand the weight of this decision. If you become a part of our family, you will undertake a responsibility to represent our name and uphold its legacy. You'll need an education. You'll have to work to build a strong reputation for yourself. You'll have to choose a good wife to marry and have children with, so our name continues generation after generation."

Max wrinkled his nose. "Sounds like a lot of work."

Aelius grinned. "Luckily that's many years off. So what do you say?"

Max chewed his lip. "All right. I'd like to be your son." A shadow crossed his face. "I would've liked to be *her* son, too."

Aelius didn't need to ask who he was talking about. "She would have liked that." A bittersweet pain blossomed in his chest. He had lost a wife, but gained an heir. At least he would have no further need to marry now that he had Max. He could spend the rest of his days as a bachelor, living in comfortable anonymity with his mother and Max. No need for another politically moti-vated marriage to an unsmiling, icy, brilliant woman who would capture his heart like an eagle captured an unsuspecting squirrel. "Well, if we're in agreement, I'll write to a magistrate and set the process in motion. You can go back to your disemboweled birds now."

Released, Max climbed off his chair and raced from the room. Aelius cast a rueful smile after him, then found a blank piece of papyrus and began to write.

Crispina stared at her reflection in the polished silver mirror. A pale, hazy ghost stared back at her, all pinched cheeks and empty eyes. A week had passed since she'd left Aelius. She refused to show her parents how deeply she was suffering, so she pretended everything was all right. She assisted her mother in planning the day's menus, helped with weaving, and gave her opinion on trivial matters like what type of fabric would be best to reupholster the dining couches. But every moment she was awake, she missed Aelius, Max, and Gaia with a fierce ache that felt like it was going to tear her apart.

How was it possible that a simple arrangement between herself and Aelius had bound her so tightly to three people? Even if Aelius would never look at her again, she would still give anything to see Gaia smile or hear Max crow with delight as he instigated some sort of mischief. Day by day, moment by moment, they had become her family. Without them, she was unanchored, a boat drifting from the harbor, soon to be swamped by a passing wave.

The days were bad enough, but the nights were even worse. She spent them staring at the ceiling, alternately racked with guilt and tormented by longing. She missed Aelius's warm body beside her, the way she would wake in the night to find that he'd pulled her closer. She missed the little touches and kisses that set her body aflame. Most of all, she missed having someone there in the darkness, someone who smiled when she was the first thing he saw upon waking.

Her guilt was compounded by the fact that once again, she had been forced to abandon her students on the Aventine. They'd been making such progress, too, and now it would all be lost.

A light knock came at her door. "Visitor for you, mistress."

She straightened. "Who?"

But the sound of footsteps told her the slave had already retreated. Who could have come to see her? Her mind immediately jumped to Aelius, but their parting had been final. Still, hope blossomed. Could Gaia have brought Max to see her?

Crispina jumped up from her dressing table, hastily adjusted her hair, and hurried from her bedroom. When she saw who waited for her in the atrium, her surprise was so great that it quashed the disappointment. It wasn't Max or Gaia, but...

"Horatia?"

Her erstwhile friend turned, hands clasped in front of her. "Crispina." She took a hesitant step forward. "I will leave if you don't wish to speak to me, but I ran into Gaius Valerius Catullus and he told me you had separated from Aelius. I knew I had to see you. I went to your home, and Aelius told me it was true and I'd find you here." Her eyes grew wide. "Gods, Crispina, what happened? The way you spoke about Aelius, I thought..."

"So did I." Crispina surveyed her friend. Horatia's disparaging words at their last meeting still stung, but that was months ago, and much had changed since then. She no longer had a husband or child who needed her to defend them. "You spoke to Aelius?"

Horatia nodded, then smiled regretfully. "He's as handsome as you said, not to mention charming, though I can tell he's devastated by all this. I should have welcomed him sooner. I'm sorry I've only realized it now."

When it's too late.

"Please, will you forgive me for my mistakes?" Horatia asked. "I wrote you a letter, but you never replied."

"I know." At the time, Crispina had been tempted toward forgiveness by her friend's apology, but had been too wrapped up in her newfound bliss with Aelius to fully contemplate pardoning Horatia.

"I want to be friends again," Horatia continued. "I want my children to know you. Paullus misses you, and little Nonus is getting so big already."

"I would like to see them," Crispina said quietly.

"And the boy you took in…will he stay with Aelius?"

Crispina nodded. "You no longer have to worry about Max corrupting your sons."

Horatia blanched. "I didn't mean…I was going to say I would be happy to invite him to play with Paullus, if the situation permitted. I regret the things I said about him. I'm ashamed that I could have been so cruel to a child who only wanted a friend." She hesitated. "You must miss Max greatly."

"Yes." Crispina couldn't let herself dwell on Max and Aelius and Gaia, the life she had lost. Horatia was offering kindness and friendship, the memory of a time before Crispina had met Aelius, when she'd thought losing a disinterested husband was the worst tragedy that could befall her. Horatia was her oldest friend, the only person until recently who knew about her secret lessons and supported her mission. Crispina might never be able to forgive herself for what she had done, but maybe she could forgive Horatia instead.

Crispina reached out to clasp Horatia's hand. "Your friendship saw me through my first divorce. I hope it can do so again."

Horatia flung her arms around Crispina in a quick, tight hug. "Yes, if there is anything I can do for you, consider it done."

Crispina returned the embrace. No one had touched her since she left Aelius's house. She'd missed the playful shoves and nudges from Max, Gaia's gentle touch, the casual kisses on the cheek or furtive squeezes from Aelius.

"Would you tell me what happened?" Horatia asked. "Only if you wish to speak of it, of course."

Crispina hadn't spoken about any of this since leaving Aelius, but maybe talking about her troubles would help. She led Horatia into the peristyle, the private garden at the back of the house, where they could speak in relative seclusion. They sat on a bench amid two flowering trees. In quiet tones, Crispina told Horatia everything that had happened.

Horatia gasped when she relayed the incident with Rufus, and let out an anguished sigh when she described Aelius's discovery of her betrayal. When the awful story was finished, Horatia grasped her hand. "I'm so very sorry. I'm sure if someone had been threatening Paullus or Nonus, I would have done exactly as you did."

"Even if it meant you would have lost Decius?"

Horatia bit her lip, her love for her husband shining in her eyes. "Yes, even then."

Crispina exhaled. She hadn't realized how good it would feel to talk to someone who understood. "So now you see why it's all over."

Horatia leaned her head against Crispina's shoulder. "You poor thing. You must be in need of a distraction. It's not healthy to sit inside all day by yourself. Would you like to accompany me and Decius to a dinner party tomorrow evening? I'm sure your parents will allow it."

Crispina hesitated. Socializing and feigning happiness sounded as unappetizing to her as cold porridge, and it would be rather odd for her to appear in public without her husband, especially since no one was supposed to know of their separation yet. But it was just one small dinner party, and she'd be with Horatia and Decius. The alternative was spending another night alone, cursing the choices that had brought her here. A distraction might do her good. "All right. That would be nice."

"Wonderful! We'll pick you up in the litter. Now, let me tell you about the funniest thing Nonus did the other day…" Horatia launched into an anecdote about her little son. Crispina smiled and tried to forget the fact that she would never again have a family whose anecdotes she could share.

Crispina secured permission from her parents to attend the dinner party with Horatia, though she had to promise to be home by midnight. That was no great sacrifice, as Crispina had no desire to stay out until dawn anyway, but having to answer for her whereabouts rankled. Yet another thing she'd left behind with Aelius.

At the party, Crispina stuck close to Horatia and Decius, trying to avoid having to make conversation with anyone else. The music and laughter cheered her, and the food was good, the wine plentiful. She noticed Catullus seated on a couch across the room, making lively conversation with their hostess. He acknowledged Crispina with a nod, which she returned before quickly looking away. She wondered what he must think of her. Catullus was a great supporter of Aelius's political ambitions, and she was the author of their ruin.

Halfway through the first course, a couple arrived late. Crispina looked up from her wine to see Memmius, her ex-husband, with a young woman on his arm. Memmius made eloquent apologies to the host and hostess for their tardiness, but Crispina's attention remained fixed on the woman, who had to be his new wife. The young woman's hand brushed her abdomen as she spoke to their hostess, causing the green dress to cling to the slight roundness. When their hostess offered congratulations to the couple, Crispina knew.

Beside her, Horatia sucked in a breath. "I'm sorry," she whispered. "I didn't know he would be here."

Crispina tore her gaze from the young woman. "Did you know…his wife…?"

"I heard he'd married several months ago. I didn't know…" Horatia shook her head. "I'm sorry."

Crispina took a long swallow of wine. She had once wondered if her lack of conception was due to Memmius, not her, but the months she'd spent lying with Aelius without pregnancy had disproven that. The fault, whatever it was, laid with her alone. So the sight of his newly pregnant bride shouldn't disquiet her.

But it brought to mind everything she'd failed at. She had never truly wanted a child, but if she had only been able to conceive, none of this would have happened. Memmius never would have left her. She never would have met Aelius, or if she did, it would have been as a passing acquaintance at a party like this one, someone she'd admire across a room.

She would have spent her life in a conventional, passionless marriage. She never would have known what it was like to belong so deeply to someone, and to feel so broken when the bond was severed.

She might have had a child of her own, but it wouldn't have been Max. And the thought of never having witnessed his antics or his horrid language or atrocious table manners was nearly unbearable. The realization hit her in a startling jolt as she stared at Memmius and his wife: *I wouldn't give a single sestertius to still be married to that man, child or no.*

Crispina took a long, shuddering breath. The weight of missing Aelius, Max, and Gaia overwhelmed her in a sudden rush.

"Are you all right?" Horatia asked.

"Excuse me a moment." She rose from the couch and left the dining room, fanning her face as if she needed air. She had left another dinner party like this long ago. Aelius had followed her, and they'd had their first ill-fated conversation. She remembered his cocky smile, and the impulse that had led her to douse him with water from the atrium pool.

She passed through the empty atrium and went into the peristyle. It was inappropriate, verging on rude, for a dinner guest to venture into the family's private garden, but if she was discovered she could claim she'd gotten lost on the way back to the dining room.

She found a bench in the shadow of a column and sat, bracing her elbows on her knees to bury her face in her hands. Would these feelings ever leave her? It wasn't just that she'd lost Aelius. The guilt of what she'd done to him crushed her like a boulder on her chest. He had a dream, and she had ruined it.

Soft footsteps sounded and she jumped to her feet, ready to make an excuse about why she was lingering here. But she recognized the lanky figure that approached.

"Good evening, Crispina," Catullus said. "May I join you?"

She sat back on the bench. "I wish you wouldn't."

He sat next to her nonetheless. "It must be difficult to see your ex-husband with a newly pregnant wife."

She shot him a sharp look. Sometimes he was too perceptive. "My first ex-husband, you mean. I have two now."

"You're not divorced yet."

"You've known Aelius for longer than I have. Do you truly think he will ever so much as look at me again?"

Catullus shrugged. "It's only been a week. Things may change."

She pivoted to stare directly at him, his profile shadowy in the dark garden. "Your optimism is naïve."

"Love is not so easy to set aside, Crispina," he said. "I believe Aelius wishes he could hate you, but he will never be able to. His love for you has become a torment."

"Wonderful," she murmured.

"I only meant that if you were to take the first step, you may find reconciliation comes easier than you'd expect."

Crispina shook her head. "I hurt him greatly. I'd never ask him to forgive me. I don't deserve that." Still, the thought of returning to Aelius tempted her, rising like a desert mirage in her mind. "Do you think there's any chance he could pull through? He must be doing everything he can in these last few days."

"I believe he is concentrating his efforts on acquiring an estate in the countryside."

Crispina blinked. "He means to leave Rome?"

Catullus's mouth pulled down into a mournful expression. "Much to my chagrin. But he's done with politics."

"You mean...he's not even going to try to win this election? He's given up?" She knew his prospects were bleak, thanks to her, but she had assumed he would keep fighting, scrape together every last vote he possibly could.

Catullus nodded.

Shock jolted Crispina to her feet. "He can't give up!"

"With respect, I don't think you're best-suited to criticize his actions here, Crispina."

She shot him a glare. "There must be something he could do. Someone he could talk to. He can't just...leave." Aelius had been fighting this uphill battle since the day she'd met him, facing every obstacle, every insult with unflagging tenacity. The idea of his capitulation was devastating.

"There must be something that can be done," she insisted.

"Even if there is, I'm not sure Aelius has the appetite for it at the moment."

She folded her arms over her chest, summoning the stubborn resolve that had seen her through her taxing first marriage and humiliating divorce. "If he won't act, then I will." She would never ask for his forgiveness, but what if there was some way to right the wrong she'd done him?

Catullus looked at her as if she'd grown two more heads. "How, exactly?"

"I'm not sure," she admitted. "But I will think of something. And you'll help me." If there was one thing she'd always been able to rely on, it was her intellect. Catullus could be a worthy ally; he wasn't stupid, even if he did botch Sappho occasionally, and he knew more than she did about the intricacies of the election.

This venture was likely impossible, she knew. But the alternative was to live the rest of her life under the crushing weight of guilt that plagued her. It had only been a week, and she could barely live with herself. She didn't want to think about the years that stretched before her, empty and alone.

Catullus raised an eyebrow. "The election is in a week, you realize?"

"Come visit me tomorrow." Crispina didn't bother to hide the tone of command from her voice. "We can talk. And don't mention this to Aelius."

CHAPTER 29

CRISPINA WAS RELIEVED THAT Catullus accepted her half-command, half-invitation and showed up at her parents' house around midday the next day. She had informed her parents he might pay her a visit to show her his latest poetry. He was well-respected enough that they wouldn't turn him away, even if he did have a reputation for writing rather scandalous verse.

He carried a sheaf of papyrus under his arm when he arrived, and spread it over the table set up in the sunlit atrium. Mother was pacing around the atrium as if enjoying the pleasant air, but Crispina knew she had one eye on the pair of them.

Crispina's lips tightened, and she reached for one of the poems. "Is this one in hendecasyllables?" she asked, pitching her voice louder than necessary.

"Indeed, you have a perceptive eye," Catullus said, following her gaze toward her mother.

They engaged in meaningless chatter about the merits of one meter over another until Mother sighed and strode from the atrium. Crispina relaxed against her chair. For once, her mother's apathy toward poetry worked in her favor.

Once they were alone, Catullus leaned toward her. "I've been thinking on it, and I cannot uncover any way to help Aelius defeat Rufus."

Crispina bit her lip. Her mind had been buzzing all through the night, and she hadn't yet come up with any insight either. "Can we not do what Rufus did to me? Find some dirt on him, something we could use against him?"

"I know all the gossip, and there's nothing on him. He's unmarried, so there's nothing even as innocuous as an affair. He's disgustingly rich, so no embarrassing debts. He honors the gods. Despite his blackmailing of you, he seems to be an upstanding citizen in every respect."

She stared at the papers before her, as if Catullus's love verses could reveal something. She willed herself to think, to use the mind she had cultivated through reading and education.

Her thoughts went to Penelope, her favorite character from literature. Penelope was as crafty as her famed husband. Except unlike Odysseus, Penelope hadn't needed something as ostentatious as a giant horse to carry out her trickery. She had only needed a simple loom and time to unravel the threads…

Maybe Crispina didn't need a complicated plan either. One simple fact coalesced in her mind. "It's not just Aelius and Rufus," Crispina realized aloud. "There are other candidates. There are ten plebeian tribunes elected, correct?"

"Yes, but Aelius chose to focus his efforts on Rufus because he had the best chance of beating him. Romans hate new money as much as ambitious freedmen."

"But in theory, Aelius doesn't have to beat Rufus. If someone else were to be vulnerable, Aelius could still win a place."

"I suppose," Catullus said with an unconvinced frown. "But we determined most of the other candidates were almost certain of winning."

"Who else is running?"

Catullus sifted through the papers he'd brought and handed her a list of names. She skimmed down it. Most of them she didn't recognize, but she paused at one name. "Epidius Verus. I recognize that name." She thought hard, trying to recall where she knew the name. Was he one of her father's friends? An acquaintance of Horatia's?

"So?"

Epidius Verus. Epidius Verus. She rose and paced, hoping the movement would jostle something loose in her mind.

It hit her with a bolt of clarity. Taurus, Cassandra's lover, had previously worked in the house of Epidius Verus. Taurus had refused to reveal why his former master had suddenly decided to sell him. There was something suspicious there, but it hadn't seemed to matter at the time.

She relayed all this to Catullus. He eyed her skeptically. "You think this slave knows something that could ruin Verus's chances in the election?"

Her heart beat faster. "I certainly hope so." It was a long shot, but as of now, it was their only lead. "If I'm right, I could force him to drop out of the race. If no one could vote for him, do you think Aelius might win a spot?"

"It's possible," Catullus said.

"Then I need to speak to Taurus." Crispina jumped to her feet, her body aflame with new purpose. She could do it. She could

find a way to win this election for Aelius. It wasn't the way he
should have won, but maybe, just maybe, it would be enough.

Crispina set her plan in motion immediately. She sent a messenger to Aelius's house with strict instructions to go to the kitchen
entrance at the back of the house and speak only to Taurus. She
didn't want Aelius to know what she was trying to do. If she
failed, he might see it as unwarranted meddling.

It took some thinking to figure out how to actually meet
Taurus. He couldn't come to her parents' house, and she couldn't
go to Aelius's house. She debated asking him to meet her in a
market square, but her parents wouldn't let her go anywhere
without an escort, and her mother would have some questions
if she was seen speaking to a strange man, especially a slave, in
the city.

Finally, she asked Catullus to send her an invitation to a fab-
ricated midday gathering of poets and intellectuals at his house a
few days later. She told her parents Horatia had been invited too,
and received permission to attend.

The messenger would ask Taurus to find an excuse to leave
the house on the given day, which shouldn't be difficult as there
were always errands to be run, and come to Catullus's house.
She knew she was asking him to take a risk by sneaking around
behind Aelius's back, but she sensed he would comply since she
was responsible for reuniting him with Cassandra.

On the appointed day, she paced in Catullus's atrium, waiting
for Taurus. Catullus sat at a small table in a shaft of sunlight,

twirling a stylus between his fingers as he glowered down at a wax tablet. He seemed to be trying to write, but didn't appear to be having much luck.

The minutes stretched on. Crispina glanced up at the opening in the ceiling, gauging the angle of the sun. It was past midday now. What if Taurus hadn't been able to get away? Or what if he had just decided not to take the risk? All this tenuous hope would have been for nothing.

She heaved a sigh and kept pacing.

"Will you please sit?" Catullus demanded. "You're distracting me."

She opened her mouth to shoot a sharp reply, but at that moment, one of Catullus's slaves entered the atrium, Taurus at his back. Crispina's heart leaped.

"Sir, this man said he was here to see the lady?" The slave glanced at Crispina before focusing on Catullus.

"Yes, that's right," Catullus said. "That will be all."

The slave nodded and departed. Crispina hurried to Taurus. "Thank you so much for meeting me here. I realize this must all seem very strange. And I know you took a risk by heeding my request."

"I'm still confused why you wanted to see me, mistress...I mean..." He stumbled over the form of address.

Crispina waved a hand, not caring what he called her. "I wanted to know about your former master, Epidius Verus. He's running against Aelius in the tribune election. I need to know if he has any weakness that might be exploited."

Taurus lowered his gaze. "I don't know anything about politics."

His voice was too careful, too measured, and Crispina knew he was keeping something back. "Why did Verus want to sell you so abruptly?" she pressed. "It struck me as unusual at the time."

He shifted his weight, passing a hand over the back of his neck, but said nothing.

"I know you know something," Crispina said. "Please, it could be the difference between victory and defeat for Aelius."

"I…" He shook his head, and his freckled cheeks reddened. "Forgive me, but I vowed never to speak of it."

Crispina reached out to grasp his hand. His fingers jerked under her touch, but he didn't pull away. "I regret it, but I must ask you to break that vow. Anything you know could be of critical importance to this election and to Aelius."

Taurus ran a hand through his reddish hair. "I do owe you both a great debt," he said quietly. "You reunited me with Cassandra, and allowed me to watch my daughter grow up." Emotion roughened his voice.

Crispina squeezed his hand. "It was the right thing to do."

He met her gaze. His brown eyes were steady, resolved. "For the sake of what I owe you, I'll tell you."

Behind them, Catullus rose from his seat and came over, his eyes alight with interest. "I hope it's sordid. This could make a good poem."

"Let him talk," Crispina snapped. Everything hinged on this. If the information Taurus knew was damaging enough, then Crispina could use it to ensure Aelius's victory.

Taurus glanced between them. "I accidentally opened a letter to my former master. I didn't know it was supposed to be private, and my master didn't know I could read. I hardly even understood it, but when my master realized I'd read it, he flew into a rage. I started to understand what the letter was about. It was from a builder, discussing the type of marble to be used for a temple my master was in charge of building."

Crispina glanced at Catullus. So far, this did not seem promising in terms of sordidness or likelihood to influence the election. "Why would he have been building a temple?"

Catullus chimed in. "I believe Epidius Verus was an aedile last year, so he would have been involved in the maintenance and construction of temples."

Taurus nodded. "Yes. What I understand is that he was taking money from the treasury to pay builders. But he had some sort of arrangement with the builder to use bad marble. The stone was taken from the top layers of a quarry, which I gather is much cheaper to procure. But it's pitted with holes, which the builders patched with wax or plaster, so no one can tell."

The pieces were coming together in Crispina's mind. "So he paid the builder for cheap marble, and then pocketed the difference from the treasury?"

"I believe so, mistress," Taurus said.

Catullus let out a low whistle. "Sneaky louse."

Crispina's heart beat faster. "So he's trying to cover up fraud and embezzlement of public funds. In addition to dishonoring the gods with a shoddily built temple. No wonder he wanted to get you out of the way, Taurus."

Taurus's lips tightened. "I swore not to speak of it. But he didn't care."

She turned to Catullus. "Do you think this is enough?"

He raised his eyebrows. "The punishment for theft is a penalty of twice the amount stolen. And given that it was a temple, it'll look like he stiffed the gods themselves. He'd be lucky to get exiled, if people don't bludgeon him in the street."

Crispina wanted to hug Taurus, but she maintained a shred of dignity and merely clasped his hand once more. "Thank you for this, Taurus. This information could change everything."

He bowed his head. "As I said, I owe so much to you both."

She released his hand. "I just have one last question. Where does Epidius Verus live?"

CHAPTER 30

WITH DIRECTIONS FROM TAURUS, Crispina climbed into the waiting litter that had ferried her from her parents' house and told the litter-bearers to take her to the Viminal Hill. No doubt the litter-bearers would relay her itinerary to Mother when they returned, as she'd only gotten permission to go to Catullus's house, but Crispina didn't care. She hadn't felt this energized since before leaving Aelius. Finally, she had a purpose, some good she could do after betraying him.

The litter slowed as it passed through a crowded square. Crispina nudged the curtain aside to glance out over the people filling the square, everyone hurrying about their business. A tall man caught her attention on the other side of the square, hand in hand with a child. Crispina drew in a sharp breath. It couldn't be them…but the sun flashed bronze on Aelius's hair, and she knew the lilt of his stride by heart.

"Stop a moment," she called to the litter bearers. They drew to a halt and set the litter down. Aelius was too far away to notice her, but she watched him and Max nonetheless, her eyes drinking in the sight of them like the sweetest wine.

Max clutched a savillum, his favorite treat, and munched it eagerly. Aelius said something to him, a grin flashing across his face, and Max laughed, mouth still full of cheesecake.

Crispina's heart twisted in bittersweet emotion. They were happy together. Happy without her. They didn't need her. If she walked up to them right now, she doubted Aelius would receive her with anything other than disdain. Some of the purposeful fire dulled within her, but she tried to remind herself she wasn't doing this to win Aelius back, only to right a wrong. Aelius might never forgive her, even if he won, and she would not beg him to.

"Proceed," she said quietly, and the litter lurched back into motion.

They crossed the city and arrived at the Verus house, which was tidy and not much bigger than Aelius's home. She would bet Verus was funneling the money from his construction fraud into a lavish country estate, so his urban neighbors wouldn't notice any suspicious increase in wealth.

Crispina dismounted from the litter and knocked on the front door. A slave answered. Crispina gave her name and asked to see the mistress of the house, apologizing for the unannounced visit. She had decided on the litter ride over to try to speak to Verus's wife. Firstly, because Verus probably wasn't even home at this hour, secondly because she had a feeling she might be able to have a more reasonable conversation with a fellow woman.

The slave showed her into a small atrium. The columns were plain, with square-carved tops, but expensive statuary lined the room. Some of them were even gilded. Crispina found it rather gaudy, but perhaps it served as further proof of Verus's illegal activities.

While Crispina was looking around, a light-haired woman around her age entered the atrium. She wore gold earrings set with pearls, and several heavy jeweled bracelets. The woman cleared her throat. "I was told you're here to see me? Forgive me, but I don't think we've met."

Crispina shook her head. "I apologize for the intrusion. I am Crispina, wife to Aelius Herminius." Her stomach clenched at referring to herself as Aelius's wife. How much longer would she be able to say that for?

"My name is Licinia, but I think you must already know who I am. May I ask why you've come?" Licinia's inquisitive gaze ran over Crispina from palla to sandals.

Crispina attempted an ingratiating smile, but feared she just looked smug. Winning others over was Aelius's strength, not hers. "Our husbands are both involved in the election for tribune of the plebs."

"Yes." A spark of pride brightened Licinia's blue eyes. "Verus tells me his chances are very good to win a place. I hope the same is true for your husband."

During the litter ride here, Crispina had wondered how to play this conversation. Should she be forthright and demanding, or try to skirt around the issue? She settled for playing the naïve young wife. "I overheard something rather troubling the other day, and I thought you would appreciate knowing. As I would, if I were in your place."

Licinia cocked her head. "Knowing what?"

Crispina tried to read her expression and tone, to get a sense if the woman knew what Crispina was about to reveal. But Licinia looked no more than innocently curious. "There are some nasty rumors out there about your husband. I fear they may be devastating if spread too far."

Now Licinia looked completely bemused. "I'm sure there are always untoward things said before an election. But I know my husband has nothing to hide."

"So he's *not* committing construction fraud and embezzling state funds?"

Licinia's mouth dropped open, shock spreading across her face. "Embezzling...what?"

Either Licinia was a natural-born actress, or she truly had no idea what her husband was up to. This was more awkward than Crispina had anticipated. She stammered for a moment, trying to figure out what to say.

Licinia drew herself up. "If you've only come here to slander my husband's good name, then I will kindly ask you to leave my home."

"It's not slander," Crispina said. "It's true. And if this news gets out, you will be ruined. Your husband needs to drop out of the election, or I will not hesitate to reveal what I know."

Licinia's eyes blazed. "Drop out? Based on the word of a woman I barely know? That is ridiculous."

Crispina opened her mouth to reply, but the sound of footsteps behind her distracted her. She turned to see a man a few years older than Aelius entering the atrium. He shed his cloak and tossed it into the arms of a trailing slave without so much as a glance.

Crispina's stomach tightened. She had not been prepared to have this confrontation with Verus himself.

The man glanced from his wife to Crispina. "Didn't realize you had company."

Licinia waved a hand at him. "Verus, come here and set this woman straight. She's spouting all sorts of nonsense about you."

Verus approached with a slow stride. "Have we met?"

Crispina inclined her head. "My name is Crispina, wife to Aelius Herminius."

His mouth twisted. "The freedman." Contempt laced his voice.

"Better a freedman than a thief," Crispina shot back.

He narrowed his eyes at her. "Please tell me what gives you the nerve to come into my house and insult me."

Crispina drew in a breath and straightened her shoulders. "You embezzled state funds during your term as an aedile by using sub-par marble in the temples you built. And insulted the gods, as well."

"Ridiculous," Licinia muttered, but Crispina kept her focus on Verus.

Anger, but not surprise, blossomed across his face. He fixed her with a scorching glare. "Is your husband so incompetent that he sends his wife to make his threats?"

Licinia interjected. "Verus, just tell her she's wrong and send her on her way. We don't have to listen to this."

"He can't send me on my way," Crispina said. "Because he knows it's true. And it's easily proven. All it takes is a cursory examination of the temples you were in charge of. Maybe you were smart enough to use good marble on the parts people can see close-up, but I'm sure the rest of the structure is cobbled together with wax and plaster." She turned to Licinia. "My sympathies. It's clear you didn't know you were married to an embezzler. And now all of this"—she gestured around at the house—"hangs in the balance. The penalty for theft is repayment twice over, and then of course there's the issue of blasphemy. A lawyer could easily argue that your husband was stealing from the gods themselves. Exile would be a mercy."

Licinia had gone paler and paler as Crispina spoke, until her skin took on a gray cast. "Verus…" the woman said uncertainly. "It's not true, is it?"

"I didn't see you complaining when I showered you in jewels and silk," Verus snapped.

"But I thought…I never imagined…" Licinia braced herself against a column. "By Juno, what have you done?"

Verus ignored his wife and focused on Crispina. "I assume there's something you want from me, or the magistrates would already be here to arrest me." His voice was flat.

Crispina nodded. "I want you to withdraw from the tribune race. And of course desist any of these fraudulent activities which may still be ongoing. In return, I'll swear to silence. You will avoid financial ruin and public condemnation."

He glowered at her. "Swear it."

Crispina raised her hand, lifted her eyes skyward, and spoke a formal oath. "I hereby swear by Juno, queen of the gods, that if Epidius Verus withdraws from the tribune election, I will never reveal his illegal doings to a magistrate or the public. May Juno strike me down if I lie. And if Epidius Verus does not withdraw from the tribune election, I swear I will do everything in my power to ruin him."

Silence fell in the atrium. She glanced from Verus, still bristling with helpless fury, to Licinia, who seemed on the verge of crumpling to the ground in shame. She addressed Verus. "I'll look forward to hearing news of your withdrawal by tomorrow."

"Get out of my house," he growled.

"With pleasure." She nodded primly, and showed herself out.

CHAPTER 31

AELIUS GAZED AT MAX, who was stuffing his face with a plate of poached pears across the dining table. Fondness swelled in his chest. As of an hour ago, Max was legally Aelius's son and heir. They had visited a praetor to make the adoption official, then met Gaia at a temple to sacrifice a brace of doves in honor of the occasion. On the way to the temple, Aelius had bought Max his favorite treat, savillum. Max had devoured an entire one by himself but somehow still had room to inhale the contents of the celebratory lunch at home.

Catullus was the only one in attendance besides family. He was as jovial as always, joking with Max and unashamedly flirting with Aelius's mother. His presence was welcome, but it didn't fill the emptiness Aelius felt on the dining couch beside him.

Crispina should be here. He had thought of her often this past week. He missed her with a keen ache. Anger still filled him when he remembered what she had done, how she had lied to him, and he couldn't yet forgive her. But by the gods, he longed to see her. To spark one of her rare smiles, to see how she cared for Max, stern and tender at the same time. And especially to hold her, squeeze her, feel her shudder against him as he…

He tried to snap himself out of it. Dwelling on the past would do no good. As of today, he had a new future to build in Max.

Max lifted a dish of fried octopus and offered it politely to Gaia—too politely. "More octopus, grandmother?" His mouth curved in a sly grin. He had been good-naturedly tormenting Gaia with her new title since they returned, once he realized how much it annoyed her.

Gaia smacked him with her folded napkin. "Maximus Herminius, you call me that one more time and I will send you to bed right this instant!"

Catullus burst out in full-throated laughter. "I never thought the day would come when I would gladly fall at the feet of someone's grandmother, if she would have me."

"Don't test me, Catullus," Gaia said. "I will not hesitate to send you to bed too."

Catullus grinned wolfishly. "Believe me, I would relish it."

Aelius threw an olive at him. "Please let us change the subject." He turned to his mother. "You'll be happy to know I've confirmed the availability of a country villa. All that remains is to decide when we leave. I feel I should stay in town at least through the election. How about the day after? Will that give you enough time to pack up the house?"

"That's only a week away," Gaia said with a frown.

"With respect," Catullus said, "don't you think you should see how the election turns out before you make plans to leave?"

"The outcome is all but certain," Aelius said. "Will you pay us a visit in the country, Catullus?"

Catullus snorted. "Fat chance. You forget I was born a rustic. I've had enough of trees and horse dung. Escaped to Rome the first chance I got."

Aelius hardly thought Catullus's sprawling family estate on Lake Benacus qualified as "rustic," but he kept that observation to himself.

"Do I still get a horse?" Max piped up.

"That sounds rather dangerous," Gaia said. "You could fall and break your neck, or get trampled."

Max glowered. "I would never fall."

An argument ensued over the relative safety of horseback riding. As Gaia and Max bickered, Catullus leaned over to speak quietly in Aelius's ear. "Do as you like, but you might find that it behooves you not to count your chickens before they hatch, as Aesop says." He gave Aelius a glance laden with some unknown significance, then turned away to take a swig of wine, leaving Aelius to contemplate what he meant.

Aelius sifted through the piles of papers, scrolls, and wax tablets in his study, trying to achieve a semblance of organization so he could pack everything into the chest sitting open on his desk.

He glanced over the tablets, using the flat end of a stylus to rub away the writing on anything he didn't need to preserve.

One tablet, covered in a few lines of neat handwriting, caught his attention. It was the letter Crispina had written in response to his apology for his awkward behavior at their first meeting. He ran a gentle thumb over the delicate writing, feeling the ridges and indentations of the wax. He'd forgotten he saved this. He thought back to those early days, when he'd been scheming to win her hand because he thought her family's clout would give him an advantage in the election. How wrong he'd been.

He picked up a stylus and rubbed away the words, returning the wax to a smooth, blank surface. He left her name for last, but eventually it, too, disappeared from the thin layer of wax. Soon, all reminders of her would be similarly erased from his life. He needed a fresh start, a new home that wasn't filled to the brim with ghosts of their life together.

He stacked the tablets in the bottom of the empty chest, then loaded in some carefully sealed inkwells and a handful of styluses and reed pens. He reached for a pile of papers, but a noise from elsewhere in the house caught his attention.

"Aelius?" his mother called, sounding alarmed.

Aelius lurched to his feet and hurried from the study. He found his mother standing in the atrium with Malchio. Malchio hefted a basket filled with eggs and vegetables, clearly just returned from the market.

"What is it?" Aelius asked.

Gaia nodded to Malchio. "Tell him what you overheard at the market."

"I don't know if it means anything, sir, but I thought…if you didn't already know…"

"Yes?" Aelius was impatient to hear whatever had caused his mother's consternation, but he tried to keep his tone mild.

Malchio took a deep breath. "People were talking about how a man named Epidius Verus has dropped out of the tribune election, sir."

Aelius blinked. "That can't be right."

"I'm only telling you what I heard, sir," Malchio said.

"Of course. Thank you for the information."

Malchio bowed his head and hurried off to the kitchen with his basket.

Aelius paced in a tight circle, running over this new piece of information in his mind. *Epidius Verus dropped out.* But why?

Gaia watched him, chewing her lip. "What does this mean?" she asked quietly.

"It doesn't make sense," he muttered. "Why would Verus drop out? He was almost certain to win a spot."

"No matter his reasons, it has happened," she said. "What does it mean for you?"

Aelius swallowed hard. "It means…I could win." Voicing the possibility aloud made his stomach lurch. A flood of excitement rushed through him. He paced even faster, traversing the width of the atrium in short, frantic strides. "With Verus out, all of those voters will have to find another candidate to give their vote to. And if enough people give it to me…"

"You would win," she whispered.

"I might." His voice was unsteady. Was it possible? *Surely not.* But numbers were numbers, and if everyone who planned to vote for Verus had to cast their tenth vote for someone else… "I'm sorry, Mama, I know this isn't what you wanted."

She crossed to him and grasped his hands. "No, my love. I want everything for you. You deserve every bit of happiness this world can give you. I only tried to steer you away from politics because I feared it would hurt you, and it has, but I know you are strong enough to overcome it." She brought his face down to hers and kissed him on the forehead. "You will win, and you will make me so proud."

Aelius retreated to his study, his mind whirling. He stared at the half-filled chest atop his desk. Already, the idea of an estate in the country seemed so far away. The news of Verus's withdrawal reignited every ounce of hope that had been crushed by Crispina's betrayal.

Crispina. Had she heard the news? Did she realize what it could mean?

An uncomfortable realization struck him. If he won, he'd be expected to host a celebratory banquet the day after the election. It would look extremely odd if Crispina was not by his side.

He dug a blank tablet out of the box he'd been packing and stared at it for several moments. Finally, he touched the tip of a stylus to the surface and wrote.

Aelius Herminius to Crispina:

As you may have heard, it seems my fortunes have shifted. Another candidate, Epidius Verus, has withdrawn from the race. Nothing is certain, but should I prove victorious, I will host a celebratory meal the day after the election. It will look strange if you do not attend. I hope you will oblige me.

He closed the tablet. The thought of seeing Crispina again added to the jangle of nerves in his stomach. If he won the election, would they still divorce? A divorce would reflect poorly on him, but he wasn't sure he could trust or forgive her. Maybe the best they could hope for was a cordial, passionless marriage for the sake of appearances. The thought gave him no joy, but it might be the best he could hope for.

CHAPTER 32

THE MORNING OF THE election dawned sunny and warm. Aelius rose from his bed with a sigh, rubbing a hand over his face. He'd barely gotten any sleep, tormented alternately by his newfound hopes for the election as well as anxiety over what his future with Crispina held.

He remembered being consumed with nerves on this day last year. He'd spent the day pacing, unable to eat, waving away his mother's attempts at conversation. But his nervousness had been mostly anticipation. He hadn't actually thought he would lose. He'd been arrogant, naïve, and had been crushed by the defeat. Now, he knew what it felt like to fail. He tried to use that to temper his hope, but the fear of yet another failure only added an undercurrent of dread to his nerves.

By now, voters would be assembling at the Campus Martius outside Rome, ready to cast their ballots. He imagined them standing in line, holding small wax tablets inscribed with the initials of the candidates they were voting for. Would his name be on enough of them?

Voting commenced at first light and would take two or three hours. Last year, it had taken ten further hours to count the votes, so there would be no news until nightfall. The day would be an agony of waiting, wondering. He tried to be rational. Voting was divided between tribes, based on the regions of the city and surrounding areas, and depending on how the tribes voted and in what order, it was possible for a candidate to win with only a quarter of the popular vote. But right now, imagining even a quarter of voters would write down his initials seemed insurmountable.

He spent the day quizzing Max on his reading and writing skills, hoping the boy would distract him with his antics.

"This is boring," Max groaned as Aelius corrected his mal-formed letters.

"You must receive a good education," Aelius said. At least Max was getting several years more than Aelius had, as his education had only begun after being freed at the age of fourteen. "It was important to Crispina, and it's crucial that you become educated if you are to honor our family name. Besides, reading will become more interesting once you master the basics. You could read about anything that interests you. Horses, boats, battles, and the like."

Max's face brightened. "People write about battles?"

Aelius nodded. "In great detail."

Max grinned and snatched the wax tablet back, poring over it with renewed enthusiasm.

As noon passed and the sky slowly turned golden later in the day, the tension in Aelius's body ratcheted up. Every sound, every murmur of someone speaking, every echo of footsteps anywhere in the house was a messenger arriving with news.

But no one came. Dusk set in. Aelius left Max in Gaia's care and retreated to his study, needing to be alone. A heavy ball of dread settled in his stomach. He'd been a fool to get his hopes up.

If he had never heard the news about Epidius Verus, he would have spent the day continuing his preparations to leave the city. Now, he had to contend with failure once more.

He sank his face into his hands, elbows braced on the surface of his desk. If he couldn't win an election after another candidate's last minute withdrawal, maybe he would have lost even without Crispina's betrayal. He was an idiot to ever believe he could have won.

Quiet footsteps sounded, and Aelius lifted his head. His mother poked her head around the door. "Dinner is ready. Will you join us?" Her voice was soft with pity.

"I'm not hungry."

"You haven't eaten all day."

"I said, I'm not hungry," he snapped, but immediately regretted his harsh tone. "I'm sorry, Mama—"

She held up a hand to silence him, her head turning toward the front of the house. "Someone is at the door."

Aelius froze. He could just hear the sound of the door opening and words exchanged between Ajax and whoever had come. A moment later, the door closed, and footsteps approached.

Through the doorway, Aelius glimpsed Ajax. "Letter came, mistress," Ajax said.

Gaia reached out to take the small scroll from him. "Thank you."

He departed, and Gaia came back into his study to hand him the scroll. Aelius took it, staring down at the red wax that sealed it. It was the seal of the magistrate's office that supervised the elections.

Aelius swallowed hard, panic suddenly rising in his chest.

His mother smiled encouragingly. "Go on, open it."

"I-I can't." His fingers were stiff, he couldn't bring himself to break the seal. "You do it." He handed the letter back.

She broke the seal and unfurled the scroll.

"Well?" Aelius asked, his heart thumping.

She smiled again. "You've forgotten I can't read, dear."

He lurched to his feet and took the scroll. His eyes skimmed over the words. *Congratulations…tribune…victory…*

He read it twice, three times. He'd done it. He'd really done it.

Aelius dropped back into the chair. Shock thrummed through him. After so much uncertainty, he could hardly believe this was really happening.

He read the letter a fourth time, just in case.

"I presume it's good news?" his mother asked, her smile growing.

He managed a nod. She crossed behind his desk and wrapped him in her arms, bending to kiss his forehead. "I am so proud of you, my love."

He returned the embrace, hugging her tighter than he had since he was a child. All he had ever wanted was to make her proud, to erase some of the pain and shame of their beginnings. Emotion choked him for a moment, and he pressed his face into her shoulder until he could master himself.

She drew back and kissed him on the forehead once more. "I will go tell the kitchen to serve our finest wine at dinner tonight."

"Make it our second finest." His voice was raspy. "Save the finest for tomorrow."

She nodded, then left. Aelius's gaze returned to the letter. It contained a list of the ten newly elected tribunes in order of votes received. His name was the last. Rufus's name was only one spot higher, which gave him a certain grim satisfaction.

They'd be colleagues now. Perhaps they could find a way to work together, as they would both face a difficult road forward. As Catullus had once said, Romans hated new money almost as much as they disliked upstart freedmen. It was a miracle either of them had managed to win enough votes to be elected.

Thinking of Rufus made his mind turn to Crispina. He would see her tomorrow at his victory dinner, assuming she showed up. What would he say to her? His heart ached to forgive her, but his mind balked. A chance victory didn't erase the fact that she had lied to him. He only had to decide if he would insist on a divorce, or settle for a distant marriage to preserve the advantage of her family's connections.

Crispina spent the day of the election consumed with powerless anxiety. She kept reading and rereading the curt note Aelius had sent a few days ago, mentioning Verus's withdrawal and his renewed hope of victory. Would it be enough?

In the morning, Mother insisted she help with the weaving, as Father needed a new tunic. She tried to expend some of her nervous energy in the push and pull of the loom, but made so many mistakes Mother started muttering under her breath about what a trial it was to have such a careless and ungrateful daughter.

In the afternoon, Crispina feigned a headache and retreated to her room to read, but even Sappho couldn't distract her. Her mind wandered from the inked words to the Campus Martius where the election was taking place.

She wondered if Aelius was nervous, or if Verus's withdrawal had instilled him with confidence. She wished she could be there to reassure him. At least he had Max to distract him. No doubt the boy's capers would be a blessing today.

In the evening, she dared to ask Father over dinner: "Have you heard anything of the election results?"

He frowned at her. "Election?"

"For tribune of the plebs."

"That was today?"

She tried to keep her face neutral as she nodded. "I was just wondering…"

"Politics are of no concern to a lady. Especially not a *plebeian* election," Mother said.

"They are of concern when my husband is a candidate," Crispina snapped.

"The *ex*-husband who threw you out." Mother shot her a glance dripping with disapproval.

"He didn't throw me out." Not literally, at least. "We decided to separate."

"Do you think he may take you back if he wins?" Mother asked. "I suppose he'll need a wife to host dinners for his political connections and such. Frankly, I think remaining unmarried for the rest of your days would be better than marriage to a *freedman*." She spat the word. "I never understood why your father even considered his proposal."

Father reached for another helping of oysters. "He made the point that it could be beneficial to have a connection among

the plebeians. They grow more influential each year, after all."
He glanced at Crispina. "Hopefully he will see the benefit of a
connection with our family and agree to take you back. It's not
as if you can expect a better match."

Crispina focused on cutting her food into tiny pieces. She
wouldn't allow herself to hope that Aelius might want her back.
But if he did, what if he thought like her parents and merely
wanted a hostess with a prestigious name?

That was our arrangement from the start, she reminded herself.
She had no right to hope for more.

CHAPTER 33

A LETTER FROM AELIUS arrived the next morning. Crispina ripped it open and read it with shaking hands.

In case you haven't heard, I've won, he wrote. *Mama is planning a banquet to start at sundown. It would be helpful if you arrive in advance to assist with the preparations. Max will like to see you.*

Crispina clutched the letter to her chest and leaned against the wall. A smile spread over her face, her first in so long. He'd done it. Aelius was to be a tribune, representing the people and working to improve their lives.

Pride swelled inside her, but she had no right to be proud of him. This wasn't her accomplishment.

Father quickly gave permission for her to attend the dinner party, and instructed her to grovel in apology for whatever she'd done to cause their separation. Crispina nodded meekly, then returned to her room to get ready.

She laid out several dresses on her bed, debating which to wear. She usually didn't spend much time thinking about her clothing, but today was important. She'd be representing Aelius at his first official engagement as an elected tribune.

After deliberation, she pushed aside her finest dresses of silk and selected a modest stola of crimson-dyed linen. The stola, a pleated, sleeveless robe layered over a tunic, could only be worn by married women. Putting it on gave her a pang of regret: for how much longer would she be able to wear this? But for tonight, at least, she was still a wife, and she was determined to look the part.

Trepidation built as she rode in the litter to Aelius's house. She ran through the things she wanted to say to him and prepared herself for the pain that seeing him again would cause. Would he be awash with joy after his victory, or would he be cold and distant with her?

No matter his mood, she was not going to tell him what she had done with Verus. Though she desperately wanted his forgiveness, she didn't deserve it just because she'd gotten lucky. If she told him, he might feel beholden to her, and she didn't want him to take her back out of gratitude or for the perceived repayment of a debt. She would keep silent in penance for her original betrayal.

A nervous shiver ran through her as she crossed the threshold of the house that had once been her home. In the atrium, Cassandra and Taurus were twining garlands of flowers around the columns, Taurus balancing carefully on a ladder and Cassandra handing the garlands up to him. They greeted her with respectful nods.

Crispina approached them. "I need to thank you again, Taurus," she said. "The information you gave me led directly to Aelius's victory."

Taurus dipped his head. "I'm happy to have helped, mistress."

Cassandra smiled. "I'm so glad we could repay at least some of what you have done for us."

Crispina let them get back to their garland-hanging and waited like a guest for someone to come greet her. Perhaps Aelius would send Gaia to meet her. Perhaps he wanted to avoid seeing her for as long as possible.

But a few breaths later, her heart leaped at the sight of the tall, lean figure who entered the atrium. He wore a new tunic of fine linen dyed a deep blue. Crispina recognized the fabric; Gaia had been weaving it around the time she left. The silver wristband Aelius wore to cover his brand shone as if it had been freshly polished.

He stopped a few paces from her and inclined his head. "Crispina. Thank you for coming." His voice was clipped, formal.

"I would not have missed it." She cleared her throat, which had suddenly gone dry. "Congratulations on your victory. It is well-deserved."

"Thank you."

Hasty, light footsteps sounded, coupled with a gleeful shriek Crispina instantly recognized. Max barreled into the atrium, heading straight for her. Crispina braced herself, expecting him to crash into her, but he skidded to a halt between her and Aelius, caught his breath, then nodded in a formal gesture of greeting.

"How polite you've become," Crispina said with a smile. She opened her arms, and he closed the remaining distance between them. She bent to wrap her arms around his small body. He smelled like herbs and honey, and she took a deep breath, as if she could imprint the scent into her lungs.

With effort, she forced away the emotion that threatened to overwhelm her and gently pulled back from the embrace, reaching out to pat his hair back into place. Keeping her voice brisk, she asked, "Have you been good to Aelius and Gaia?"

"He makes me read *all the time*." Max shot a glare at Aelius. "And practice writing until my fingers are about to fall off!"

Crispina dared a grateful smile at Aelius. "Thank you for keeping up with his lessons. That means a great deal to me."

"I didn't do it only for your sake." Aelius stepped closer and laid a hand on Max's shoulder. "It's important for him to have the best education if he is to uphold the legacy of his new family."

"His new...family?" Crispina glanced between them, not ready to let herself believe what Aelius seemed to be suggesting.

"I adopted Max last week," Aelius said. "He is now officially my son and heir."

Max grinned. "And Gaia is my *grandmother*."

Aelius swatted him lightly on the head. "We've talked about this."

Adopted. Crispina gaped, and tears sprang to her eyes, breaking the composure she'd fought so hard to maintain. Aelius had truly accepted Max, whom he'd once seen as nothing more than an unruly inconvenience. They were a family now. Without her.

She pressed a hand to her mouth, but a sob of bittersweet joy still escaped. "I can't believe it," she whispered haltingly. "I can't believe you did that for him."

Aelius met her gaze. "Whatever may have happened between us, you gave me a son, Crispina."

That undid the last of her control. A wave of sobs overtook her, releasing all the sadness and regret pent up inside her.

"You made her cry," Max complained.

"I'm sorry, Crispina, I didn't mean to upset you..." Aelius began.

"Upset me?" She took a gulping breath. "This is the most wonderful thing I've ever heard." She scrubbed a hand across her eyes. Luckily she hadn't worn much makeup today.

"I should have written to tell you," Aelius said. "It was wrong to keep it from you until now."

She shook her head. "You owe me nothing." Her breathing steadied, and she dabbed at her damp cheeks with the edge of her palla.

His lips parted, as if to say something, but then his head jerked up as another set of footsteps sounded.

Gaia entered and surveyed Crispina, hands clasped as she approached. An uncommon coolness cloaked her, evident in her formal posture and distant gaze.

"Gaia, how good to see you," Crispina said. "I've missed you so much." She took a step forward, wanting to hug her mother-in-law, but drew to a halt when Gaia didn't move to meet her.

"How nice of you to come," was all Gaia said, her tone chilled.

Crispina's lips pressed together. This austere welcome from Gaia, who was usually overflowing with warmth and kindness, tempered her momentary happiness at the news of Max's adoption. "I know I owe you an apology, Gaia."

Gaia lifted her chin. "You caused a great deal of pain. You broke my son's heart."

"Mama—" Aelius interjected, but Gaia held up a hand.

"I am not sure what the future holds between the two of you—that's for Aelius to decide—but know that my first concern is his happiness. You took that from him, so forgive me if I am not overjoyed to see you."

Crispina bowed her head. Gaia's words cut deeper than any snide comment from her own mother. "I understand."

A throat cleared, and Crispina turned to see Ajax entering the atrium from the front antechamber, Catullus behind him. "Gaius Valerius Catullus is here, sir," Ajax said.

"Forgive me for the early arrival," Catullus said. "Ah, Crispina, you're here already. Have you told him yet?"

Aelius frowned. "Told me what?"

Crispina bestowed her iciest glare on Catullus. Trust the chatty poet to immediately reveal what she wanted to keep hidden. "I wasn't going to."

Catullus rolled his eyes. "Exactly as I suspected. For such an erudite woman, you can be remarkably stupid, Crispina." He addressed Aelius. "Your wife—with my help, of course—is the reason you won yesterday. I had a feeling she was going to affect some misguided humility and not tell you of her efforts, so I knew I had to come set things right. What the two of you would do without me, I haven't a clue."

Aelius looked as befuddled as if Catullus had made an obscure literary reference. "What are you talking about?"

Catullus gestured to Crispina. "I will let your wife tell it."

Crispina bit her lip. "I don't seek your forgiveness. I only wanted to right the wrong I did you." She swallowed hard. "Epidius Verus withdrew from the election because of me."

The confusion did not lift from his face. "I don't understand."

"And because of Taurus." She glanced around the atrium to find Cassandra and Taurus, but the two had slipped out, perhaps not wanting to intrude on this conversation.

"Taurus?" Aelius squinted at her as if she'd started speaking Aramaic.

"Taurus used to work for Verus. He found out that Verus was involved in embezzling and construction fraud. That's why Verus was so eager to get rid of him." She gave a brief description of how Verus had been stealing money from the state, not to mention dishonoring the gods. "I threatened to reveal what Verus was up to if he didn't withdraw from the election."

"Great gods, Crispina, you blackmailed Verus? Haven't we had enough of that sort of thing?"

"Well, it worked," Crispina said.

"Infernal Dis," Aelius breathed.

Max wrinkled his nose. "You said I can't say 'Dis' because it's rude."

"It's very rude," Gaia said, casting a disapproving glance at her son.

Aelius stared at Crispina. "So you are the reason I won."

Crispina shook her head. "You would have won if I had not interfered. I had to do something to fix the mess I'd made."

Aelius stepped closer to her, putting their bodies a handspan apart. His gaze traced her face as if he'd never seen her before. His proximity made warmth rush through her, heating her cheeks and spreading over her skin. After several weeks apart, his effect on her had only strengthened.

Out of the corner of her eye, she saw Catullus offer his arm to Gaia. "Perhaps we should remove ourselves to give these idiots privacy."

"Excellent idea." Gaia took his arm, and the two left the atrium. Max had scampered off to the back of the room, and was occupied in wrapping himself in the unused garlands Cassandra and Taurus had left behind.

The movement didn't break Aelius's focus on her. "I think we have much to discuss."

Crispina couldn't decipher his tone. Was it hopeful, or resigned? "We do." She closed her eyes briefly, gathering the strength to utter the words she knew she needed to. "My father suggested that, in light of your victory, you might see the benefit in the continued connection between our families. If you do seek a reconciliation on those grounds alone, then I'm afraid I must refuse."

He blinked, confusion returning to his face. "Refuse?"

She nodded. "I know we began as something simple. Something with boundaries and limits, something to do with mutual benefit, not love. But somewhere in the midst of all that, I fell in love with you, Aelius. And if you can't love me or trust me because of what I've done, I don't blame you. But I refuse to live as your wife merely for the sake of who my father knows or the dinner parties I can host. I refuse to live half a life with you. I want all of you, Aelius, or none of you."

There, it was said: the words that could seal her future as a woman twice-divorced, twice-rejected, doomed to a lifetime of regret and loneliness.

Aelius lifted a hand to brush her cheek. "Have all of me, then." He dipped his head and pressed his mouth to hers.

Disbelief seized her for a moment, then joy blossomed in her chest like a flower bud stretching toward the sun. She reached for his shoulders, anchoring their bodies together as she opened herself to their kiss.

Max made a vomiting noise from where he was entangling himself in garlands. "Blech!"

Crispina pulled away and laughed. Aelius chuckled too. She gazed up at him, still unable to fully comprehend. "Do you mean it? Can you truly forgive me?"

His arms encircled her waist. "I've been looking for a reason to forgive you ever since the moment you left. You gave it to me today." He kissed her again, which sparked another round of disgusted noises from Max.

"Perhaps we should finish our conversation somewhere more private," Crispina whispered.

Aelius grinned, took her hand, and led her away.

CHAPTER 34

C RISPINA FOLLOWED AELIUS INTO their bedroom. It hadn't changed, and memories surfaced of all of the nights they had spent within these four cozy walls. Desire bloomed within her, rendering her dry-mouthed and sending a shiver down her spine.

Aelius shut the door, then stepped close to her, filling her vision with the breadth of his chest and the lustful promise in his gaze. "I'm afraid I don't have much conversation left." His voice was the low, husky rumble she remembered.

"Nor do I," she breathed, then tilted her face up to kiss him. She did have more things to say to him; she needed to broach the topic of continuing her lessons on the Aventine, but that could come later. No more words, for now. All she cared about was the way his hands grasped her body, the press of his mouth against hers.

Aelius seemed to be of a similar mind. His lips skimmed her neck, and she gasped at the feel of stubble against her throat. She angled her hips against his, and found him hard and ready. He let out an appreciative growl. He untied the sash beneath her breasts, then unclasped the brooches securing the shoulders of her stola. The fabric fell to the floor, and she pulled off her undertunic.

Cool air whispered over her skin, but the heat of Aelius's gaze warmed her straight through. The tips of his fingers caressed her collarbone, traveling lower. She arched toward him as his fingers trailed over her breasts, longing for a firmer touch, but he didn't give it to her.

In retaliation, she reached under his tunic and gave him a single slow, light stroke. He throbbed in her hand, growing impossibly harder. His mouth fell open as desire rippled over his face.

"Bed," he grunted. "Now."

She grinned smugly and ambled over to the bed, casting a glance back at him. He yanked his tunic over his head and tossed it to the ground. She drew in a sharp breath, catching her lip between her teeth at the sight of his lean, golden-skinned body. She had come so close to losing all of this—losing him.

She perched on the edge of the bed. He walked over to her, then bent down, slid his hands beneath her bottom, and tossed her lightly into the middle of the bed.

"My hair," she whispered as her head rested on the bedcovers. "It will be ruined for dinner." She had chosen a more elaborate style than usual for the occasion, and it had taken nearly two hours to curl, braid, and pin her hair.

His body covered hers. "How I want to ruin it," he murmured against her neck.

A thrill shot through her, but she tried to keep her head. "There will be time for that after dinner," she promised. "Until then…" She rolled onto her stomach.

"Mm." He traced a finger down her spine, making her shudder. "I think this will do." He gave her bottom a firm squeeze, then grabbed her hips and pulled her to him.

She arched her back, seeking the hardness that thumped against her, but still he made her wait. His fingers delved between her legs, dipping into the wetness that had already gathered. He remembered exactly how she liked to be touched, how to make her writhe and gasp.

She closed her eyes, basking in the pleasure that arose with each stroke—only for him to pull his hand away much too soon. She let out a frustrated growl, but eagerness took over once more as she felt him shifting behind her, adjusting the positioning of her hips. The blunt, warm head of his arousal pressed against her. Her body welcomed him, and he let out a rough sigh as he sank all the way in.

Crispina lowered her forehead to the mattress, arching her back to take him even deeper. She loved the way he filled her like this, primal and possessive. He bent to drop a kiss between her shoulder blades, then his fingers closed around her hips, holding her steady as he thrust. He set a hard, fast pace, rougher than usual, but her body thrilled at every movement. She dug her fingers into the mattress as each thrust jolted her body.

"Harder," she gasped. She needed to feel him in every inch of her body, needed him to make her entirely his once more.

"Are you sure?" His voice was breathless and unsteady.

"Oh, yes." She wanted everything he could give her, wanted to take every bit of the anger and pain he must have felt over the past few weeks. This coupling would cleanse her, absolve her. It would serve as the final proof of his forgiveness that she desperately needed.

"Give me your hands."

At the raspy command, she laid her cheek on the mattress and stretched her arms back toward him. He clasped her wrists in one hand, gripping tightly where they rested on her back. With his other hand, he reached around her hip to rub between her legs, somehow keeping pace as he continued to ram into her.

Crispina squeezed her eyes shut, overwhelmed with sensation. The pleasure drew tight, almost painful in its intensity. "Aelius!" she gasped.

"Too much?"

"Don't stop," she begged. The knot of pleasure exploded, and she lost herself to a wave of blissful shudders. Moans burst from her mouth, gasping and keening as the climax ripped through her.

Aelius released her arms to take firm hold of her hips, holding her in place as her body convulsed against him. His fingers dug into her flesh, and his breathing grew ragged. He groaned her name amid a few final hard thrusts, then withdrew, panting, and collapsed on the bed next to her.

Crispina rolled onto her side and nuzzled his chest, her mind still foggy with pleasure, her body aching but satisfied. Aelius pulled her to him, wrapping her in his arms. Their lips met in a long, slow kiss.

"Do you think it's mandatory for a victorious candidate to attend his own banquet?" Aelius asked in a drowsy murmur.

Crispina chuckled. "I fear it is." She wanted nothing more than to bask in his warmth for a few more delicious moments, but unfortunately, they had obligations. She poked his shoulder. "We should make sure everything is in order out there."

He groaned, but hauled himself into a sitting position. Crispina slid out of bed and went to retrieve her clothes. Other thoughts intruded as the bliss of their coupling receded. She remembered what she still needed to broach with him: her lessons.

She bent to pick up her discarded clothing. "There is one other thing I wanted to discuss. I became rather distracted earlier."

Aelius eyed her as she shook out her undertunic. "You're going to need to put something on if you don't want me to get distracted once more."

"I will be extremely impressed if you can manage any *distraction* after what we just did," she joked, but she pulled her undertunic over her head anyway, covering herself from neck to ankle. "It's about the lessons I was giving to the children over on the Aventine. I'm sorry I kept that secret from you, but I'd like to continue them. The children deserve that." She hated that she'd abandoned them again, even though she had no choice.

Aelius rose from the bed and donned his tunic. When he didn't answer right away, anxiety flared, twisting in her stomach. What if, after all they'd been through, he denied her something that meant so much to her?

He cinched a belt around his waist. "You must understand that it's highly inappropriate, not to mention dangerous, for a tribune's wife to visit such impoverished areas."

Her stomach plummeted. "They are the people you were elected to represent." She would not let this go. She had only married him in the first place to gain the freedom to pursue her lessons. If he tried to prevent her...

"You misunderstand me." He met her gaze, a small smile playing around his lips. "I think it would be better if you invited your pupils here, to take lessons in our home."

Her mouth dropped open.

"But only temporarily," he continued. "As soon as it's feasible, I'd like to introduce a bill to dedicate some funds to the creation of a school, where parents of any status who can't afford tuition may send their children. It may be difficult to convince the Assembly to spend money on educating the children of the poor, especially the girls, but I trust you can help me build a compelling case as to why increased education will benefit the entire Republic."

"Oh," she breathed. "Oh, Aelius. Thank you." Joy surged within her. He not only understood her mission, but he was prepared to use his newfound power to extend it in ways she could only have dreamed of. She launched herself at him and threw her arms around him. This meant everything to her.

He gave her a deep kiss which made her want to drag him back to bed. "I love you, Crispina," he murmured, leaning his head against hers. "And I will do whatever it takes to keep you by my side."

Aelius lingered with Crispina in the atrium after bidding the last guest goodbye. The dinner party had been a success, but the congratulations heaped on him by his guests paled in comparison to the joy he felt whenever he glanced at Crispina sitting beside him. His face hurt from smiling.

Now, the guests were gone. His mother had just bid them goodnight, and Max had been put to bed hours earlier, which left Aelius alone in the atrium with his wife. He plucked a rose from a garland and tucked the crimson bloom behind Crispina's ear. Next to her fair skin, it looked like a flower that would decorate a goddess's statue during a festival. "Do you remember the first night we met?" There had been a dinner party then too, and a quiet, empty atrium.

"I splashed you." She smiled. Once, he hadn't even known if she was capable of smiling. Now, though it was still a relatively rare occurrence, each one felt like a blessing.

"Catullus warned me away from you that night, you know," he said.

Her eyebrows lifted. "The nerve. On what grounds?"

"Your intelligence. Apparently he was bitter that you had pointed out an error he made once. He thought our courtship would end in disaster."

She chuckled, and the sound warmed him like a flame. "It very nearly did."

"For once, I'm glad I didn't listen to him." He pulled her close and lowered his head to kiss her forehead. She rested her cheek against his chest, her body warm and solid. Contentment washed over him as his arms encircled her.

Nothing would ever be better than this moment, not even if he won the consulship ten years from now. None of that mattered without her by his side.

A memory came back to him, from the night a year ago when he'd lost the election. Sitting in his bedroom with his mother, devastation heavy in his chest. His mother's gentle hand on his shoulder, the concern in her eyes. *I question if this will make you happy*, she'd said.

He hadn't known the answer then. Now, though he would never stop striving toward his dream of a consulship, he knew he had found true happiness with Crispina.

Crispina let out a quiet yawn. "To bed, husband?"

He released her from his embrace and took her hand. "To bed, wife."

EPILOGUE

Ten years later

ON THE STEPS OF the temple of Jupiter, Crispina stood with Max and Gaia on either side of her. A huge crowd gathered at their back. In front of them, Aelius stood beneath the temple portico with a group of priests, his co-consul beside him. An acolyte grasped the lead of a brilliant white ox, its horns gilded and its neck wreathed in flowers.

Crispina could hardly believe this day had arrived. Ten years had passed since the tribune election, and now Aelius had achieved his ultimate dream: becoming Rome's first freedman consul.

His co-consul was none other than Rufus. They had been rivals in nearly every election over the past decade, but had learned to work as allies during their terms. Now, they would serve in Rome's highest position together for a year, each with the power to veto the other. A freedman and a baker's son, effectively ruling the Republic. The patricians might take back power next year, but until then, Rome was in the hands of plebeians.

Like Rufus, Aelius wore the consular toga of white striped with rich purple, a mark of his new status. Rufus's arms gleamed with his usual array of gold bracelets and rings, but Aelius's arms were both bare. That morning, he had taken off the silver wristband that covered his brand. "I have nothing to hide anymore," he'd said, and tossed the wristband into a chest, locking it away.

As she watched him, standing tall and proud before the city, pride swelled and fluttered in her chest like a baby bird breaking out of its shell. Once, his freedman status had been a bane, a shadow that would never stop following him. But since becoming tribune, he'd used his newfound prominence to benefit all freedmen and women. He'd created a network of former slaves who met for dinner once a month, building alliances and supporting each other. Their household purchased flour only from freedman-owned mills, and Crispina wore jewelry crafted by freedmen artisans. As Aelius's power grew with each successive election he won, he hired freedmen to work in his offices as clerks and scribes.

She glanced over at Gaia, whose eyes shone with tears as she watched the priests prepare the sacrifice to bless Aelius's term. Crispina clasped her hand. "He did it," she murmured.

Gaia nodded, speechless.

Crispina looked to her other side, where Max stood. He'd grown into a gangly seventeen-year-old who now loomed over her. His attention was not rapt on the ceremony, but instead he grinned foolishly at a pretty young woman on the other side of the steps, standing next to Rufus's wife. The young woman acknowledged him with a shy smile, then returned her attention to the proceedings.

Crispina elbowed him. "Pay attention," she hissed. "And stop mooning over Rufus's stepdaughter." The young woman was beautiful, with rosy skin and hair the color of dark honey. Rufus had married the girl's mother, a widow, shortly after the tribunal election. His wife seemed to have a good influence on him, as he'd later apologized to Crispina for the way he'd treated her. But he still regarded Max with nothing but disdain, and Crispina knew he'd never let Max within an arm's length of his precious stepdaughter.

Max let out a sullen sigh, but directed his gaze back to the ceremony. Crispina allowed her gaze to rest on him for a moment longer. He had grown into a fine young man. True, his Greek was atrocious, he hadn't abandoned his penchant for foul language, and he was prone to sneaking out of the house at night to gamble and carouse with his friends, but he'd avoided getting into any real trouble. Max was good-hearted and gregarious, and he had a knack for horsemanship. He planned to join a cavalry unit in the army next year, once Aelius's term was finished. It pained Crispina to think of Max leaving, but military discipline would benefit him, and he'd bring honor upon himself. Maybe one day he'd command a legion.

The crowd quieted as Aelius and Rufus stepped forward. The priest raised his hands to the sky and intoned a chant to Jupiter, asking for divine blessing on the new consuls. Then, in a clear, strong voice, Aelius spoke the oath of consular office, swearing to protect Rome from foreign enemies and allow no man to become king. Rufus did the same.

Another invocation followed. Aelius and Rufus bowed their heads as the priest produced a shining knife. In a quick, clean strike, the priest flashed the knife across the throat of the ox. It bellowed and sank to its knees, blood gushing into a deep bowl held by the acolyte.

The crowd roared. Aelius and Rufus clasped arms formally. They might never be the best of friends, but at least they were no longer brawling in the Forum.

Men stationed on the tops of the neighboring buildings let fall a cascade of red and white petals which shimmered in the air before blanketing everyone's heads and shoulders. Crispina plucked several out of her hair, not envying whoever had to clean up after this.

With the ceremony concluded, the crowds began to dissipate. Several acolytes dragged the body of the ox into the temple. It would be cooked and served at a banquet that evening.

Two dozen burly, toga-clad men emerged from the temple and split to surround Aelius and Rufus, twelve each, escorting them down the temple steps toward their families. These were the lictors who would accompany each consul wherever he went for the next year, responsible for protection. Their constant presence would no doubt be an annoyance, but every consul had enemies, and Aelius's safety was well worth the inconvenience.

Aelius, smiling, waved away the lictors as he reached Crispina, Gaia, and Max. The twelve men retreated a few paces, standing at attention. Their gazes flicked around the dispersing crowd, already searching for hidden threats.

Gaia stepped forward to fling her arms around Aelius, her cheeks wet with tears. "Oh, my love, I never imagined I would see this day."

Aelius grinned. "You had such little faith in me, Mama?"

She wiped her eyes with the back of her hand and shot him a good-natured scowl. "You know that's not what I meant."

Aelius turned to Max, reaching out to ruffle his hair. Max dodged, batting away Aelius's arm, but allowed himself to be embraced. His face bore a distinctly mournful look as he looked at his adoptive father. Crispina poked him on the shoulder. "Can't you summon a smile on the happiest day of our lives?"

Max grimaced. "*Your* life, maybe. I have a feeling being a consul's son is going to be as boring as a eunuch at an orgy."

"Max!" Gaia smacked him. "That's no sort of language for a consul's son."

Max gave Crispina a significant look. "See what I mean?"

Crispina rolled her eyes.

"Remember our bargain?" Aelius said. "Spotless behavior for one more year, then you can ride off to join the army and wreak as much havoc as you want in Gaul or Germania or wherever you end up."

"Right," Max said unenthusiastically.

Aelius chuckled at his son, then turned to Crispina. Their gazes met, and in his hazel eyes Crispina saw a reflection of the past ten years: their triumphs, their struggles, and the love that had endured through it all.

It hadn't all been easy. Though Aelius had legislated a tax break for landowners who employed free laborers instead of slaves, it was later reversed by a future vote. He did, however, succeed in introducing a hefty tax on the sale of female slaves who were visibly pregnant or who had birthed a child in their master's home, meant to deter the separation of families.

His bill to create a state-funded school had also failed. But with Horatia's help, Crispina had secured a slew of donations from wealthy families, enabling her to hire a group of tutors and hold a rotation of free classes in her home.

With the proper investment and continued donations, Crispina hoped the school would eventually be self-sustaining. She had her eye on a vacant lot, the site of a collapsed apartment building, that she wanted to buy to build a permanent school as her group of students grew.

Her earliest students were already flourishing. Aelius had hired Sextus, one of her pupils from the Aventine, to work as his secretary, and her other pupil Silus had become a mathematics tutor at the school.

Aelius wrapped Crispina in his arms, squeezing her so tightly her feet lifted from the ground.

"Congratulations, my love," she whispered in his ear.

"For a moment, when I was standing up there, I thought it was all a dream, or a mistake," he said. "I was waiting for someone to come drag me away. But then I saw you and Max and Mama, and I realized if my life with you is real, then the consulship has to be. Because nothing could be more of a dream than the fact that I get to wake up beside you every day."

His face blurred before her, and she blinked away tears. "It's going to be a busy year," was all she could manage.

His mouth curved in a grin. "The busiest." He swept her into a kiss.

She kissed him back, lifting a hand to caress his cheek, as Max made vomiting noises next to them. It would be a busy year, a stressful year, maybe even a dangerous year. But they would face it together, and their love would endure.

Thank you for reading! Want more Aelius and Crispina? Scan below or head to jennabigelow.com/tribune for a spicy bonus scene. You can also download *The Merchant Match*, a free prequel novella about Gaia's love story with Aelius's stepfather.

Turn to the next page for a sneak peek of Book 2, *The Legionary Seduction,* which catches up with Max—all grown up and ready for his own happily ever after.

SNEAK PEEK: THE LEGIONARY SEDUCTION

Ten years of longing. A second chance at love. One shot to catch a murderer.

Max joined the Roman army in search of glory and adventure, but thanks to his dislike of punctuality and penchant for foul language, he's stuck in the provinces, unable to land even one promotion. When his latest punishment lands him on guard duty at the governor's residence, the last thing he expects is to come face-to-face with the girl he loved ten years ago. Only now, she's married to the governor.

Volusia has long resigned herself to a passionless marriage, as her husband prefers to spend his nights with his private secretary. Seeing Max again throws her orderly world into chaos, and finally she remembers how it feels to be loved, desired, and protected.

When Volusia's husband mysteriously dies, she's convinced he was murdered by the corrupt legionary commander. The only person she dares trust is Max, and she begs him to help prove her husband was murdered. Max knows speaking against his commander will risk his position in the army—not to mention his life—but if Volusia asks, he can't say no. The two become embroiled in a dangerous world of deception and corruption. Their love is strong, but can it withstand a killer's blade?

CHAPTER 1

Outside Narbo (Narbonne)

Max crossed his arms over his chest and took a deep inhale of the air, tinged with the scent of woodsmoke. Chainmail armor laid heavy on his shoulders, but after ten years in the army, he barely noticed its weight.

Tax day was everyone's least favorite day, from the provincial citizens who had to turn over their hard-earned profits, to the legionaries tasked with the tedious collection. Until a moment ago, the day had been painfully boring but peaceful. Max and five other legionaries had traveled from village to village around Gallia Transalpina, watching the tax collector tally careful figures and weigh sacks of grain.

Now, a complainer had emerged. Finally, something interesting. A large man, sporting the mane of fair hair common to the provincial natives, approached the tax collector. He braced his weight against a tall walking stick and spoke Latin with a lilting Gallic accent. "I'll ask again for an explanation. Why have our taxes nearly doubled?"

The tax collector, seated at a table piled high with wax tablets, twirled his stylus between his fingers. "And I'll tell you again. The tax rate is set by acting governor Gaius Galerius Petronax."

The man raised a bushy eyebrow. "That's not an explanation. If we're to hand over nearly twice a share of our income, we deserve to know why."

Murmurs of agreement sounded from the crowd behind him. The tax collector fixed the man with a dispassionate stare. "It's not for you to ask questions. Only to pay the lawful taxes that are due of every man who has the honor of calling himself a citizen of Rome."

The man glanced behind him, as if gauging the support of the others. He turned back to face the tax collector. His hold on his walking stick changed from a casual grasp to the sort of grip that could wield the staff as a weapon if required. Max tensed, his hand going to the sword hanging at his hip. Out of the corner of his eye, he noticed the other legionaries making similar moves, chainmail rattling as they shifted.

"I reckon we could go to Narbo and ask Governor Petronax ourselves," the Gallic man said, the threat clear in his words. The men behind him shifted forward, fanning out at his back.

Metal rasped as the other legionaries drew their swords. Max kept his in its scabbard. He had only the haziest understanding of the intricacies of provincial tax code, but he did understand frustration. And he was no mathematician, but the arithmetic of this situation was clear even to him. There were at least thirty men of the village, against five legionaries. The legionaries had swords, armor, and training, but the villagers had numbers and righteous anger. If this turned to violence, it wouldn't go well for either side.

Max jumped in front of the tax collector's table, between the legionaries and the villagers, his hands raised. "Let's all take a moment before we do anything we might regret." He used the same tone of voice as when he was trying to calm a skittish horse, and glanced from the other legionaries to the villagers, making it clear that his message was for both groups. "We don't want any trouble."

The blond man walked forward to meet him, planting his walking stick into the ground at his side. "All you Romans are is trouble."

"Insolence," one of the other legionaries growled.

Max merely rolled his eyes and ignored the insult. It wouldn't help to appear as over-sensitive as some of his colleagues. "Listen, I won't pretend to know exactly how your tax money is going to be spent." Max hesitated, trying to summon the right words. He had no gift for rousing men with words or giving eloquent speeches—that was his politician father's skill, not his. But maybe he didn't need to be an orator here. Maybe nothing more than calm, reasonable words could defuse the tension humming in this situation. "I do know that the province's taxes have gone to building a bunch of roads here. Travel is safer, and Narbo is connected to Hispania as well as Italy. I bet your wife enjoys all the goods she can buy at the market from around the world at decent prices. And she can visit her mother in the next village over without fearing that her wagon will lose a wheel to a muddy road. All because everyone pays their taxes."

The man surveyed him. Max wasn't sure if his words would be enough to avert violence, and his shoulders tensed. He forced himself to adopt a casual, relaxed posture, hands loosely clasped in front of him, as if they were chatting at a tavern. Usually, Max was getting chewed out for looking too casual—"slovenly," as his centurion was fond of putting it—but today, his natural ease might be useful.

The Gallic man glanced from Max to the other legionaries, their swords still drawn. He must have realized, as Max had, that even if the thirty villagers succeeded in overcoming the handful of legionaries, the might of the entire legion would crush them. It wasn't fair, but it was true.

The man hefted his sack of grain and dumped it on the tax collector's table. The legionaries sheathed their swords. Max caught the man's eye and gave him a small nod, hoping the man could sense his gratitude that he'd chosen peace. It wasn't right to make people give up their money without explanation, but today, it seemed more important to keep the peace than to question the entire system of government.

An hour later, Max helped load the last of the tax payments into a large cart, to be taken back to Narbo. He mounted up on Elephant, his gray mare, and took up the rear of their little caravan.

Elephant was his favorite being, human or animal, in the entire world. His adoptive parents had gifted her to him as a filly when he was seventeen, just before he joined the army. She'd carried him all over the Republic, kept him safe in battle, and was always there to lend a listening ear.

As they left the village behind, riding single file on a narrow road, Max pulled Elephant to a stop and hopped down from her saddle. The legionary riding in front of him noticed and slowed his own horse. "Everything all right, Legionary Maximus?"

Max bent to lift one of Elephant's hooves, frowning as if concerned. "I think my horse has taken a stone in her hoof. You all keep going, I'll be right behind you."

The legionary shrugged. "Don't forget, we're expected back in Narbo for the arrival." He continued on.

Vesta's tits. Max had forgotten all about the event later today. The province's new governor was arriving this afternoon, and the legion was expected to assemble to welcome him. Max glanced at the sun's position in the sky and calculated that he had a bit of time. Worst case, if he was late, he'd just have to sneak into formation without attracting his centurion's notice.

Max pretended to diligently check all of Elephant's hooves until the other four legionaries had vanished around a bend in the road. Then he grinned in triumph, mounted back up, and steered Elephant off the road and down a small path between the trees. This was one of many paths he'd discovered that led straight to the beach. A gallop on the beach would be the highlight of his week, and he wasn't about to give up his chance, even if he was risking another punishment for tardiness.

Soon, Elephant's hooves pounded on flat-packed sand. A vast expanse of glimmering water shone to their right. Wind whipped at Max's hair. He let out a whoop of delight as Elephant effortlessly jumped a log of driftwood lying on the beach. Her hooves slammed down on the other side with only a minor jolt, her strong legs absorbing most of the impact. Waves crashed beside them, and flecks of sea spray cooled him.

He'd needed this, needed the freedom, the exhilaration. Army life, though it offered opportunity for adventure, was constricting. He should be grateful that Narbo was peaceful, far from the civil war that was currently seething in Greece, but sometimes he longed for a bit more excitement. Everything was rules and duty and saluting, and sometimes only the chance to gallop his horse on an empty beach made it worth it.

As the beach began to curve, he gently guided Elephant into a measured trot and lifted a hand to squint at the sky. The sun was much too close to the horizon. Oh yes, he was definitely going to be late. Fuck.

He wheeled Elephant away from the water and found the trail back to Narbo. Elephant snorted at the interruption, but allowed herself to be coaxed back into a canter once they hit the wider road.

"Sorry," he murmured to her. "Glabrio will skin me alive if I'm late again, and then who would spoil you?"

She flicked her ear back at him in a gesture that was the horse equivalent of an eye-roll.

Max practiced excuses in his mind as they approached Narbo. Punctuality was not his strong suit, but he'd resolved to do better. He needed to do better if he was going to make decurion, after all. Then, he'd be responsible not just for himself, but for a squadron of thirty men. He should have been promoted already, given his ten years of service, but too many incidents of lateness or accidental impudence had held him back.

When they reached the stables, Max untacked Elephant, brushed her down, and released her into the pasture as quickly as he could. Then, he jogged outside the walls of the city to the field before the eastern gate that the legion used for drills and assemblies.

Shit, he was definitely late. The whole legion was assembled already, facing the road on which the new governor would arrive. Max held his breath and tried to make himself as unobtrusive as possible as he slipped through the ranks to find the spot that had been left for him in his cavalry unit. His height was usually an advantage, but today, he was fairly sure that all five thousand men of the legion were watching him fumble around.

He finally found his spot next to his friend and bunk-mate, Drusus, and slipped into it.

"Where in Dis have you been?" Drusus breathed.

"Riding," Max replied.

"Idiot."

Max nodded in agreement. His one consolation was that Glabrio, his centurion, was at the front, facing forward, so might not have noticed Max's tardy arrival. Then again, the man seemed to have eyes in the back of his head, so Max doubted he'd get off easy. Besides, someone else would probably rat him out to curry favor.

Between the heads of the men in front of him, Max could just glimpse the legion's commander, Petronax, pacing before the ranks. He wore a bright white cape, and sunlight glanced off the gold filigree in his ceremonial breastplate. Petronax had been acting governor of the province in the months since the previous governor finished his three-year term. Petronax probably wasn't looking forward to giving up the power and prestige that came with governing a profitable and peaceful province like Gallia Transalpina.

They waited for several minutes. Then, a scout on a fast horse came riding down the road, hooves thumping, and relayed a message to Petronax, likely announcing the imminent arrival of the traveling party. At the front of the legion, trumpeters lifted their instruments and launched into a loud, jaunty tune.

Moments later, a small procession rounded the curve of the road and came into view. A few men rode horses in front, followed by a small enclosed carriage. Several carts packed high with crates and boxes brought up the rear.

The frontmost rider surveyed the assembled legion with an air of command as he drew his horse to a halt. He must be the province's new governor. His close-cropped hair was graying at the edges, but he sprang down from his horse with energetic ease. He patted the horse on the nose before handing the reins to an eager legionary. A good sign—Max liked men who were kind to their animals.

Petronax stepped forward, ready to greet the new governor, but the other man turned toward the carriage, which had pulled up behind them. He waved away another attendant and opened the door himself, extending a hand up to assist the woman inside the carriage.

A jolt of shock pulsed through Max. He sucked in a ragged breath through his teeth at the sight of the woman who emerged from the carriage.

Over the past ten years, he'd often had moments like this, where he'd thought he'd seen her. But it was always just another woman with the same shade of dark-honey hair, or a build similar to hers, petite and slender.

Though other women might share the same hair color or figure, no one had ever matched her bearing: prim but not haughty, dignified but not cold. She'd carried herself like that even when they were adolescents, and the woman who stepped down from the carriage moved with the warm grace he remembered.

It was Volusia, his childhood friend and source of deep infatuation. He hadn't seen her in ten years, not since one disastrous kiss had ruined everything between them. He knew she married shortly after they had parted. He hadn't known her husband would become the new governor of Gallia Transalpina, or that she would accompany him all the way from Rome.

He swallowed hard. Petronax and the governor were exchanging a formal greeting, but Max couldn't tear his gaze from Volusia. She stood patiently behind her husband, glancing over the ranks with a small smile. A fair-haired attendant stood at her side, and Volusia leaned over to whisper something to her.

His chest felt tight. He had never expected to see her again, had resigned himself to it, despite comparing every woman he flirted with or the few he bedded to her. Now, she was to live here, in the same town.

But they would probably never see each other. He didn't often cross paths with the governor's household, and Volusia would have no reason to venture outside of the comfortable house she'd soon be installed in. She was married now—to a governor, no less—and he was just a soldier who couldn't even land one promotion.

Regret pulled at him. Once, they were the best of friends. But fate had torn them apart, and they'd never be able to recapture what they once had. He'd keep his distance, and she'd never even know he was here.

To keep reading, go to jennabigelow.com/tribune for purchasing information!

ALSO BY JENNA BIGELOW

THE IMPERIAL GAMES SERIES

Set in the early days of Caligula's reign, the Imperial Games series follows three gladiators during a stretch of games held to celebrate the new emperor's accession. Win or lose, one thing is sure: love will be found where they least expect it.

Gladiator's Embrace (Book 1)

A retired gladiator reluctantly returns to the arena for one last series of fights, only to fall for his manager's ambitious niece when she hires him to train the up-and-coming gladiator she's taken on.

Gladiator's Beloved (Book 2)

She's Rome's most feared female gladiator. He's the emperor's personal physician, commanded to heal her latest injury. Sparks fly when they're together, until the machinations of the imperial court threaten to tear them apart.

Gladiator's Touch (Book 3)

A former Vestal Virgin seeks out the gladiator-turned-sculptor whose life she spared. He wants nothing to do with her after she ended his fighting career, but the heat that blossoms between them is impossible to escape.

THE ROMAN HEIRS SERIES

The Roman Heirs series follows the love stories of three generations of an unconventional family in the last decades of the Roman Republic. There's a politically motivated marriage of convenience, forbidden pining between a soldier and a governor's wife, and a pair of business rivals who somehow find themselves trading sex lessons for a truce.

The Merchant Match (free prequel novella)

After gaining her freedom from slavery, Gaia will do whatever it takes to build a new future for herself and her son—even infiltrate a dinner party under an assumed identity to extort money from her former mistress. There, she meets Herminius, a wealthy merchant in search of a respectable bride. Despite her subterfuge, Gaia can't ignore the heat that sparks between them. She knows she should keep her distance, but what's the point of freedom if she can't enjoy the pleasurable attentions of a man who makes her heart flutter every time they touch?

The Tribune Temptation (Book 1)

In the cutthroat world of Roman politics, family is everything. Aelius, a freed slave turned ambitious politician, enters into a marriage of convenience with a disgraced patrician divorcee, hoping her powerful family name will bolster his chances in his next election. Prickly one moment and icy the next, Crispina is determined to keep her charming husband at a distance. That is, until Aelius undertakes a campaign to win not just the city's vote, but his wife's heart.

The Legionary Seduction (Book 2)

Max joined the Roman army in search of glory and adventure, but soon finds himself stuck in the provinces, unable to land even one promotion. During a stint on guard duty at the new governor's residence, he comes face-to-face with Volusia, the girl he loved ten years ago. Only now, she's married to the governor. But when her husband mysteriously dies and she suspects foul play, the only person Volusia dares trust is Max, and she begs him to help investigate. Their love is strong, but can it withstand a killer's blade?

The Fortune Flirtation (Book 3)

After losing her husband to a shipwreck, Lucretia has devoted herself to keeping his shipping business afloat. Felix, her scheming rival, strives for a monopoly on trade, which requires seizing Lucretia's ships for himself. Unfortunately for Felix, it's not just her ships he desires. Even worse, he's been too busy building his business empire to dally with women...*ever*. When Lucretia discovers both how much he wants her *and* that he's as inexperienced as a Vestal Virgin, she decides to use this to her advantage—proposing a truce in exchange for initiating Felix into the ways of the flesh.

OTHER WORKS

A Princess's Ransom (Tales of Timeless Romance anthology)

After the sack of Rome, Galla Placidia, the emperor's sister, becomes the Goths' most valuable hostage. While awaiting ransom, the ambitious princess, tired of living in her brother's shadow, realizes the Goths could be the key to the power she craves. Allying with the Goths could also allow her to indulge her forbidden attraction to her captor—the stoic, noble, and irritatingly handsome Athaulf. Placidia must decide how far she'll go to secure both the man and the future she desires, and if she's willing to turn her back on Rome forever.

Acknowledgements

Thank you to all of my fellow writers who provided invaluable feedback on early drafts of this book, including Maggie Sims, Anne Knight, Sarah T. Dubb, Meredith Crosbie, Amanda, and Irene. Rachel Shipp provided excellent editorial feedback and guidance.

Thank you also to the members of the SF 2.0 Discord server. Your advice, encouragement, and the examples that you all set have been integral to my journey of bringing these books into the world.

Finally, thank you to Frankie, my loving husband, valiant proofreader, and self-professed #1 fan. I could never have done this without you.

ABOUT THE AUTHOR

 Jenna Bigelow is a historical romance author based in Wilmington, DE. She has eleven years of Latin classes under her belt, as well as a minor in Classical Culture and Society. When not writing, she enjoys sewing, especially recreating historical fashions of the 18th and 19th centuries. She thinks about the Roman Empire every day.

Connect with Jenna at her website, jennabigelow.com, or on Instagram/Threads at @jennabigelowwrites.